Dear Reader:

It gives me great pleasure to welcome Ahyiana Angel to the Strebor Books family. Her debut novel, *Preseason Love*, is all about the choices we face. Sometimes making decisions can lead to life-altering consequences.

It follows the journey of Scottie and her relationships and encounters with several men. After leaving Ivan in L.A. suddenly for New York, Scottie connects with the lovable Kari, and after landing a coveted position as an NBA publicist, she falls into secretive liaisons with a pro baller, who is full of surprises.

I'm sure you will enjoy this fast-paced page-turner told through the eyes of a savvy, adventurous woman who discovers how finding romance can be challenging and what glitters is not always paradise.

I appreciate the love and support shown to Strebor Books, myself, and our efforts to bring you cutting-edge stories.

Blessings,

Zane

Publisher
Strebor Books
www.simonandschuster.com

ZANE PRESENTS

PRESEASON
Love

A NOVEL BY

Ahyiana Angel

SBI

STREBOR BOOKS

NEW YORK LONDON TORONTO SYDNEY

Strebor Books
P.O. Box 6505
Largo, MD 20792
http://www.streborbooks.com

ISBN 978-1-59309-612-0
ISBN 978-1-4767-8291-1 (ebook)
LCCN 2014935327

First Strebor Books trade paperback edition October 2014

Cover design: www.mariondesigns.com
Cover photograph: © Keith Saunders/Keith Saunders Photos

10 9 8 7 6 5 4 3 2 1

Manufactured in the United States of America

For information regarding special discounts for bulk purchases, please contact Simon & Schuster Special Sales at 1-866-506-1949 or business@simonandschuster.com

The Simon & Schuster Speakers Bureau can bring authors to your live event. For more information or to book an event, contact the Simon & Schuster Speakers Bureau at 1-866-248-3049 or visit our website at www.simonspeakers.com.

For my grandparents—
Velma Long, Aznell and Wilfred Francis.

Prologue

We are all faced with choices and decisions in life. Keeping secrets makes things more complicated and your actions will always have consequences.

Kari's Secret:

"I tried to warn you, man!" Kelvin shouted at Kari through the phone. "That night at dinner, I predicted this would happen, son. She left you for one of them ballers, didn't she, B?"

"Look, bro, it's not like that," Kari insisted. "Scottie's a good woman. It's not like we broke up because she was cheating on me. I didn't say that, did I?"

"Not that you know of, son."

Kari huffed. "We simply needed to take a break."

"According to who? Her?" Kelvin shook his head in disbelief at the naiveté of his friend. "Son, she hit you with the okie doke. And you fell for it, B."

Kari tried his hardest to explain the status of his relationship in a favorable light to his childhood friend, but Kelvin wasn't buying it. They had been on the phone less than ten minutes, and Kelvin had all the facts he needed to conclude that Kari had gotten played. What he saw with his own eyes convinced him that Scottie was definitely sleeping with Byron Stalling. He knew that she saw him backstage the night of the Jay-Z concert, but she ran behind a black curtain before he could confront her.

"I can't even front," Kari said. "I'm hurt."

"You're my boy, son. No matter what, you know I got ya back," Kelvin preached. "You can't be worried about Scottie shady ass. I bet she doing her. You gotta do you."

"I know, man. I need to be alone. Clear my head. I'm gonna go over to Slate and have a drink."

Devin's Secret:

The upper level of Slate in the Flatiron district was dimly lit as usual and packed with trendy people. Of all the faces in the crowd, Dev spotted a familiar mug coming her way from across the room: Kari. It was too late to duck and act like she didn't see him. She could only brace herself and prepare for a potentially awkward exchange because they had not seen each other since his breakup with Scottie.

"Hey, Dev. How have you been?" Kari said as he smiled and greeted Dev with brotherly love like always.

This might not turn out that bad, Dev thought. "Hey, Kari, it's good to see you."

"Yeah, it's good to see you too, Dev." His smile quickly faded. "I'm glad I ran into you," Kari added as he turned to walk away.

Dev thought that was a strange way to end an extremely brief encounter with her girl's ex. Dev knew that it must have been difficult running into her. He had to pretend like everything was normal. Either way, Dev couldn't wait to call Scottie in California and tell her who she'd just run into.

Dev dipped into a corner to dial Scottie's number on her cell phone. Getting no answer, she left a voicemail message, then turned to go and meet up with her girls. But Kari was standing directly in her path.

Kari was rubbing his forehead vigorously. "Dev, I really need to speak to you. Can we go somewhere and talk for a minute? I'll buy you a drink."

Dev didn't know what to make of his request, but it was Kari. Of course she wouldn't turn her back on him.

Scottie's Secret:

Scottie Malveaux sat behind an airtight conference room door exchanging intense glares with The League's legal watchdog in addition to the most useless human resources representative ever, Caroline Stinger.

"Ms. Malveaux, I'm going to ask you one last time."

Spit gathered at the corners of the lawyer's squirmy mouth, creating saliva piles that resembled a foam party. He used his right index finger to slide the silver, wire-frame specs up over his nose, aligning perfectly with his dark, beady eyes. His scowl grew closer to Scottie's face as he leaned over the pressed-wood table, violating Scottie's comfort zone.

"Were you or have you ever been involved with a professional athlete?"

Scottie's nude lip-gloss made it easy for her lips to slide apart in an attempt to formulate the same answer that she had so graciously provided the first three times the attorney asked. She sat back, folded her perfectly manicured hands across her chest and batted her long, jet-black lashes with an innocent smirk. Before she could respond, however, Caroline interjected.

"What he means is, were you, or have you ever been involved with, a professional athlete employed by The League?"

Scottie rubbed her palms against the dark-gray woven material of her chair to try to wipe away any signs of her increasing discomfort.

The balding lawyer tapped his pen on his tablet awaiting a response. "We received a tip regarding suspicion of an inappropriate relationship," he offered after a moment. "Do you have any explanation?"

"Nope," Scottie politely replied.

Chapter 1

Relocating Love

His eyes opened at the touch of my lips, and knowing glances and unspoken words filled the silence. The past was officially being put to rest and the future was to begin without us. There would only be me.

It was the morning of my transition. Cali girl to the core, born and bred, but it was time for me to test myself and make the biggest move of my life—New York City.

My phone buzzed with a text message, but I didn't bother checking the screen. It was typical of me to be running late, and Nikki was probably patiently waiting out front with her foot on the pedal. She was likely wondering if she had wasted a trip driving to Ivan's house.

Ivan was the beginning of my flawed relationships with men. I liked his style. He moved with a distinct confidence that drew women to him. Always known for reveling the female gender with the intriguing details of his life, he kept women hanging on his every word. That was one of his specialties. Not to mention, one of my problems.

He and I had been seeing each other, minus any form of exclusive commitment, since the latter portion of our college years. You know how that goes. Guy wants to keep girl around and continue having sex with her, but guy does not want to bother with a title so girl goes along with the bullshit excuses. The initial hookup was unintentional, but every late-night call, sexy text message, and rendezvous that followed was completely deliberate.

Ivan dressed fly but at times almost too fly. It felt like we were in constant competition with each other when we stepped out together. His closet was stacked to the ceiling with perfectly lined boxes of shoes. From hard bottoms and loafers to retro Jordans and Air Maxes, he had them all. The man shopped more than most women I knew. His slim frame allowed for clothes to drape his body like a showroom mannequin. I loved to see him rocking a fresh pair of Jordans, fatigue cargo shorts and his signature GVG-brand tees.

Our chemistry was undeniable and everyone in our circle knew it. Ivan's soft, sandy-brown locks and butter-toffee complexion had me wide open. A little charm and a likable persona—that's how we lasted so long. His endearing touch was the best, and at times the worst. We both craved attention and especially loved it from each other.

Ivan shunned commitment and unlike some girls, I had too much pride to try and manipulate the situation to make him see things my way. Consequently, I repeatedly felt empty and desperately unfulfilled by our relationship, which brings me to my final night as a California resident. The Test.

Unfortunately, The Test wasn't a new concept for me. I'd played a similar game with myself many times over, but in this instance, it wasn't a test for him. Rather it was a test for me.

During my final twenty-four hours as a California resident, I moved with an air of confidence. Everything was on my terms. The Clique, my group of girlfriends, threw me an amazing going-away party, complete with all the liquor a person could dream of. Hennessy, Patrón, Belvedere, Maker's Mark, and Grand Marnier filled our glasses.

New friends and old friends from college and beyond were in attendance to celebrate the new adventure that I was determined to embark on. The Clique rented out a few lanes at an upscale bowling alley in Santa Monica, but because of the size, it felt like our own private party and we had a blast. With all the shots we consumed, there were shenanigans everywhere. And at the end of my festive night, my highly inebriated self decided to go home with Ivan. I wanted him to hold me like he couldn't stand to ever let me go. I wanted to feel passion and sincerity in his touch. I wanted him to surrender himself to me for once. And then I wanted to disappear. That's how I would be absolutely positive that I was ready to leave him in my past.

On countless mornings prior, Ivan had fled the warmth of my bed to gallivant the streets, leaving me emotional and confused. I would lie there and stare off into the distance feeling warm and tingly inside and daydreaming of the time that we'd just spent together. However, in the same moment, I would always feel a sense of loss and sadness knowing that our quality time was inconsistent and never guaranteed. He dictated our arrangement, leaving me to fumble around my apartment, wondering and waiting with my little cracked heart in my hands.

On my last night in Cali, I wanted something different. And I got it.

Ivan held me tightly. His grip was like a man in love. He whispered all of the right things, though I knew that it was for all of the wrong reasons. So there I was in Ivan's plush, king-sized bed on a sunny Los Angeles morning, grappling with the fact that if I couldn't pry myself away from his embrace right then, I would miss my opportunity for a fresh start, along with my flight.

Naturally, I did what any woman in her right mind would do. I wiggled from Ivan's grasp as fast as I could. Ivan's hollow, hazel eyes gazed up at me as I spazzed out, shoveling clothes, heels, makeup, accessories, and everything else strewn about into three huge, red suitcases sprawled out on the bedroom floor of Ivan's swanky bachelor pad.

Looking past the cocoa-brown curls that were continuously falling into my eyes, I spun around in a frenzy only to witness the reality of what was now disbelief on Ivan's face. His expression called out to one-fourth of my heart, begging and pleading with me to stay. But the pain in the other three-fourths said, "Don't walk, girl. Run! Run away from this self-centered, sexy yet sorry excuse of a man."

As Ivan stood by with glassy, somber eyes watching what must have seemed like a blurry image fumbling about, I got dressed in my flyest flight fashions, complete with four-inch, green, leather, military-inspired booties. Then I hit the front door, but not before giving him a gentle kiss on the forehead and pulling a Chris Brezzy and waving my hand in the air. *Deuces. I'm out*, I thought to myself.

I heard Ivan calling to me through the closed door. "Scottie, wait! Don't leave me like this."

I picked up my pace, sliding each suitcase down the staircase faster than the one before.

Nikki, who stayed dripped in designer fashions, was parked along the palm tree-lined sidewalk tapping her perfectly manicured nails on her steering wheel. She couldn't wait to hear "the juice," as we referred to it in The Clique.

I hit the last step on the staircase and she hopped out of the truck with her luxurious twenty-seven-inch Brazilian weave swaying. A sisterly hug ensued but before we could get what was left of my belongings into her trunk, she turned to grill me. "Spill it! And please don't try to be cute and leave out details, Scottie Malveaux. I want *all* the juice."

"What juice?" I said, acting like Stacy Dash in *Clueless.*

Nikki shot me a glace with her head cocked to the side and her hand on the bedazzled key ring sitting in the ignition. I had better say something quick. "You can already imagine what type of wild, passionate, bon voyage sex we had."

"Well no shit, Sherlock. I knew that. But what I really wanna know is what his whack ass face looked like right before you bolted out of his front door?"

We laughed hysterically, so much so that I doubled over.

Among our friends, it was no secret what everyone thought. They were certain that I couldn't break away from Ivan's spell, and they were positive that Ivan would pull some sort of trick to get me to stay in Los Angeles. People were probably taking bets that I wouldn't make my flight when they noticed me leaving my farewell party trailing behind Ivan. What they didn't know was that I was tired. Tired of talking, tired of getting let down, tired of playing the fool, and tired of giving my emotions to someone that was not emotionally available to me. I hadn't valued my own happiness in the past few years and it was time for me to get a grip, take back my control, and explore new possibilities.

Los Angeles held so many amazing memories. My girls from college and their infamous annual Halloween party; the nightlife and living it up with celebrities; underage drinking at The Gate, the Garden of Eden, the Goodbar, and countless other Hollywood hot spots; and doing all of that when I should have been studying for my college courses.

I would always have the memories, but other than great friends, there was nothing keeping me in Los Angeles. I would miss The Clique like crazy, but I was single by the government's standards, had no kids and my job basically sucked. Luckily, the entertainment PR agency I worked for agreed to let me relocate and even paid to have some of my belongings shipped to my new apartment. But the nature of the agency was sneaky and underhanded at best. I only planned to use the transfer as an opportunity to get to New York.

In a whirlwind of last-minute Craigslist sales and friend-of-a-friend deals, I parted with everything that represented the familiarity of a life that I created. I was never really one to fall into the materialistic category, but there was one major possession that I almost shed a tear leaving behind. It was a birthday gift to myself. I was turning twenty-four and fed up with rolling "smash-it or trash-it," a white Mitsubishi Mirage. It earned the name due to the massive hit-and-run dent left on the rear bumper by an inconsiderate U-Haul driver. My first car and I had history, but I was sick of wishing that I could fade into the darkness of the Hollywood Hills when the valet would bring around my hooptie after the club. It would essentially yell at me by making this awful, loud squealing sound. Even the valet would look embarrassed for me in the midst of the other partygoers' staring and pointing.

So for my birthday I'd decided it was time for an upgrade. I purchased a matte-black Mercedes-Benz CLK with butter leather interior. Clean. You couldn't tell me a thing when I rolled through the streets of Los Angeles. I loved the feeling of knowing that I'd made the decision to purchase that specific car and solely relied on myself to make it happen.

I would miss the days of riding through my Beverly Hills neighborhood with the sunroof open and my tinted windows down, hair blowing in the wind while people looked at me like they couldn't imagine that I was actually their neighbor. Now that I would be living in a city with more modes of public transportation than days in a week, I had no need for my luxurious birthday ride.

That's how I ended up rolling in the passenger side of Nikki's SUV praying that I wouldn't miss my flight and listening to tales from her encounter the previous night. Her long-time secret crush made an appearance at my going-away party and, per the usual, they were pretending like they were not checking for each other. But to my surprise, her crush decided to step it up.

"Scottie, I was in complete shock. I knew that he had a lil' gangsta in him, but I never woulda thought that he would follow me into the ladies room." Nikki shifted her eyes to me. "He took control and pinned me up against the stall. Then he looked into my eyes as if to dare me to say stop. His kiss was so intense that I had no choice but to kiss the mothafucka back!"

"Oh whatever! Don't front. You would have kissed him back regardless," I screeched with excitement.

"True," Nikki conceded.

"Was it good? Was it everything you fantasized about?"

"Uh, who said that I fantasized about that?"

I had to give her the side eye because I knew and she knew that she had whipped up a fantasy or two at some point.

"Anyway," Nikki said with a giggle, "good is an understatement. I couldn't have dreamed up a better scenario. The shit only got better!"

"Shut up!"

"The next thing I knew, our hands were touching places on each other that I didn't even know could make me feel that good." Nikki slapped me a high-five. "You know me, I go commando on any given Sunday, and not knowing this, he grabbed my dress and hiked it up leaving me totally exposed and secretly loving it! The bathroom was a bit dark, but I was able to see all of our movements in the mirror behind him, which turned me on even more."

"You little freak nasty!"

"Don't judge."

"Hush and finish the story," I demanded.

"Once he lifted my dress, it was a wrap and I did not object."

My mouth dropped open. "Wait, so you guys got busy in the restroom?"

"If you felt what I felt, you would have done the exact same thing, girl."

Nikki was right. I loved the idea of undeniable passion, and I was definitely a sucker for a man who knew exactly when and how to take control.

"So now what?" I asked.

"Afterwards, we made a quick exit and went back to my place. We finished what we started five times over!"

"Stop lying!" I said with a laugh.

"Naw, girl. As for what's next, we'll see," Nikki said, not even holding back her grin. "Only time can tell, but right now I know that he's still laying in my bed and I would be snuggled up with him if I didn't have to chauffeur your ass around."

"Well damn, I'll miss you too," I said.

"I'm playing. You know I love you. Now get out and get New York ready for my return!"

Before I knew it, we were pulling up to the airport. I was so caught up in Nikki's story that I didn't realize we were making record time. I wondered if she was using her turbo speed to ensure that I made my flight or to get back to the naked man waiting in her bed.

We smiled at each other. I would miss having scandalous chat sessions with my girl in person. Given her frequent trips to visit her many "Lil' Daddies" in the city, I knew that I would see her soon enough.

I gave my girl a big hug, hopped out of her ride, hastily dragged my bags out of the trunk, in an effort to make a mad dash for the ticket counter. There was just one problem. How the hell was I going to manage with three suitcases that felt like body bags? I had no choice; Nikki kept an eye on my bags while I ventured over to get a tourist luggage cart.

After paying what seemed like my life's savings in luggage overage charges, I was finally on my way to my gate. My big move was really happening and it felt more real than ever. I was nervous, scared, and excited all at the same time, so I did what I always do: dialed up my Jolie.

My Jolie had always been like a best friend and a confidante. Sometimes mother and daughter relationships could be trying, but I couldn't ever recall a time, from youth to young adulthood, where she and I had a conflict or a fight. She was always very straightforward and honest. That transparency nurtured a positive relationship. The day that she found out that she was pregnant with my younger brother, she sat me down on the bottom bunk of my bed—the "My Little Pony" characters staring up at me from my comforter—for a girl's chat.

My mother said, "I want you to know that I'm having a baby, and when the baby comes things are going to seem a bit different at first. But I really want you to understand that I love you, cherish you, and I'll always be *your* mom."

I didn't quite understand the change she was talking about, but from that moment on, she became *my* Jolie.

My Jolie was hands down one of the coolest mothers a girl

could ever have. She was always understanding and respectful of my decisions, which translated into her being very supportive. When I made the announcement that I was moving to New York, she didn't give me any drama about not wanting me to go. I'm sure that a piece of her was scared as hell for her oldest child and only daughter to pick up and move across the country, especially with all of those potentially crazy people that she watched on *Law and Order: SVU* every week. But she masked her fear so that I could do what my heart desired.

"Hi, my Jolie." I could sense her smiling as if she had been waiting for this call.

"Baby, don't be nervous." Her words were comforting. "This is your time for a fresh start. Enjoy the new experiences."

"You always know what to say." I smiled. "I love you."

"I love you too, baby."

I made it to the gate without a moment to spare. The ticket agent clicked the boarding passes under the scanner like rapid fire, and my heart was racing as I continued inching forward in line. I had to tinkle, but I figured it was my nerves. That was pretty standard when my anxiety kicked in. But there was no time for hesitation or bathroom breaks, no time for second thoughts or an emotional breakdown, which was probably best because my track record as a crybaby would almost guarantee a waterworks show.

Instead, I click-clacked down the runway corridor in my heels and dug through my ridiculously big purse to check my phone one last time as I headed toward the airplane. Devin, my girl from college and also a member of The Clique, had texted me, "Hey chick! Can't wait until you touch down! Safe travels." She was my soon-to-be new roommate and sole friend in New York. I looked at my boarding pass with a sense of disbelief. And I whispered, "I'm finally on my way."

Chapter 2

Jungle Dreams

"Sir, honestly, if you don't stop slamming on the brakes, you're gonna smell a sour stench coming from the back of your cab."

The cabby responded with a loud silence and a glare in the rearview mirror.

Did this idiot just look at me like I was crazy? As long as he stopped the madness that he was attempting to pass off as driving, we would be cool. On the positive side, he seemed to be going the right way, according to my MapQuest directions. It didn't appear that he was attempting to go off course and take me to some deserted warehouse to lock me in a dungeon as his sex slave like Liam Neeson's daughter in *Taken*.

I had traveled to New York quite a few times before I decided to make the move, so I wasn't a complete newbie to the city. My first visit was through an internship program and that's when I fell in love. I got a high from the hustle and bustle. I was drawn in by the feelings of excitement and independence that I gleaned from roaming the streets.

My decision to move to New York was solidified a few months back while on a trip visiting the city with Dev. We both wanted a drastic change. She found a job and moved into temporary housing a month before my arrival, so naturally she did all of the research in finding a suitable apartment for us to share. Although our plan was to live in Manhattan, it was crazy expensive, so she found what she described as the best place she'd seen in her hunt for an apartment…right across the river…in New Jersey.

My Los Angeles apartment was a spacious studio in Beverly Hills that I lucked up on through a friend. I had not lived with a roommate in years. It was going to be interesting to see how things would work since past roommate situations had always ended in drama. My fingers were crossed. Regardless, I was about to embark on the biggest journey of my life, and I was quickly approaching Dev and our new place.

The cab driver zoomed down a street lined with apartments and homes on one side and the Hudson River flanked by the Manhattan skyline on the other side. I had a sudden urge to squeal with excitement. This was hot! I felt like I was in *Sex in the City* except on the other side of the river. I was going to be living in an apartment with a view of Manhattan. It couldn't get much better.

While I was busy daydreaming out the window, the driver hit a sharp left turn, then a quick right, causing me to slide to the right of the backseat along with the vision of my fantasy apartment. We were no longer on the skyline street. He pulled up to a new-looking building with a top-to-bottom brick finish. I glanced down at my paper—*1721*, it had to be my new home. I got out of the yellow cab and pushed the buzzer. I heard Dev's voice. "Who is it?"

Like she was expecting a ton of people at that time of night.

"It's me."

"Hey, girl! Do you need help?" Dev yelled through the intercom.

"Uh yeah, that would be nice, boo!"

While waiting for Dev, I paid the cabby and he swiftly took off, leaving me standing on the curb with all of my belongings. I felt like Eddie Murphy in *Coming to America*.

Dev finally made her way outside, and we dragged my body bags into our new apartment.

The building had an inviting atmosphere. Neutral-colored, tile floors in the entryway, a fresh coat of warm, yellow paint on the walls and black iron accents along the corridor leading to our apartment door. From the looks of things, Dev had made a good selection—not that I ever doubted her taste.

Once inside, I realized that we really had lucked up. The apartment had stainless steel appliances, granite counter tops, and it even included a finished basement with a private patio and an additional bathroom. The spot was sick. I roamed around in awe. I quickly began to take mental notes in preparation for the sassy decor of my new boudoir.

A brand-new city, brand-new apartment, brand-new furniture—at that moment standing in my new space, my completely empty oasis, I decided that this would be the start of a brand-new me.

"What's in the pile over there?" Dev asked, as I flipped through clothes that were still in a suitcase.

"Nothing cute enough," I said. I was in search of a jazzy outfit for the evening.

"You're trippin'." Dev rolled her eyes and left me sitting on my bedroom floor surrounded by clothes.

Lucky for me, I had been blessed by the gods with the best-of-both-worlds: nice, firm breasts and a well-proportioned derrière. However, picking out the clothes that would hug my curves could sometimes cause a dilemma because I was indecisive when it came to fashions. But once they hit my five-foot-eight frame, they would always fit like a glove.

I glanced at the pile that Dev had pointed to. It was steadily growing in height next to my window. There wasn't a single thing that caught my eye. We were on our way to a cover party for *Vibe* magazine and I needed to make a statement with my outfit. After all, this was a brand-new Scottie.

Dev and I had been running nonstop since my arrival. Hence, I hadn't made time to pick up some of the essentials like clothes hangers or a winter coat. Hell, I didn't even have a bed. I had been sleeping on an air mattress for ten days. But my plan for the weekend included shopping for all of the must-haves, first and foremost a comfortable place to lie my head at night.

The city hadn't been our playground for long, but Dev connected with a new flame, Mel, whom she'd met in Washington, D.C. a few months earlier. Mel was a Queens, New York native and he certainly knew all of the hot spots in the city. Mel knew that his most desirable trait was his tendency to spend money with abandon. We began to roll with him on the regular.

"Scottie," Dev called out from her room.

"Yeah?"

"Mel called. He's about fifteen minutes away."

"Shoot!" I said to myself as I started scrambling. "Are you ready?" I asked Dev, already knowing the answer.

"You know it," she said, walking past my room to obsess over her reflection in the full-length mirror.

She was definitely ready and looking cute in a skin-tight, burgundy dress with burgundy and cream python pumps that brought her petite stature up a notch. Mel mentioned once to her that he loved to see her in dresses and that's all she needed to hear. She worked it out and showed off her best assets in a dress every time that he came around.

And then there was me. Always the last to get ready though I despised being rushed, go figure. Before Dev alerted me to the sudden need to scurry around, I was fairly close to getting it together. I'd already straightened my hair. It was full of body and flowing. The hair gods were showing me love.

I decided to rock my new dark denim skinny jeans. They were one of my latest bargain finds in SoHo. I narrowed down my options in tops to a purple silhouette blouse with gold accents, which gave me the perfect dose of cleavage to get the boys excited. My last order of business was shoes. I decided to throw on my nude pumps from Bloomies, which set my whole look off.

Before I knew it, we were strolling out of the apartment and hopping into one of Mel's many rides. He was profiling in the Infiniti G35 sedan. I jumped in the backseat and Dev followed my lead. To our surprise, there was an unannounced gentleman in the front seat.

Mel was a very quiet, mellow type of guy. So imagine my shock when we were met by the roaring sounds of his passenger's voice projecting into the backseat. He introduced himself as Mel's cousin, Que. I could tell that he was going to work my last nerve. As we headed to the city I checked him out from the side view and decided that my first impression was right. The huge Gucci sunglasses that were covering his chubby face shielded his eyes, but it was nighttime: automatic fail.

Normally when we rolled with Mel, he always had the latest music. We would vibe and have a good time, but that night we were clearly going to be subjected to the soundtrack of his cousin's yip-yapping. The guy talked nonstop. I guess he thought that the lame, flashy dialogue he offered would entice us to think that he was "the man."

He bragged about living in Miami, and asked if I wanted him to fly me out for a shopping spree, in addition to a bunch of other nonsense. He was basically trying to sell me a dream, and he was completely unaware that I was not in the market to buy bullshit.

It was music to my ears when we arrived at the club, a trendy new spot in midtown. Finally, I could escape the chatterbox and do my thing. The vibe was totally different from what I was used to in Los Angeles. Fly girls with designer outfits from head to toe, big butts, yet mediocre weaves strutting around looking pressed for the attention of overhyped block boys vying to be the next Jim Jones.

Then there were the buttoned-up "industry executives." They talked fast and played the part but could offer nothing of real substance. Either way, the excitement of it all had me at hello as I made my way through the crowd. The DJ had the party rocking, so I chatted it up with what could one day prove to be a few promising business connections. Eventually, I made my way back to where I left my crew. They were living it up. Mel, in his usual style, ordered bottle service.

I slid into the booth, intentionally not sitting next to Que since he would not stop giving me the eye. I tried to ignore him, but honestly he was starting to annoy me even more than before. Dev and Mel were in each other's space like teenagers on a first date, completely oblivious to their surroundings, but she looked happy and I was happy for her. Dev could be hard to crack for men and even harder to entertain, so Mel seemed to be doing something right.

"Are you comfortable?" Mel asked Dev.

Dev replied with a simple, "Yes."

"Do you want me to mix you a drink?" Mel asked Dev.

With a coy smile, she nodded yes. I sat back and watched this little love fest unfold. He sure didn't ask if I was comfortable or parched.

In an effort to avoid any potential awkward advances from Que, I politely excused myself from the booth and headed to the second level. I caught a glimpse of what looked like a cutie making his way up the stairs. Since I had nothing better to do, I decided to do what I did best: investigate.

He had a deep, flawless, black-onyx complexion, pearly whites, heart-melting smile, and the body of a lean, chiseled gladiator. I thought to myself, *now what the hell do you do?* He had to be a model. I'd never been the forward type—only when intoxicated—so to think that I would saunter up to a man and strike up a conversation was unlikely. I needed hints, cues of interest, a hand gesture telling me to come hither, something. So I decide to play it cool and scope him out from afar. After two whole minutes of that game, I was bored. I took a long sip of my drink and forced myself to walk into his line of sight. I felt a tap on my shoulder. I quickly snapped my neck to the right expecting to see Que the bug-a-boo, but it wasn't him.

"He's calling you," said a man wearing a hunter-green lumber-jack-esque shirt and matching hat. He informed me of something that I had clearly missed.

I gave him a puzzled look, then he pointed in the direction of my new crush. He appeared to be signaling me to come over to him. *Get it, girl!* This was not the normal way that I liked to be engaged by a man but what the hell, a brand-new city, a brand-new me. With the speed of light, I straightened up my posture, flipped my hair over my shoulder and put a swift strut in my peep-toe pumps. I made my way toward the bar where he was standing.

Anxiety filled my body at the unknown, but there was no time for fear or doubt. I was less than three feet away from saying hello to my future love, but for some reason his eyes were not exactly meeting mine as I thought they would be, or imagined they had been. I continued toward him and as I said hello and extended my hand, he reached past me. He fell into a sensuous embrace with an extremely tall brunette who had a true model figure. After their long hello, he turned to me with a puzzled look on his face and asked, "Do we know each other?" I guess he noticed me staring. The woman was standing there waiting to hear my answer as well. Hell, I was standing there waiting to hear my answer too. In a split-second decision, I determined that I would not make an even bigger ass out of myself by trying to explain this natural disaster caused by a lumberjack. I simply flashed a polite smile and made a swift exit toward the stairway.

I was humiliated. I felt like I was just written into an old episode of *Ugly Betty* as her uglier twin. The night could only get better, but I did not want to stick around and take the chance that it could get worse. When I got back to the table, I gave Dev the un-spoken signal that I was ready to go and figured I'd explain why once we got home.

On our way to the car, I secretly asked Dev if Mel was planning to drop us off at our house. She quickly assured me that he would. However, for some reason I had a strange feeling about her answer. She didn't make me feel confident in her response, but since Mel was Dev's boo, I let her take the lead and coordinate our trans-portation.

After riding for some time, I noticed that we'd left the city, which was essential to getting to our apartment in Jersey. But something was off. I wasn't a native New Yorker and I had only been living in the area for a minute, but the route definitely did not seem like the way home.

"Where are we going?" I said finally.

Mel swiftly replied, "Back to my place in Queens."

I shot Dev a glare that could have pierced through an ice sculpture had there been one in the backseat with us. She shrugged her shoulders as if she was slightly clueless and that's when I really started to get pissed. All I wanted to do was go home and be in my own space and use my own bathroom and sleep in my own makeshift bed.

"I don't feel like driving back to Jersey tonight, then going all the way back to Queens," Mel stated. "You guys can stay at my place and I'll take you home in the morning."

I sat in silence. I could not respond without rambling profanities. By that time, we were on some highway or another and basically out of the city and sure as hell out of my comfort zone, so what was I to say? I felt like I had a one-way ticket to hell.

After roughly five minutes of silence, I blurted out, "Well, do you have some place for all of us to sleep? How is this going to work?"

I knew that Mel had an extra bedroom, but in the few times that I'd gone to his place, I never saw him so much as crack the door open. It was always closed. I joked to Dev once that he was probably hiding a huge weed-growing operation.

"Don't worry, you and Dev can share my bed. Que and I will sleep on the futon." Clearly, Mel had everything preplanned and mapped out.

I thought to myself, *yeah right*. Since when have you known a grown man to give up his bed to a chick that he is trying to get with and her friend; only to have to turn around and sleep on the futon. I don't think so. At that point, all I could do was take his word for it and keep my eyes on Que who was not to be trusted.

Mel lived among a sea of apartments. Each one looked like the next. When we finally arrived at Mel's apartment door, I wanted to go to sleep as quickly as possible. Mel gave us T-shirts and shorts to sleep in and he was very hospitable. However, it didn't take long to figure out that the plans had changed yet again. Dev and I would be sleeping on the futon in the living room. After Mel gave me a blanket, I grabbed my purse, went into the bathroom and hastily changed, obviously leaving on my bra. When I climbed on the futon and into my corner for the night, I could hear Que still running his mouth and trying to get some attention. Needless to say, I had no intentions on being polite and entertaining his ass. It was four in the morning, the sun would be coming up soon and all I wanted was sleep.

The last thing that I remembered before dozing off was Dev lying on the futon next to me. Mel was sitting on the floor by Dev and they were watching TV, chatting it up about the night. I must have been extremely tired. Normally I could not fall asleep with so much activity going on.

I had been sleep for what felt like hours when all of a sudden, either I was dreaming or actually feeling hands touching me. A warm body was attempting to spoon me.

My reflexes shot into action and I jumped up. "What the hell are you doing?"

Dev and I didn't get down like that so I knew it had to be Que. I could barely make out his face in the darkness of the living room. I was instantly livid.

"Shhh! You know what's up. Why you think you here?" Que exclaimed in a hushed tone.

"You better back up off me, that's what I fucking know!"

"C'mon, girl," Que cooed.

"I don't know what you thought this was, but do not touch me." I seethed, pushing what I could of his chunky body and stubby fingers away from me.

He snatched my arm. I quickly felt his strength and the intensity of his grip.

"You acting like you don't know what the deal is," Que whispered as he grew agitated.

I had been known to talk a lot of shit and most of the time I could back it up, but to say that I was not afraid at that very moment would have been a lie. Crazy thoughts were going through my head during those few seconds: *Where the fuck is Dev? What if this drunk fool won't listen to my objections and he continues to try and force himself on me? Damn it! I don't even have my mace. Okay, I gotta pull it together and show no fear.*

"I do know what the deal is," I said, as I snatched my arm away using a thumb-breaking self-defense technique my dad had taught me. "I'm trying to sleep and I wake up to some perv trying to feel me up. I don't know you and I don't know what you think I'm about. But I'm not the bitch to be fucked with. Yo' best bet is to back yo' ass up ASAP!"

He was buying into my confident act, so I continued. "What I suggest you do is take yo' ass to sleep 'cause ain't nothing going down over here. Understood?"

I swear I tried to give him the death look that said if you touch me, I will rip your balls off and feed them to you. It must've worked because his face changed and he backed up in silence. Who knows? He had probably done this before. I guess he thought that he was going to somehow punk me into having sex with him or letting him take advantage of me, but he'd picked the wrong one on the wrong night.

To make matters worse, there was no other couch in the living room. Only some antique-looking chair that was uncomfortable to sit in, let alone sleep on.

I knew that there was no way that he would waddle his big ass over to the chair to sleep, so I informed him of my rules. "I better not feel you so much as brush up against me if you plan to stay on this futon."

He mumbled something slick under his breath before rolling over in the opposite direction. I let out a slight sigh of relief but that was the worst night's sleep I ever had. Technically, I did not sleep because I was too paranoid to actually close my eyes for more than a minute. There I was, lying in some dude's house in Queens, in a desolate area, next to his lightweight rapist cousin, who was way larger than me. I had no clue how to get home even if I said "fuck it" and left. We were miles away from any main road where I could potentially have an opportunity to flee. I faced the wall and my mind kept replaying the incident. Each time I came up with other comments that I should have or could have said. My anger forced a stream of tears to drip down the side of my face. I felt trapped, vulnerable, and violated. My legs were clutched tightly to my chest. I mapped out my plan of attack in the event that he tried again. I could not put my finger on the one thing that made me feel the most uncomfortable, but the feelings were all too familiar and I never wanted to feel like that again.

The next morning, I was mute. We piled in Mel's car around nine. I had nothing to say to anyone during the ride to Jersey, Dev included. I was beyond pissed and they must have sensed it, so everyone left me alone. When we pulled up to our apartment, I hopped out, slammed the door, and made a beeline straight for the shower. I wanted to wash that night away. I was safe, but the reality was that things could have easily taken a turn for the worst.

After my shower, I went straight to Dev's room. "So what the fuck happened last night?"

"What, what are you talking about?"

"Look, don't ever put me in a situation like that again. I trusted you to take care of things and make arrangements to get us back to the apartment, but you didn't do that. We ended up in Queens hella far out, no train station in sight, and I fall asleep with you on the futon only to wake up to Que's fucking ass trying to take advantage of me in my sleep. To top it off, he got aggressive when I rejected him. Where the hell did you go?"

Dev batted her long, black eyelashes and stared at me confused. "What do you mean?" she asked. "After you fell asleep, Mel told me to come in the room for a minute which turned into me staying in there. When I left the living room, Que was asleep in the chair."

"Well, at some point, he decided that he was going to climb on the futon with me. He tried to push up on me and then snatched my arm hella hard when I objected."

"Oh hell no, I did not know all of that." Dev folded her arms across her voluptuous chest.

"I'm sure you didn't because you were in there doing you, but that's exactly why I wanted to make sure that Mel took us or at least me home. I knew that if we stayed over his house, it would make for an uncomfortable situation for me. Maybe not for you, but for me."

"I'm so sorry, chick. I didn't know he was a creep. That was totally out of line!"

"I felt extremely uncomfortable. It was a horrible night. I basically had to lie there next to this perv, hoping that he would not try something again."

I never told Dev—frankly, I never told anyone—but there was an incident with Ivan, which was the only other time in my life when I felt sexually disgusted and violated. Que had no clue that his actions triggered negative emotions from the past.

Ivan's house was somewhat of a social hotspot. We had just come from having dinner and his roommate had a few friends over. When his place was packed with people, it was natural for us to head straight to his room. We were watching TV for a bit before deciding to get in bed.

Of course Ivan and I had a sexual relationship, but that night was different. We ended up falling asleep with the TV watching us. As usual, he woke in the middle of the night horny and looking to me to satisfy his sexual craving. His signal was always the same. He would cuddle up next to me so that I could feel his bulging penis pressing up against my lower back. Then came the touching and soft kisses. That night I did not feel like having sex. I wasn't in the mood. I was asleep and I wanted to stay that way.

They say that when you are married, sex is an obligation for a woman, but hell, we were not married and barely even dating exclusively. Our situation was complicated at all times and that night was no different. I always had my reservations about whether or not to be with him sexually. Who wants to readily give all of their self to a person sexually when that person barely acknowledges them emotionally?

The next thing I knew, we were kissing, which was by force of habit and not the excitement of passion. Ivan was clearly turned on but despite the kissing, I did not feel the same way. He had nothing but boxers on, so his fully erect penis was already peeking out of his shorts. My T-shirt had started to creep up my stomach and Ivan began to pull at my panties. Through intertwined lips I told him to stop and suggested that we go back to sleep. He kept kissing me and eventually I pulled my head away and turned my face toward the wall. I did not want to make him feel rejected, but I really did not want to have sex.

Maybe he thought that I was joking when I said no or maybe he didn't care. He was tugging at my panties, pulling them down to my knees. I squirmed and asked him to stop. Ivan began thrusting his penis inside me anyway. I could feel his manhood pounding away at me as I lay there wishing he would hurry the hell up. Soon his thrusting began to burn for the lack of moisture between my legs. It blew my mind that he could not sense that I wasn't into it. I said no several times more, but he kept pumping.

Once he was finished, his sweaty palm touched my shoulder, he kissed me on the lips, and then he rolled over. I did not feel a sense of fear, but I was definitely confused. *What just happened? Did I have sex with my lover or was I raped?* I had no clue.

I quietly crept into the master bathroom to clean myself up. Looking at my reflection in the mirror, I felt like a pitiful mess and I looked the exact same way. I wasn't battered or bruised, but my body and spirit felt abused. I didn't know what to say or do next, so I turned off the light, opened the bathroom door, and walked into the darkness to lie beside the man that suddenly felt like a stranger.

Only in the days that passed did I realize that I had, in fact, been raped. It stayed with me tucked away in a tiny dark corner of my soul. I was confused because I still had feelings for Ivan. I never told my girls from The Clique because I felt silly and I did not want them to judge my relationship. Essentially, I blocked it from the forefront of my thoughts. After a few weeks, I guess you could say I acted as if I'd gotten over it, but I promised myself that, if I could help it, I would never let anything like that happen to me again.

Chapter 3

New Life

The morning of my first day in the New York PR office, I was a nervous wreck, but I tried to play it cool. *Am I ready for the hustle and bustle of the city? Will I get on the right train and get off at the right stop? Will my new colleagues like me?*

Eighth Avenue and Fiftieth Street was my destination. I had to hop on the New Jersey Transit, then transfer to the C train at the Port Authority terminal in the city. I'd been haunted by dreams of riding the subway. In California, the closest I'd been to taking public transportation was the occasional bus ride in junior high. The overall concept was basically foreign to me.

I finally made it to the C train. Once I stepped inside the train car, I felt like the other passengers could sense my insecurity. I felt as though they were looking at me like I didn't know where I was going. In reality, they probably couldn't have cared less about my insecurities and didn't even notice me.

I could hear Mary J. Blige blasting from the earphones of the hefty woman in hospital scrubs sitting beside me. I started to jam along to her music until I realized that I looked like an idiot. However, I would have been in good company since the man sitting directly across from me in the cramped, bench-style seating started showing his ass. Out of the relative silence on a crowded morning train, he started rapping what seemed like an impromptu performance of the most vulgar, explicit, and raunchy lyrics that his simple, ignorant brain could think up. I knew rap, and this man's foolish nonsense came straight from his personal collection of bad rhymes. After the initial shock wore off, it was almost hilarious how serious he was about the crap he was spewing.

I casually looked around the train car to gauge the reactions of other passengers. Most people totally ignored him. Their facial expressions remained stoic. That must have been a sign that you were a true New Yorker. Thankfully, the train started to slow down. It was so crowded that I was having a hard time seeing the signs at each stop. I shifted my body and leaned my head to the right in order to peek through the people that were standing. I could see enough to figure out that it was my time to depart this unsolicited show. I exited stage left of the train car.

After navigating my way through the massive complex of buildings, I finally found the entrance for my office building. It was nothing spectacular and quite frankly, it looked like my co-workers had been working out of a temporary space. No décor on the walls, a drab paint job, and standard light-brown, yucky indoor/outdoor carpeting. Little did I know this would be even more temporary for me than it seemed. My first meeting of the day was with my new manager, Barbra. She was oddly petite, super chic, and wore red, cat-eye frames. I admired her bold style. I'd met her once before when she briefly came through the Los Angeles office on business.

The new situation was a complete contrast from my former manager in Los Angeles who turned out to be an insecure bitch who carried herself like a mix between a frumpy Wicked Witch of the West and a homely, wannabe, redheaded version of Carrie Bradshaw. She was a sad sight.

The Los Angeles Hollywood entertainment scene was large but small at the same time. I'd heard outrageous stories about my old manager before deciding to work with her. She used to fight with her subordinates, even going so far as to have screaming matches, which is completely unprofessional. But I needed the experience the job offered and I was up for the challenge. I gave my all on the job, following the lead of my Jolie. But the one thing that I would never do was allow myself to be disrespected.

I managed to do my work, fly under the drama radar, and stick it out in the Los Angeles office long enough for my boss to go on an unexpected leave of absence. That's when I saw my opportunity to flee to the New York office. And I took it. The Wicked Witch of the West wasn't around to object to my transfer request.

Before my departure to New York, I was in the office working on a project when one of the partners in the agency called in from the road. He needed a favor. This was typical since he was rarely ever in the office. He asked that I go into his office and retrieve specific information from his computer. I thought nothing of it and gladly agreed. He gave me his password and told me to call him back once I had the information. I rushed into his massive corner office with floor-to-ceiling windows and sat at his spacious, modern, glass desk to retrieve the files. I phoned him from his desk and supplied the information requested.

When I hung up the phone, I clicked on the start menu to log out of his computer, but my curiosity got the better of me. *I wonder what that wicked witch has been saying about me?* My boss was a habitual shit talker.

I had great intuition and when I followed it, I was never steered wrong. At that moment, alone in the partner's office, it was all too easy. His email inbox was already open, so I hit the search button and began to look through the emails that were from my manager. I was on edge and my eyes were scanning the screen at a rapid pace. Any one of my coworkers could've walked in without notice and caught me in the act.

My hands were slightly shaking, but I clicked through as much information as I could as fast as I could, skimming through the emails that caught my attention. It didn't take long to find what I was looking for. What I read blew my mind! The woman was crazy and insecure, but I did not know that she was actually out to sabotage me.

The first email, from only two days prior, read: "So now you are letting her transfer to New York. I thought that you were going to fire that bitch?" *She actually referred to me as a bitch!* I was in shock. His response, "If she requested to go, then I'm going to let her go. We can take care of everything else later."

This was my first lesson in how truly treacherous and foul people can be in the business world—especially in entertainment. Oftentimes, it's not about the work that you do. It's about how much ass you kiss to make people like you.

I finished scanning a few more scandalous email messages and ultimately read enough to know that my time at the agency was coming to an end. I was fine with moving on as long as I made my way to New York first. I knew I could brace myself for whatever came later. But first things first; I had the New York office to deal with.

After enduring a few more meetings on my first day, it was time to head to happy hour with Dev. We'd heard about a sexy spot in SoHo with great drink specials and yummy-looking men. Dev and I linked up at the N train in midtown and headed downtown to see what type of shenanigans we could get into.

The walk from the train station to the lounge wasn't too bad. I was still trying to get used to all of the walking required in the city.

Before we approached the lounge, I shook my head and finished touching up my nude lip-gloss. Dev shimmied down the street in her four-inch stilettos adjusting her tight, royal blue pencil skirt while simultaneously tousling the front of her shiny black asymmetrical bob. Dev was a trip. She loved to get dolled up every single day. Me, on the other hand, since I've always worked in entertainment, dressing in corporate attire had never been my thing. I simply dressed according to my mood. Sometimes I would feel like rocking a cute little black dress and "come fuck me heels." But the very next day I could be on my B-girl swag with a sexy pair of skinny jeans and some fly, limited-edition kicks. Either way, I would still feel as sexy as the next chick.

The scene in the lounge was inviting. The candlelit tables were filled with men and women who wanted to see and be seen. My girls were propped up nicely, and I was ready to mingle.

Dev and I headed to the bar in the rear. I set my sights on a seat next to a well-dressed man with a lean, basketball build. I walked up and tapped the gentleman on the shoulder. He spun around and my face turned into absolute shock. They must have deleted the dental plan from his benefits package because this man's teeth were jacked up.

I can deal with dudes of all sizes and complexions, so long as they are taller than me and have good teeth. But this guy's grill was crisscrossing with a few teeth running to the left and the others fleeing to the right. "Oh hell no!"

"Excuse me?" he said.

He was confused. I had tapped him to get his attention, but I didn't realize that I had blurted out what I was thinking. Some-times my face would say what I was thinking, but this time my vocal cords backed it up.

I cleared my throat and managed to mumble, "Is this seat taken?"

With an agitated look on his face, he shook his head, and I politely slid onto the stool.

When I looked over at Dev, she had the stupidest look sprawled across her face. I could tell that it was taking everything in her power not to burst out into a roar of laughter. I gave her the squinted evil eye and proceeded to order a drink, which I desper-ately needed.

The music was so loud that I unintentionally yelled at the bartender, "May I have a glass of Riesling, please?! Actually, make it a double!"

Dev finished up her conversation with a possible suitor, then met me at the bar. We were swapping stories about our day and gossiping a bit when we noticed a young lady who seemed out of place looking suspiciously in our direction as she walked across the room. Her tan Timberland boots let me know that she was at the wrong happy hour. She was glaring with disdain like one of us had stolen her man. Dev and I looked at each other puzzled. We didn't know many people in the city and we definitely didn't know her. The woman finally looked away once she realized that we were staring back at her. We dismissed her petty antics and continued our conversation.

After a few cocktails, Dev and I decided to head to another spot since the night was still young. It was a Tuesday and my first day of work in the city was complete. I was feeling light as a feather and carefree. We were walking down the sidewalk pointing out silly observations and giggling when I suggested we hail a yellow cab. As the cabby sped off, Dev and I flew back in our seats trying to ramble off our destination. The cabby was driving like he was in the Indy 500. "Can we please make it to our destination alive?" I whispered to Dev.

No sooner than the words left my lips our cab swerved. The sound of tires screeching rang out. Our driver had cut off another yellow cab. Thankfully the other driver had reacted quickly to avoid smashing into us. The profanities and yelling started almost instantaneously—right after the radical horn blowing.

The driver that our cabby cut off was now on the side of us, my side to be exact, and he was furious. He looked like a sixty-year-old grandfather that should not be cursing like a lunatic. He rolled down his window and started screaming at our driver in a language that I could not understand. There was only one word that I did recognize: "Motherfucker!"

They are making me lose my buzz.

Our driver yelled back. He had some nerve, considering that it was his fault.

Suddenly we felt our cab shift erratically to the right and "BOOM!" Our driver smashed up against the other cab and swiped his side mirror off. Fragments of mirrored glass and yellow plastic went flying.

"What the hell is wrong with you?!" Dev shouted. "Stop this damn cab right now and let us out!"

"You must have lost your damn mind!" I chimed in.

"But…miss…did you see him? I apologize, miss. I apologize," the driver pleaded.

"Oh no, it's way too late for that!" Dev shouted.

We jumped out of the cab, slamming the door behind us. If that reject thought that he would get a single cent from us, he was sadly mistaken. Like Thelma and Louise, we walked away from the scene of the crime and never looked back. We let the cabby's fussing and yelling fade in the distance.

That debacle was almost enough to stop our fun for the night. But we were getting used to the crazy happenings in the New York streets. Instead of going home, we quickened our strides with the frigid winter air whipping against our cheeks. Our destination was only a few blocks away at an underground spot Dev's hairdresser had told her about. Questlove of The Roots was DJing.

New York was known for having its hidden gems, so we giddily walked down an unassuming street on the Lower East Side looking for a red door. When we walked up to the mystery door, Dev tugged at the handle with a bit of hesitation. We crossed the threshold and it was as if we had entered a different world. Black velvet lined the walls and a "barely there" light fixture gave the doorman *just* enough glow to check our IDs. After he signaled the thumbs-up, we hit the stairs heading down into the abyss. The spot was small and crazy crowded, but the scene was dope, and the secret underground feeling gave me a rush.

Casually pushing my way through the crowd, I spotted a tall, clean-cut Idris Elba look-alike heading in my direction. He looked fly so naturally I wanted to see how he moved. I posted up on the wall and watched him work.

He walked through the room with a sense of confidence that I was definitely digging. I saw him speak to a few people, both male and female, but it was obvious that he was rolling solo. Showed independence, I liked that. Never one to seem pressed, I inadvertently glanced in his direction. Not to my surprise, he was looking in my direction as well. I was standing next to an oversized gold Buddha—don't ask—and we caught eyes. Of course, this was not a love-at-first-sight type of situation, but he had my attention and I hoped that I had his. In any event, I would not be a fool again and walk up to some strange man in a club thinking that he was looking in my direction.

Dev and I grabbed drinks and mingled throughout the scene. I met some interesting people. A part-time DJ and dog walker, a girl who was out with her friends because she just broke up with her boyfriend Gino, and last but certainly not least, the Idris Elba look-alike named Kari.

Kari was super sexy and there was no denying it. Through our conversation, I learned that he was around my age, worked in midtown as a publicist—crazy coincidence—and he was born and raised in Brooklyn.

He fidgeted with his black, button-down shirt as he cracked corny jokes and talked about his love for travel. Beyond the physical, I thought he was endearing.

We both scanned the room and bobbed our heads to the music. I tried not to stare at him when he wasn't looking.

"So did you leave a man back in California?" he asked after a long stretch of silence.

His chocolate, flawless complexion and sensual, brown eyes had me mesmerized. "Well, uh, I wasn't really…short answer, no." I didn't expect that question and I had begun fidgeting myself.

"Perfect. So can I take you out sometime?"

I was concentrated on his full, kissable lips, but I managed to respond, "I'd like that."

"Are you available Thursday after work?" he inquired, looming over me roughly at six feet two with excellent posture.

"Yeah, I'm free." I was definitely intrigued by Mr. Kari.

Normally you had to play the game of giving a guy your number, then he would wait the obligatory two days to call, only to end up playing a game of phone or text tag. Then you finally established firm plans for a date roughly two weeks later, only to realize that he wasn't as cute or interesting as you remembered. It could really be a waste of your time. So Kari was an introduction to a new way of doing things. Like I said: brand-new city, brand-new me.

Chapter 4

New Lust

To my surprise, the next morning I received a text message from Kari. This naturally made me smile like a kindergartner with a cookie. But a million thoughts also went through my head. I was used to the typical Los Angeles men who played entirely too many games and almost acted as if you were supposed to chase them. Despite my reservations, the new approach from Kari was refreshing.

I responded to his message with a safe, "Morning, sunshine." He wished me a lovely day and that was the end of the communication—which was fine with me. Sometimes too much too soon could be a bad thing.

Admittedly, my day was a bit brighter since I had someone handsome to daydream about. New like was always the best phase in a relationship. You're in a state of endless possibilities. You could create whatever story, fantasy, or background you wanted to dream up because you hadn't had the opportunity to experience the new person.

"Scottie!"

I was quickly snapped out of my thoughts.

"Have you had a chance to start working on the RSVP rundown for the Sting event?"

It was Barbra, my manager.

"Yes," I said, suddenly alert. "I've established the email address and drafted the copy. I'll email you the copy for review right now."

"Perfect! Thanks, hun!"

Barbra was so cheerful, it seemed as though she didn't have a care in the world.

I was actually excited about working the Sting fundraising concert. It was my first event in the city and it was at an amazing loft space in Tribeca. I had worked plenty of events in Los Angeles, but I wasn't quite sure what to expect from the New York scene.

As I clicked back into the screen with my personal email open, an Instant Message popped up. My heart paused. It was Ivan. I had forgotten to block him.

11:02 AM IVANdaMan: What's up? How is New York treating you?

11:07 AM SassyScottT: Great so far.

11:08 AM IVANdaMan: So why did you leave me?

11:08 AM SassyScottT: Contrary to YOUR popular belief, not everything is about you, Ivan.

11:10 AM VANdaMan: You know what I mean. You know that I really did want to be with you.

11:11 AM SassyScottT: How many times have we been through this?

11:11 AM SassyScottT: I'm gone now and you were never willing to give me what I wanted or needed so I moved on.

11:12 AM IVANdaMan: But you had to move so far away?

11:13 AM SassyScottT: Absolutely.

There was a long pause in the conversation. My stomach was in knots and my silk blouse suddenly started clinging to my body in what felt like a restrictive hold. My temperature had risen and sweat beads were forming on my neck. I could only imagine that he was trying to decide what to say next. I repeated to myself over and over, *whatever he has to say it does not really matter.* My life was moving on and his problem was that he thought I would be around forever for him to string along, but I got smart and got out.

11:20 AM IVANdaMan: Well, I guess there is nothing left for me to say.

11:21 AM SassyScottT: Take care, Ivan.

On the outside, I tried to act tough like I was happy not having Ivan in my life, but if I were to be honest, it hurt. Of course I thought about him. I remembered the fun times and I fantasized about what it would have been like if he had stepped up to be the man I wanted him to be. I probably wouldn't have moved to New York. I was fully aware that in leaving Los Angeles, I was running from my past and trying to start over with a clean slate. Maybe I'd admit it to him one day, but for now I'd chat with Dev.

I grabbed my cell and went to the lobby downstairs to call Dev's office. She worked as a buyer in women's apparel. It was the perfect job for her since she could out-shop Ivana Trump. I felt sorry for her husband-to-be.

Dev was normally pretty accessible on instant messenger, but this warranted a phone call and I didn't want my new coworkers all in my business. The phone only rang once. "Devin speaking.

"Guess who just hit me up?"

"Who, Scottie?" Dev quickly responded.

"Ivan," I snapped.

"What the heck did he want? What did he call to say?"

"He didn't call. You know he could never bring himself to do that. He popped up on IM asking why I left and as usual, making it about him. I shut him down and quickly ended the conversation."

"What does he want from you at this point? Chick, you should have blocked his butt," Dev said, with a devious laugh.

"I thought the same thing, a moment too late, though."

"Don't let it worry you. He is trying to stay relevant in your thoughts and in your heart, so don't play into it. You did the right thing by not letting the conversation drag on."

"Yeah, you're right," I responded.

Dev was the listener in The Clique so when she spoke, I listened. The four friends and I that comprised The Clique had been hanging together since our college days rolling around the malls of Southern California luring in cuties. We fell into each other's worlds in school and remained tight like sisters. Everyone played a role. Dev was the mellow, easygoing one and I was the sassy one. According to our friends, I always offered my unsolicited advice and opinion. I accepted that as essentially an accurate assessment, so I owned it.

After Dev's pep talk, I decided to reach out to Kari. Even though we had exchanged text messages a few hours earlier—and I potentially ran the risk of looking pressed—I wanted to hear his voice. I needed to see if a simple phone interaction with him could help push Ivan out of my mind.

As the phone began to ring, my heart simultaneously started to pound. *Is it too late to hang up? Shit, my number probably already popped up on the caller ID. Suck it up, girl.*

A strong baritone voice was music to my ears. "Hey, Scottie."

"Hi, Kari. Did I catch you at a bad time?"

"No, no, not at all. It's nice to hear your voice."

He invited the conversation so I continued. "I had a moment to spare, so I thought that I'd give you a call."

"I like that. So are we still on for Thursday?"

"Definitely...yes...yes, we are."

There was a brief moment of silence, so I decided to end the call on a high note. "Well, I'm about to run into a meeting so I'll talk to you later, okay?"

"Go handle your business. I'll see you soon."

Having been knee-deep in site visits, press releases, media advisories, and guest lists, all in preparation for the Sting event, I did not have time to get nervous for my date with Kari. He reached out Thursday morning and let me know the exact time and location of our date. His grown man-style was really winning me over. I guessed it was time-out for the boys, and game-on for the men.

I walked up to Fig & Olive in the meatpacking district rocking peach-colored skinny jeans that highlighted all the right areas of the hips and butt for prime male observation. My light-blue, jean-distressed sweetheart corset top with the peplum waist gave my girls the platform that they needed to be on display. My favorite necklace of the moment was chunky and gold, so I mixed in a few delicate gold bangles with a splash of ivory accessories to balance my look.

As my steps brought me closer and closer to the restaurant, I started to slightly panic. *What will I say? How will I greet him? How will he greet me? Will he be as charming as he seemed upon our first meeting? Does he have a girlfriend?*

"Oh shit, I didn't ask." I had to pull it together because now the thoughts were rattling aloud and I probably looked like the crazy lady walking down the street talking to herself.

I arrived at the front entrance of the restaurant, hand on the handle, no choice but to go forward. I walked inside the establishment where a pleasant young man with black thick-rimmed stylish glasses greeted me. He had a slim build with a very structured yet edgy haircut. He must have been an aspiring actor or maybe even a model since he was gorgeous. I informed him that I was there for a 7:30 reservation. "Mr. Kari's party?" he said.

"Yes," I said politely, trying to mask my face from revealing what I was thinking. *How do you know? Does he bring all of his dates here? Is he a regular?*

The host showed me to a cozy booth big enough for two. It was near the front window of the restaurant. Kari stepped out of the booth, greeted me with a smile, a sweet hello, and a pleasant hug. His cologne smelled amazing, but I tried to play it cool.

As I sat down, I glanced over. Kari was clearly getting a better look at me outside of the dungeon club lighting where we had met. Normally, this would have made me a bit shy, but for some reason, I instantly felt comfortable around him.

"Glad that you found the place okay."

"Thanks to your precise directions."

We smiled at each other. *Taking the care to give a woman excellent directions. Was that the New York equivalent to picking a lady up in your car?*

"You have amazing eyes," Kari commented.

I was hoping that I didn't blush. "Thank you."

"Are they gray?"

"Yes, my Jolie, I mean my mom, says that I get them from my great-grandmother."

Not wanting to talk about myself too much, I quickly changed the subject, though I didn't know what to say. "I love the décor in this place. Very light yet comforting."

"I'm glad that you like it. The restaurant is actually one of my clients', so I frequently have meetings here and everyone seems to love it. I don't regularly mix business with pleasure, but I thought that you'd like it, being that you are new to the city."

"Well, I definitely appreciate your thoughtfulness."

Kari nodded and grinned. "So how was your day?"

Interesting, he wasn't quick to revel me with the tales of his day before asking a word about mine. Kari and I chatted for hours while nibbling on appetizers of samosas and tiger shrimp. We feasted on delicious seared salmon and grilled lamb chop entrees. Kari's drink of choice was Scotch on the rocks. I kept it simple and sipped Chardonnay.

After an excellent dinner and unlimited, engaging conversation, we had a brief moment of intense silence as we stared into each other's eyes. I caught myself and blurted out an awkward, "We should probably go."

As we exited the restaurant, he hailed a cab for me. Standing on the curb, I thought to myself that I could get into this guy. He was sweet, attentive, charming and he knew how to take control. *He is probably nicknamed the "panty dropper,"* I thought to myself as he gave me a soft kiss on the cheek accompanied by a firm hug goodnight. I slid into the cab and he closed the door.

As the cabby sped up Eighth Avenue toward the Port Authority bus station, I thought about Kari. I felt that tingle in my stomach and a slight sweet feeling between my legs. Being so high off of my date, the hassle of hopping on the New Jersey Transit and rolling through the Lincoln Tunnel to finally arrive at home almost an hour later did not bother me in the slightest. I fantasized my way across the river. I swore that I could still smell the sandalwood hints from his cologne lingering on my new coat.

Chapter 5

Hidden Gem

The Sting fundraiser was set to start in a few hours and we had just finished the final walk-through when my phone buzzed. I never kept my phone on ring at work because the excessive noise was simply rude.

I glanced down to see Kari's name on my screen. My stomach started to get the jitters. His text message was sweet: *"Just wanted to wish you a successful event tonight. Hope all is well."*

I wasn't sure if it was game. But whatever his angle, he was good. Remembering about my first big event in the city spoke volumes. That sweet and simple message was all that I needed to put an extra pep in my step and knock out a crazy fabulous event. The red carpet was jam-packed with an eclectic mix of celebrities, from Sting himself to Russell Simmons and supermodel Petra Nemcova. One of the main stars from *The Wire*, Omar, was also in the house and I liked his style. He was a very humble man.

When the concert started, I decided to duck off to the restroom for a moment of peace. I made my way through the crowded venue and began walking down an empty hallway. It was strangely dark. *Maybe one of the lights blew out.* Suddenly I felt a slight pull at my wrist. A million things ran through my mind before I could turn to acknowledge what was happening. I was freaked out—likely because I had been watching way too much *Law & Order*. *Was I about to get attacked in public at an event? Scottie! Remember the self-defense moves that Dad taught you. Where should I aim first? The groin or the eyes.*

I quickly snapped back into reality and spun around in a flash. I heard the sound of a man's voice mid-spin. *Where is my mace? This is the second time!* As I was about to scream, the shadow in the corner grabbed me and put his hand over my mouth in one swift motion like a skilled ninja. My body completely tensed up and I was ready to piss on myself. Then he said my name. *Oh shit! A stalker, already?* The voice in the dark was damn near breathing on me and it sounded vaguely familiar.

We were so close now that I could smell him. He didn't smell like a killer. He took his hand away from my mouth and I turned, then backed up to get a better look, as well as a head start if I needed to run. Just then, I realized that it was Kari. I felt slightly calmer as my eyes adjusted to the darkness. The height, the silhouette, the voice, and the cologne all seemed about right. Then finally, once he realized that I had actually been terrified, he said, "Scottie, it's me, Kari."

If I hadn't been feeling him, I would have tried my best to beat him senseless. Before the curse words could leave my mouth, his breath was flowing in and his lips were covering mine.

"I hope I didn't startle you too badly," he whispered. "My friend had a plus-one at the last minute and I wanted to see you. I thought that I would surprise you."

A nice big hello in an adequately lit section of the venue would have been sufficient too. But hell, who was I kidding? Now that I knew I wasn't in danger, his approach was kind of spontaneous and sexy.

He grabbed my waist and slowly moved in to kiss my lips for a second time. We stood in the corner kissing like two high school kids at a dance. In my wildest daydreams, I could not have imagined that he would show up at my event, let alone take control of me. I was turned on and soaking in every moment.

I stopped kissing back when I heard the clicking of high-heels approaching rapidly. I saw out of the corner of my eye that it was Barbra passing by in a hurried state. Luckily, we were tucked away in the dark.

"Oh shit!" I said after she passed.

Kari had no clue who Barbra was, but I was nervous inside. All I needed was my manager to catch me playing kissy face while I was supposed to be working my very first event on her team.

"That was my manager!" I said frantically, "I hope to hell she didn't see me."

In a surprisingly calm tone, Kari said, "She barely even looked this way. I'm sure you're fine."

I gave Kari a quick peck on the lips and told him that I would catch up with him a little later.

I went back to the party and all seemed to be going well. Drinks were flowing, the concert was still raging on, and the client was visibly pleased. I caught up with Barbra to check in and to gauge her mood to see if she had seen what I was up to.

She asked me to walk with her to the green room to help facilitate a few interviews for Sting. As we headed toward the backstage area, there appeared to be no tension in her demeanor so I was in the clear.

After fifteen minutes of media interviews, Barbra dismissed the team and we were free to enjoy the remainder of the party. I texted Kari to see if he'd left.

"*Waiting on you, beautiful,*" was his reply. "*I'm by the bar if you want me.*"

I could feel my cheeks turning red. Normally, I would have

deemed his response majorly corny, but I guess with a new life and a new lust, I was feeling it. Hell, I decided before I left for New York that I was throwing my normal caution to the wind and going with the flow. The text was clearly a call to action so what else could I do? I had to step it up and put on my big girl panties.

Kari was facing my direction looking suave and edible when I spotted him. He extended his hand to pull me into his personal space. Our eyes were entranced as we leaned against the bar. The rays of physical attraction were shooting beams of horny all throughout the atmosphere.

I looked at the bartender. "May I have a Scotch on the rocks for the gentleman and a glass of Riesling for me, please?"

"I thought you didn't drink at work events?" Kari asked with a smirk.

Oh, I'm drinking tonight.

"I'm only having one glass. It's about moderation," I rationalized with a smile. I had a new life, a new lust, and a new me.

I had to text Dev to see where she was. If I brought Kari home, she couldn't be there. That would mess up all of my first-time sexy time with him.

Dev hit me back quickly with an "out of office" reply, a good sign that Kari and I would have the place all to ourselves. It was no mystery that she was likely with Mel. I was so excited to get my freak on with Kari that I almost busted out into the Cabbage Patch.

We were finishing up our drinks when Kari gently touched my face and asked if I was ready. I could feel the rush of wetness hit my panties as I struggled to reply. He took my hand in his and we made a beeline for the exit.

The cold air hit my face and that was exactly the slap I needed to calm my ass down. Kari mentioned that he drove into the city so we headed for his car. I was so hyped and ready to go that if he played his cards right, we might have gotten busy in the middle of the parking garage.

The music was on in the car, but it was really for background noise. We chatted nonstop until Kari hit a straightaway. That's when he firmly placed his hand on my knee. His manly touch slowly ran up my inner thigh, hiking my dress up in the process.

Kari continued to caress my inner thigh, teasing me. His fingers ever so slightly grazed my sweet spot and I could feel my pressure rising. I started to pant softly from the anticipation. Then he cupped his hand in between my legs, gripping my moist panties as he looked at me with a slight smile. He knew he had me.

Moving my panties to the side, Kari slid his fingers into my slippery warmth. It felt so good. I began to moan from the rubbing, touching, and moving of his fingers in and out. I yearned to know what this man had in store for me.

He leaned over and kissed me on the cheek. I slowly opened my eyes. I wasn't sleep, but it felt like I was in a dream state and I hadn't noticed that we had gotten off at my exit. After a few turns, we pulled up to the apartment and Kari unbuckled my seat belt before placing his soft lips on me again.

Once we made it inside my apartment, our hands were scouring each other's bodies searching for everything yet nothing in particular. I opened his shirt, exposing his bare chest. His physique was something to savor. Kari's skin was extremely soft and his chest surprisingly smooth, I wondered if he got it waxed.

Those thoughts quickly went away as he pushed me up against the wall and put his lips on mine, sucking deep and almost taking my breath away. His strength and control was sexy. His large hand cupped my ass perfectly. We moved onto the couch where he laid me on my back and began kissing on my breasts.

"Aaaah!" I squealed. My nerves had karate-chopped me in the stomach and suddenly I had to shit!

Oh no! I can't be this scared. I want this. No, I really do. I actually want this. What's wrong with me?

I felt my stomach rumbling and my insides churning. I hoped that Kari couldn't hear what I was feeling.

Was it something I ate at the party?

He was kissing on my neck and it felt amazing, but my sensations were conflicted. This was not good timing!

What am I supposed to do? I have to go now before I embarrass myself even more.

I jumped off the couch and ran toward the downstairs bathroom yelling, "I'll be right back!"

I almost missed the last step and busted my ass in the darkness because I was moving so fast, but it was a 9-1-1 situation. The only thing flashing in my head was *WARNING! WARNING! YOU ARE ABOUT TO SHIT ON YOURSELF, SCOTTIE!* I slid into the bathroom just in time.

I sat on that toilet for what felt like a century when you have a sexy new lover waiting. I prayed that he didn't get spooked and leave.

By the time I emerged from the bathroom and headed back upstairs, Kari was sitting on the couch watching TV. He had the dumbest look on his face, but he did not say a word. He opened his arms as I walked over to him. I laid my head on his chest and that's how we fell asleep, in each other's arms.

During the wee hours of the morning, he woke me to say that he was heading home to get ready for work. He kissed me softly on the lips and walked out the door.

Chapter 6

High Life

Dev and I were obsessed with roaming the streets of the city shopping and exploring hidden gems. From macaroon cafes to underground spoken word poetry lounges, we wanted to consume every unique aspect that the atmosphere had to offer. The trash-laden streets could conjure up a stench like no other, but I gave it a pass because the mesmerizing sights, sounds, and people somehow made it all worthwhile.

Sometimes Dev and I would stop in the middle of what we were doing to say, "Can you believe that we live in New York! Aaahhh!" Then we would both giggle with excitement. This was exactly the type of invigorating experience I was longing for. I felt like I needed someone to pinch me.

Things with Dev and Mel were gradually growing more intense. During a chat one day, she even mentioned that he might be "the one." If she didn't show up to the apartment on any given night of the week, my safe guess was that she was with Mel, which gave me time alone that I loved. Consequently, everything in the world of roommates was going smoothly.

Meanwhile, Kari and I had been consistently spending more time together as well. But after the awkward first attempt at taking our relationship to the next level, we had not gotten back around to sealing the deal.

"Do you think Kari could be gay?"

"Uh, where did that come from?" Dev looked at me puzzled as we walked crosstown on Fourteenth Street. "I thought you liked him. And no, I don't get a gay vibe from him."

"Do you think he could have a secret girlfriend?"

"No!" Dev looked at me. "Again, I thought you liked him? Why the suspicion?"

"Surprisingly, I do like him, Dev."

"You should. He is sexy as hell."

"But you know me." I shrugged my shoulders and rolled my eyes.

"Continue, chick, because you and I know how quickly you cut people off. I'm glad he made it this far," Dev said, her big brown eyes giving me a wary look. "Are you trying to find a reason to get rid of him, Scottie?"

"No! I'm confused, I guess. He really hasn't tried to push up on me since the incident at the house. And that was weeks ago."

"Wait, you mean the incident when you probably grossed him out with the bubble guts?" Dev laughed hysterically. "You're lucky he's still talking to you!"

I had no choice but to laugh. The situation wasn't funny at the time, but it was hilarious looking back. Dev putting things in perspective made me feel slightly silly. Kari was obviously interested in me.

"He probably thinks that you got scared the last time and he's waiting for your cue. Maybe he's trying to be respectful in letting you take your time," Dev said.

"You could be right. I hadn't thought of it that way."

"If you tried to jump his bones and he straight up rejected you, then maybe you would have a reason to be suspicious. Plus, does he really strike you as even possibly being gay?"

"No," I said sheepishly.

"I know you. If you thought even for a second that he was actually gay, or had a girlfriend, you would have dropped him."

"True, nothing worse than everyone except you knowing that your man likes men."

"Exactly. So stop being silly and if you want it, then take it!" Dev said firmly as she puffed out her chest, then laughed at her own forcefulness.

"I think that's the spot ahead on the left," I said, totally ignoring her last comment.

We were meeting up with a friend from college at a Hot 97 radio event. It was work for her, but all play for us.

The music was blaring and the after-work crowd was live. I couldn't get Kari off of my mind, but I decided that I needed to, at least for the evening. It was time to drink up and dance the night away. We caught up with our girl who introduced us to what seemed like the entire HOT 97 staff. To my surprise, there were actually a few cuties roaming around. One cutie could always help me get my mind off of another. Hell, I wasn't in a relationship so it was time to rotate and mingle.

I could see Dev from across the room showing off her moves on the dance floor. Her song must have come on. She was fresh out the hair shop, so her bob was bouncing from side to side with every move that she made. It was extremely entertaining watching guys try to keep up with her. If it was a booty-popping song that she really liked, she would need to do a solo to show off her dance skills. Dev was no stranger to freestyle dance or formal dance training, but I don't think that she ever believed in her skills enough to try to take it all the way to the professional level.

Eventually, I made my way to the other side of the club where I made friends with a couple of men at the bar. Nothing special.

We'd done a few shots together, so I was a little buzzed when Dev found me. Dev must have decided that she was finished with her talent showcase since she informed me that Mel was on his way to pick her up.

"Look, chick, if you're not trying to do the public transportation thing tonight, then you should hop in with Mel and me."

My tipsy meter was at its peak, so I made a hasty decision against my better judgment. "All right, I'll roll out with you guys."

"That's what I thought," Dev said.

About fifteen minutes passed before Dev gave me the signal. We said our goodbyes and we were on our way toward the door when a sleazy-looking guy grabbed my arm. "Why are you leaving so soon, gorgeous?"

Is he serious?

"I'm on my way out the door and you decide to speak now?" I asked, without really wanting an answer as I snatched my arm back. "Have a good night!" I quickly shouted over the music and continued out the door. Some guys were laughable.

When we walked out, to my surprise, the line of people waiting to get in was stretched around the block. Mel was sitting right out front, VIP-style, in his black-on-black Mercedes-Benz G-Wagen. Dev knew how to pick them, and we still had no clue what he did for a living. I could have told her my guess, but she didn't ask for my opinion.

Evidently, Que was back in town. Just my luck. His thick neck was posted in the passenger side as usual. When I saw him, my initial thought was to tell Dev that I would pass on the ride. But then I realized what I would have to do to navigate my tipsy behind to Jersey by myself and I got in the truck. I spoke to Mel and barely mumbled two words to Que. I think it was safe to say that he knew I wasn't feeling him. We had a nonverbal understanding.

Mel mentioned that he wanted to take us to this spot in Queens. I didn't like the sound of going back to Queens with him, but my head was spinning so my senses were not on high alert. Dev was down without hesitation. She would use this as her chance to see a bit more about him, like where he hung out when he was not with her.

We rode out to Queens chitchatting and blasting the music. When we exited the freeway, I could instantly tell that we were in the 'hood. You could see trash strewn about the streets, people hanging out on the corners, and abandoned buildings for blocks. Of course I didn't say anything.

As we made a few turns and rolled onto a well-lit block with quite a few bars lining the street, I saw a black car with extremely blacked-out, tinted windows swoop in front of us abruptly. It made a sharp *Fast and Furious*-type move, cutting Mel off and making it impossible to pass. Mel slammed on the brakes.

Dev and I both flew forward, and my head smacked against the headrest.

What the hell is going on? Are we about to get kidnapped or robbed or, shit, killed?!

All I saw was my life flash before my eyes. I started to sober up pretty quick.

Mel, still inside the truck, yelled out, "What the fuck?!"

Before he could finish his rant, the truck was surrounded by at least fifteen men with guns drawn. They looked like undercover cops and they were everywhere. I was secretly relieved. Cops were a better option than some relentless enemy of Mel's unloading an Uzi clip on us like a reenactment in a gangster film.

So many thoughts went through my head in a flash.

"Get out of the fucking car with your hands up!" screamed the officer with the gun pointed directly at me.

I was in shock. All I could focus on were the guns. They kept yelling at us to get out of the car with our hands up in what sounded like a cadence. I had no clue how to get out of a car with my hands still up. This could not be my life. I had no idea where I was, let alone what type of illegal activities Mel was into. As far as I was concerned, we were all fucked.

The officer on Dev's side yanked her door open. She hesitated initially, then decided that she better go ahead and cooperate. They had already snatched Mel out of the truck, and his face was pressed up against the steaming hot hood of the car, and they were handcuffing him.

Dev, Que, and I were instructed to go to the rear of the truck and put our hands on the back window. It was freezing outside, but the truck was still running so luckily, we could feel warmth on the windows.

We watched as they tore through the glove box, side-door panels, seats and everything else. Mel's Mercedes was a wreck. They searched every inch of it. I watched fearfully. I had no idea what they were looking for or what they might find.

I asked the officer closest to me why they stopped us, and he said that Mel failed to stop when an officer signaled him to pull over. I found that hard to believe. Out of four people in a car, not one of us realized that there were lights flashing behind us and that we were being signaled to pull over by the police. I called bullshit. I looked toward the front of the car, and Mel was still in handcuffs.

"What the hell did we get ourselves into?" Dev whispered to

me with a shaky voice that was likely a combination of fear and the chills from the frigid temperature outside.

"You tell me. That's yo' boy and they got his ass handcuffed. This was no accident or coincidence," I said through clenched teeth. I could see the white fog from my breath disappearing into the night sky every time that I spoke.

"Yeah," Dev said. She was confused, angry, and scared. That made two of us.

For a moment it seemed as though Que had lost his mind. He adjusted his slightly sagging pants under his belly and made a hasty move toward the front of the truck. I froze in fear thinking for sure that I would hear a shot ring out. I heard a commotion and I realized why he had made a move. They were about to put Mel into the back of a marked police car. With a hand on his gun, an officer near us yelled for Que to stop moving and stay back. Que didn't stop. He threatened to arrest Que if he did not stay right where he was.

For a split-second you could tell that Que had every intention of going to Mel's rescue.

Dev and I sprang into action and grabbed Que on either side to try to calm him down. He resisted, but we managed to pull him back.

"There's nothing you can do!" I screamed. "Do you want to get shot over nothing?"

I didn't know if Que was aware or even cared, but I definitely noticed that the officer had his hand on his gun, and although Mel wasn't resisting arrest, it took what looked like four cops to rustle him into the back of the police car. For the short amount of time that I'd been in New York, I'd heard too many news reports where cops were using excessive force or killing innocent people over their reckless mistakes. I didn't want to end up on the nightly news over some bullshit that had nothing to do with me.

After things calmed down, one of the arresting officers came over and told us that they were taking Mel into custody. He wouldn't tell us why or what the charge was. He informed us that we were free to go, and he handed Que the keys to the Mercedes.

I walked a few feet away and immediately called Kari. It was 1:00 a.m. and I knew that things could potentially get awkward since we were not dating exclusively. But I did not care. I was so shaken up that I needed him. I needed to feel safe.

Kari answered on the first ring. "Hey, babe, what's up?"

"Can you please come and get me?"

Kari's husky tone immediately changed. The bass in his voice became deeper and he was serious. "Are you all right? Where are you?"

"I'm in Queens," I replied, hesitant as to what his reaction would be. I expected him to be mad.

"Do you know where you are?" Kari asked. "If not, ask someone and text me. I'm on my way."

I told Dev that Kari was coming to get me. She was still visibly distraught. She decided to ride with Que to the police station to find out the status on Mel. I wanted to insist that she stay out of the drama and come home with me, but I knew she would have gone with Que anyway. I surveyed my surroundings for a moment, then decided that I would go into one of the bars on the block to get my exact location, text Kari, and call The Clique while I waited.

Since Kari lived deep in Brooklyn and not too far from where I was, I hadn't been in the bar fifteen minutes when he called. He was outside. I cut my update short and let The Clique know that I would call them back with more details. The girls could always arrange a conference call quicker than lightning.

I hurried toward the door of the bar with my coat fastened tight and my gloves on. I couldn't get out of there quickly enough. I practically ran out of the door to meet Kari. He was standing outside of the car and I fell into his arms. I could tell that he was still extremely confused, but he did not say a word. He just held me tightly.

Once we were on the way back to my place, I gave him the highlights from the night. He resisted saying that I was silly for even getting myself into that situation, but I knew what he was thinking.

Kari covered my hand with his hand off and on throughout the entire drive. It seemed like he wanted to reassure me that he was there for me. That felt good. I had been so used to men not being there for me that this was almost a foreign feeling. I texted Dev to make sure that she was okay. She replied that they'd made it to the police station and she was fine and waiting on answers.

Once we arrived at my apartment, it was super late and since it was a Friday night, or technically Saturday morning, I asked Kari if he wanted to stay over. He gladly agreed and we made our way inside.

Being a classic overthinker, and despite all of the drama of the night, my mind was racing about how I should handle the situation.

I'm positive that I want to have sex with him. Do I know for sure that he wants to have sex with me? I know that he is into me, right? Well, if he doesn't want to have sex tonight, then he is definitely gay.

Referencing my conversation with Dev, I wondered whether it was better for me to take control or wait for him to make a move. I had to think fast and act fast. I excused myself. I had to tinkle something fierce after all of the alcohol that I'd drunk earlier in the night.

While I was in the bathroom, I decided to freshen up a bit,

which pretty much solidified my decision to put a plan into action. My nerves were playing games with me as I tried to wash up. I kept letting the soap slip out of my hand. I could still taste alcohol and my mouth was extremely dry. I brushed my teeth and tongue to ensure that everything was minty fresh. I sprayed a soft scent in all of the important places and last but not least, cleaned behind my ears. Men always liked to go for that spot so I had to make sure that it was right and ready.

Kari was already in my room lying across the bed when I came out of the bathroom. His long legs were dangling off of the edge and I thought about how good he looked. His hair was freshly cut with his goatee lined properly. I could already imagine his soft, juicy lips licking and sucking on mine.

He watched as I walked over to the bed. *This is the moment of truth.* I placed one knee on the bed and crawled on top of him. His eyes were locked with mine, making the moment intense. Before I reached his lips, I could smell his cologne, the distinguished scent of Creed. I loved every second of it. I rubbed my lips against his lips. That was our thing. Of course we hadn't had sex yet, but we'd certainly had some great make-out sessions.

Our kisses were intense. We had waited so long for this time to come; there was no rush on either side. Kari caressed my back while he slid his tongue past my lips. We kissed passionately for what seemed like an eternity. I could feel Kari's sex bulging through his pants.

He tugged at my top a few times before finally managing to get it off. This gave me a little chuckle so I sat up and straddled him with my eyes still locked in his gaze. I unhooked my black, lace, Calvin Klein bra in a sensuous motion to expose the mini-twins, and I watched his eyes light up. He leaned forward rapidly and started kissing my body as if he could not wait to devour me.

Kari took the first nipple in his mouth and I lay back enjoying the pleasure. His free hand cupped my butt and he pulled me closer to him. *I like this man.* I could tell the difference with Kari; we were making love and not having sex. I was used to sex, but lovemaking was a bit foreign.

He was having too much fun with my breasts so I gently pulled his head up to kiss him. I loved the intimacy of kissing. Our breathing was rapid and deep. Kari flipped me over and slid off my bottoms. My panties were drenched. I was ready to consume all that he had to offer. I snatched his belt open and unzipped his pants going for the one thing that I knew would be waiting for me. Once I had his penis in my hands, I couldn't believe how hard it was.

Kari moved down south kissing and licking on my inner thighs. I was glad that I'd decided to get a fresh wax the day before. The universe was on my side.

Kari had serious technique. He used his fingers and his mouth to make me experience sheer orgasmic pleasure. As my moans grew louder, Kari became more excited. I took his index finger in my mouth and began to simulate what I planned to do with his penis. I motioned for Kari to come up so that we could be face-to-face. Our kisses had an added flavor this time and they were even juicier now with the anticipation.

I pulled on Kari's bottom lip with my teeth and my tongue as I slipped down his chest making a slight detour to suckle on his hard nipples. Once I reached my destination, I could appreciate that he was very well-groomed. I really expected nothing less based on his outer appearance and what I knew about him up to that point.

When I took Kari inside my mouth, I felt like I had the ultimate control. I was about to make him moan and squirm. That was my mission. I licked the head of his penis in a playful motion a few times before getting to work. Between the sucking and spinning motions, it must have been more than what Kari bargained for because he pushed me away.

I was so confused, I thought that I'd done something wrong. As the thought entered my mind, Kari grabbed my arm and pulled me close. We were lips-to-lips and he whispered that he was sorry. He said that he wanted to delay his climax; he wasn't ready to cum yet. "I want to cum inside you," he said.

I had never had anyone say such a thing to me and it freaked me out for a brief second, but I did not want to overthink things. I asked Kari to get a condom. If he did not have one, I sure did. He pulled out the "gold wrapper," and I put it on him. Honey dip would not be taking any chances. This was all a part of foreplay but also a method on my behalf to ensure proper use and my protection.

Kari flipped me onto my back with an execution that gave me thoughts of porno action. He slid his hand across my sweet spot to see how juicy it was before his entry. Once he felt the proper welcome, Kari slid his thick penis inside of my pussy and looked me dead in my eyes not wanting to miss a single reaction. This lovemaking session proved to be one of the best in my life. I had never felt so connected to anyone during sex and those feelings heightened the intensity. The entire experience was unbelievable.

The following afternoon, I woke up in Kari's arms. I caressed his chest to see if he was awake. He responded with a kiss on my forehead.

I smiled to myself. When I was about to daydream and doze off again, my phone buzzed. I realized that I had not heard from Dev, so I jumped up to grab the phone from the nightstand.

"Hey girl, where are you?" I asked in a raspy voice.

"I'm at Mel's. They finally released him a few hours ago and we came back to his place."

"Oh good," I said, relieved.

"I'm guessing that you made it home okay. The last text that I got was when you guys were on the way back to the apartment," Dev said.

"Yeah, I'm fine. Kari stayed over." I tried to slide that in. "Have you slept at all?"

"Nope, not a wink. I'll probably go shower and take a nap right now. I'll be home later," Dev said very matter-of-factly. "Oh yeah, and I'll get your story later too."

I couldn't help but laugh. "Okay, call me if you need anything," I offered before we hung up.

I looked over at Kari. He had fallen back asleep. I was on a high, floating on clouds and feeling extremely nice. So I decided to get domestic and headed into the kitchen to whip up a little breakfast.

Either the sound of clinking pots and pans or the smell of yummy food summoned Kari to the kitchen about twenty minutes later. He tried to mask the look of surprise on his face. I guess he didn't take me for the cooking type. He walked up behind me and put his hands on my waist. I could feel his manly physique against my body and his calm breathing on my neck as he leaned in to me. He whispered "thank you" and kissed my lower neck, then softly pecked my shoulder. His touch felt so loving. It almost made me uncomfortable.

I didn't know if he was thanking me for the previous night or for the breakfast. But either way, I accepted it. He probably thought that my cooking for him was a stretch, and in some ways it was. Not technically speaking, but more emotionally. I wanted to like him and let him in, but it wasn't that simple for me.

"Breakfast is served," I said.

"That's so sweet, babe," Kari replied, as he walked over to the bar to take a seat.

I reached over and set Kari's plate and silverware in front of him, but I could not look into his eyes. I was sure that he noticed because I felt him piercing a hole in my body.

I ignored the awkwardness and sat down next to him to eat. After his first bite, he rubbed his hand on my thigh and said how good the food was. *Where did this guy come from?*

Chapter 7

Low Life

After the events of the weekend, I felt like I needed a vacation, but I had to go and slave at a desk for eight to ten hours. Working in PR, you never knew what the day would bring, especially at an agency like mine. A client could have a crisis that needed immediate attention. Breaking news could hit that could turn your world upside down. Or one of the senior publicists could go on a tirade and start berating everyone that works on the team. Talk about a potentially uncomfortable and hostile environment. All of the day-to-day drama really created a lot of unnecessary stress and pressure, but after a while you would adapt and get used to it.

I got a call late in the afternoon from my girl Latina in the Los Angeles office. She instructed me to go into one of the conference rooms and call her back. I hung up the phone and I felt my stomach begin to tighten and turn over. I didn't know what she was about to tell me, but I did not have a good feeling. She wasn't the messy type and the tone in her voice was very serious. It wasn't a case of some silly gossip.

When I got her on the line, she spoke very calm and almost in a hushed tone. The first thing that she said was, "Watch your back."

The pause after her first statement kicked up my anxiety another notch. "What do you mean? Tell me what is going on." I didn't have time for speaking in code. I needed specifics.

"I overheard a conversation. Steve asked one of the vice presidents how things were working out with you in the New York office, and the VP basically said that you had not been reporting to him, so he didn't know what you were working on and in fact, he didn't know who you were reporting to. He essentially made it as though you are in New York doing what you want and not working very hard."

I sat there for a moment in disbelief. I couldn't find words past my anger.

"Scottie, are you still there?"

"I can't close my mouth," I finally responded. "I'm in shock."

"Girl, I know. They are so sneaky and backstabbing. That's why I wanted to give you a heads-up. It seems like something shady is going down."

"Thank you. I really appreciate it. You're right, something shady is definitely going on."

"If I hear anything else, I'll be sure to let you know," Latina said.

"Thanks again, girl," I said as we rushed off the line.

When I got back to my desk, I started clicking around on the computer screen to appear busy, but I could not concentrate. I was furious that someone was blatantly lying on me. I was told when I got to New York that I would report to Barbra and work on her team. I was never supposed to be reporting to anyone else. However, I had heard the day prior that the company had lost one of its largest entertainment accounts to a competitor. I was sure that somehow it was all connected. I did not know if I should mention what I'd found out to Barbra or wait a day to see how things started to play out.

I sat at my desk for about thirty minutes, ultimately doing nothing, when my phone rang. The caller ID showed a Los Angeles phone number. I answered. I heard a male voice on the other end.

"Hi, Scottie. This is Roger."

Roger was one of the partners in the agency. I spoke to him in passing whenever I saw him in the Los Angeles office, but I never worked with him directly. Out of all the partners, I knew Steve the best and I worked with him the most. So I was a little confused as to why Roger would be calling me and why Steve was talking to VP's about me behind my back. The day was getting stranger by the minute.

"Hi, Roger. How are you?" I said.

"I'm well, thank you," he said, before delving straight into the reason for his call. "I know that you recently relocated to the New York office and I'm not sure how things have been going, but I'm calling you because some changes have been made and we will no longer be in need of your service."

I couldn't believe that he called me to deliver this type of news. I was sitting at my desk, which was out in the open with no walls, no doors and no privacy. I had never been fired before, but I couldn't imagine that this was a standard way of it happening.

My eyes bugged out, and I did the only thing that I could do. I said, "Okay."

Roger continued to talk and I started to sweat. My stomach felt uneasy again and I wanted to hang up. He went on to say that I could finish out the day and work through the remainder of the week.

Is this mothafucker crazy?!

I politely told him straight up, "No thank you. My last day will be today." Then I hung up.

As soon as I got off of the phone with Roger, I walked out of the office and headed downstairs to call Dev.

"Guess what the fuck just happened?" I said to Dev in an exasperated roar.

"What?"

"Roger, one of the partners from the Los Angeles office, called to tell me that I'm being let go."

"What?" Dev exclaimed. "Are you joking? Can they do that? What happened?"

Dev sat on the other end of the line silent as I recalled the story. Once I finished, Dev said, "I'm coming up there. Let's pack up yo' shit and you out."

Dev had a calm to her voice before we hung up; she meant business. In the meantime, I went to talk with Barbra. She claimed that she did not have any prior knowledge as to what was going on. She said that the Los Angeles office called her right before Roger called me and that she had no say-so in the decision as it had already been made. According to Barbra, the powers that be didn't even ask her about my performance on her team.

Everything seemed overtly shady, but then again, this was a company that didn't even have a real Human Resources department. What more could I expect?

Dev showed up about twenty minutes later and we did as she'd said. We quickly packed up my minimal belongings and got the hell out of there. It was funny, though. While we were packing up, I told Dev that I actually felt good, and I did. For a brief moment after the initial call, I got in my feelings. My pride and my ego had been wounded, so I let a few salty tears stream down my cheek. But soon after, I had a moment of clarity and I felt free. Like a huge weight had been lifted off of my shoulders. Working at a PR agency was too much stress for not enough money. It's not like we were saving lives. Images maybe, but lives not so much.

When Dev and I hit the streets, we didn't have a plan. We had no clue where we were going or what was next. We let the cool evening breeze take us downtown on Eighth Avenue while we chatted about all of the drama that had unfolded in our lives over the past few days.

She gave me the update on Mel. He had a court date in the coming weeks. She still wasn't exactly sure what they'd found in his car since he refused to tell her anything. He said that he did not want to involve her. I cut my eyes at Dev.

"You need to be careful being around Mel."

"I know, I know." She nodded. "I spoke to The Clique and everyone else said the same thing."

"I'm serious. You don't know what he is into. You have a lot to lose if you get caught up on a drug charge dealing with his bum ass," I said. "He is cool to party with but nothing more."

"I get it, Scottie. Speaking of losing it, someone has been prank calling my cell phone lately," Dev said. "It's been happening more frequently now, and I have no clue who it could be."

"Really. Are you scared?"

"Not really. More concerned."

Dev was the type to remain cool with most of her ex-lovers, so she highly doubted that it was one of them playing games. She had a likable personality and in all of the years that we had been friends, I never met a single person that did not like her. I didn't have any suggestions for her.

"Enough about me. What's up with you and Kari?"

"I'll cut to what you really want to know, yes, we finally had sex."

Dev gave me a pinch on the cheek and in true girlfriend fashion,

I gave Dev the entire juicy scoop on the unexpected developments between Kari and me. She was so excited and didn't hesitate to pat herself on the back for suggesting that I take charge.

"Okay, now that we've walked and talked our way through solving the problems of the world, where are we going?" I asked.

"What do you want to do?" Dev said, "It's pretty much your call since you had the roughest day."

"At this point I think I need a drink."

"Well, let's do drinks and wings. Are you down for Buffalo Wild Wings?" Dev blurted out.

"Let's do it!"

"Brooklyn, here we come!"

Dev was such a sweetheart and a supportive friend. Before we got on the train to Brooklyn, she arranged an impromptu call with The Clique. All of my girls offered their encouragement and tried to assure me that things would work out for the best. I needed to hear their sweet voices.

Once at Buffalo Wild Wings, we ate and drank and drank a little more. We called Dev's dad before we were too tipsy to tell him about my getting fired. He was, of course, shocked. He gave us a pep talk and told us not to let the big bad city bring us down. He also told us to put our food and drinks on his tab, which was beyond nice. Dev knew what to do since her American Express card was under his account. When major changes in life occur, whether expected or unexpected, they help you to see who's in your corner.

When I got home that night, I was tipsy, but as long as I didn't slur my words, I had to call my Jolie and fill her in. I couldn't bring myself to call her earlier because she was a feisty little lady, and I knew that the news of my layoff was sure to rile her up.

My Jolie answered the phone in her usual form. "What's going on, honey? How you doin'?"

Shockingly, my voice showed no signs of distress. Maybe it was the alcohol. "I'm okay. So let me get right to it. I got let go today."

"What! From your job?" she asked. Like I could have possibly been talking about something else. But I got it. She was in shock.

"So what the hell happened?"

I told her to tell Dad to get on the line, too. Then I proceeded to run down all of the shady events from the day. As I suspected, they wanted to come to New York and inflict pain on someone. After the initial anger died down, they let me know that they would help me however they could.

I loved talking to my parents. They were always encouraging and offered amazing advice when I encountered tough situations. That night, I sat on the line and talked to them for more than an hour while they both reminisced on stories about their past work histories. Talking with my parents always eased my worries and gave me a renewed positive outlook. At that point, I wasn't sure what type of help I would need, as I was still in a daze. But I knew that they always had my back.

As the next few days went by, I got in touch with the unemployment office in California to request my dollars and cents. As I felt more comfortable with my reality, I slowly began to tell people about my situation. It was kind of awkward at first and slightly embarrassing, but I was not exactly sure why. It wasn't like I'd been terminated for poor performance or doing something illegal.

Almost a week had passed before I finally got around to telling Kari. We were on our way to a movie. While we were riding in the car, I sort of just said it. He was pissed that I had not mentioned anything sooner.

"Why would you wait to tell me?" Kari asked. "You know I'm here for you and no matter what happens, I have your back."

"Thank you," I said, not sure what else to say.

"Do you need anything? Are you all right?" Kari asked, as he looked at me with concern.

I nodded my head as I pretended to listen to him go on and on. But that phrase, "You know I'm here for you and no matter what happens, I have your back," kept ringing in my ears. I honestly wasn't certain what that meant coming from him.

I felt the tears welling up in my eyes, but I tried my hardest not to let them fall. I guess I was so used to looking out for myself and taking care of myself that I couldn't imagine a man who I liked having that much regard for my well-being and my feelings.

Chapter 8

Whose Life Is This?

This was the life: party all night and sleep all day. The first few weeks of being out of work were reminiscent of my college days. I had no desire to look for a job. Lounging around the apartment was like a staycation. This was the first time in years that I'd had a significant amount of free time at my disposal.

During the good days, I would sit around in my pajamas watching HGTV, entranced by every program on the network. I think the creativity and designs fostered nostalgia. Working with my hands was something that I learned from my maternal grandparents. When I spent time with them as a kid, they always had a project for me, whether it was helping my grandmother paint her patio furniture on a sunny afternoon, or sawing and sanding down two-by-fours of wood for a ramp that my grandfather was building at the church. They were old-school, Southern, do-it-yourself-type people, and I enjoyed every minute of the work because there was a connection and a bond that we established. The projects were a team effort and I learned what I came to know as valuable life lessons of independence, dedication, and accountability.

I had no clue what my next move would be careerwise, but I would never work at an agency again. As the days turned into weeks and I found myself in similar, if not the same, routine, I began to wonder about the purpose of my existence. Then came the bad days. Where was my life going? There were times when I would lie across my bed in the silent apartment—pajama-clad with my hair uncombed and no desire to get dressed—wondering what was next, wracking my brain for answers.

I wanted to call Kari every second of every day, especially when the boredom and stir-crazy feelings would set in. But I had to restrain myself. I didn't want to come off as a lifeless stalker. Although he had been extremely supportive, I could not be in the business of depending on any man. It wasn't like he had to be there for me. We were not married—hell, we weren't even officially together for that matter. I needed to be realistic with my expectations.

Over the next few weeks, we met in the city on occasion for dinner, art gallery openings, the occasional concert, or a movie night, but eventually I came to realize that my trips to the city had to be rationed. The costs of commuting in and out of the city were out of my budget. The unemployed life quickly became less than glamorous.

Some nights I would stare at myself in the mirror looking for answers, only to realize that I was alone and extremely lonely. The reality was that I was scared. I was in a place where I did not have any of the comforts of home, and even if I desperately needed to cry on my Jolie's shoulder, she was 2,000 miles away. I regularly ran short on covering my monthly expenses so I rationed dollars like it was the Depression era. Despite my best efforts to scale back, I still had to lean on my parents for extra cash. I felt like a dependent teenager again.

Snacking and surfing the web became my new best friends and

we spent way too much quality time together. Some days, I wouldn't even allow the sun's rays to shine through my bedroom window. The dark days matched my spirit. It was hard for me to express my emotions to those close to me. I wore my strength like a badge of honor. People say that we all go through a quarter life and a mid-life crisis, but I think there are many more crises in between that we don't ever hear about.

My emotions stayed unpredictable. Dev was constantly back and forth between our place and Mel's, but she never questioned my employment situation. By the time I hit the three-month mark of unemployment, self-help and empowerment books had become a staple in my daily routine. However, that didn't stop people from offering their advice and sending me crap jobs to apply for. That got old really quick. Didn't they understand that I did not ask them for their help? Every single person that I knew in California asked when and if I planned on moving back. It was as if they thought that moving would be the answer to all of my problems. *Hell no I won't go!* That's what I wanted to say, but I bit my tongue and let them know that I planned to stick it out. I wasn't a quitter.

Kari picked up on the negative energy that I was giving off and he requested that I meet him in the city. I decided to get super cute for our date, even though I had no clue what we were doing. Kari was guaranteed to show up looking fly, so I had to stay on point. He had a very mature, *GQ* style and I couldn't have women giving my date the eye while I sat there looking like a sack of rotten potatoes. I may have been unemployed with my life in shambles, but that didn't mean that I had to look that way when I went out.

Spring was in the air, so I slipped on a pastel-colored spaghetti strap dress that I had been longing to wear. It being my first spring in the city and a beautiful day, I arrived a bit early for my date and strolled around by myself. Since my trips to the city had become less frequent due to budget cuts, I missed roaming around. Groups of friends and couples alike were frolicking around and enjoying libations at restaurants with sidewalk seating, people were biking through the streets, and there were fewer layers of clothing on everyone. Manhattan was alive with free and happy inhabitants.

Time slipped away from me as I wandered the streets day-dreaming. I put a-pep-in-my-step and headed crosstown on Forty-second to meet Kari. He wasn't the type to get pissed about me being a little late, but I did not want to be rude. I zigzagged through the crowded streets as fast as I could. Having already changed into my heels, my pace was slightly limited, but my dress flowed with every movement making it easier to maneuver swiftly.

In finding your way about the city, you get used to physical contact with strangers. People were always bumping into you or sideswiping you as you walked down the street, but when I felt what seemed like a hand actually grabbing at my butt, I almost lost it. *This is so out of line!* Before I could rationalize how to react, my anger turned me around with my fist in motion. Kari jumped back to avoid my first swing and he chuckled a little as I stumbled. Luckily, he caught me. I felt slightly foolish.

I gave him a smack on the chest for scaring the crap out of me, then we leaned in for a hug and his athletic build consumed me. It felt so right to be in Kari's arms. He kissed me on the cheek and we strolled up the street hand-in-hand. He told me that we were headed to the Dream hotel, which was in midtown. Getting there would be a bit of a hike in my heels—twelve blocks—but it was spring and they were wedges so I would survive. On a nice day it was kind of romantic to walk with your man friend through the city streets looking at the sights and letting the sounds be your soundtrack to life.

This was my first time going to the Dream, but I'd heard great things about the rooftop ambiance. I came to appreciate hanging out with a man who took the time to explore new locations with me or introduce me to those that he was familiar with. Kari was thoughtful in that way.

When we walked into the hotel lobby, it was stunning. Everything about the place was sexy or maybe I felt sexy.

Kari took my hand in his and we headed to the rooftop. The scene wasn't too crazy, so we snagged a table nestled in a corner. While I got situated, Kari ordered drinks at the bar. From across the room, I watched a woman with jet-black hair down to her butt and legs like a goddess saunter over to Kari. She tried to spark up a conversation. From what I could tell he politely responded to her and proceeded to collect the drinks that he ordered. As he walked back toward our table, I had a silly smirk on my face. Clearly, he realized that I saw the exchange. Kari was very respectful when it came to our situation, so I never worried about his eyes wandering or him being too flirty with other women in my presence. This was a dramatic difference from my previous situation with Ivan.

After we finished our drinks on the rooftop, we decided to head to SoHo to shoot pool. I liked shooting pool with a man whom I was attracted to. The game allowed for a woman to be a bit seductive which could lead into some sassy flirting and serious sexual foreplay. If you were planning on going home together, the stage was then set for a nightcap full of fuckery and fun. On our way downtown, I may have talked up my pool game a tad bit, but as it turned out, I only won one out of four games so my shit-talking had to be kept to a minimum.

The pool hall was blasting light-rock songs from a jukebox on the far wall, however, that didn't prevent me from hearing my purse vibrating on the stool to my left. I reached in to grab my phone. When I saw the name on the screen, a rush of nerves filled my stomach. Telling Kari briefly that I would be back, I slipped away to the restroom.

Once inside the small cramped space, I held the phone in my hand staring at it with disbelief. Ivan had impeccable timing. He didn't leave a message. I called back.

"Scottie, I'm so glad that you called me back."

"What's up, Ivan? Why are you calling?"

"Look, I won't bullshit around. I want you back."

The sounds of the music rumbling in the distant background invaded my mind. I couldn't comprehend what was being said on the other end of the phone. I had a moment of disarray.

"This, this is not a good time for me. I'll call you back." I hung up my cell phone before Ivan could respond. I looked in the mirror covered with graffiti to try and compose myself. I couldn't let him continue to manipulate my world. I was no longer within his grasp and I had moved on.

When I came back from the restroom, Kari was sitting on a bar stool and he signaled for me to come to him. I was smitten with his sexy aura. He still gave me butterflies. I sauntered over to my handsome date and when I got close enough, he lightly grabbed my wrist and pulled me in to him. I was standing between his legs. I could feel my knees becoming a little weak and shaky. We were eye level with each other. He grabbed my waist and pulled me in for a passionate kiss in the middle of the pool hall. His breath was giving me hints of spearmint and his lips, soft and sweet to the taste.

"You look really sexy tonight," Kari confessed after our kiss.

I blushed. "Thank you, babe," I responded in my sweetest I-like-you tone.

"You know that I really like you, and that you're special to me, right?" Kari said.

Generally I wasn't good with expressing my feelings or talking about them. I was one of the most talkative people ever. But when it came to topics of the heart, I would get lockjaw and my lips would clamp shut. That had always been a challenge for me, but I had been working on doing better. Writing was my thing. I could pen my feelings via text, email or even old-fashioned pen and paper with minimal effort. That's probably why Aaliyah's song "4 Page Letter" spoke to my heart. In any case, I saw this as my opportunity to try to step it up.

I worked up a nice big smile to mask my trepidation and went for it. "I know, Kari, and you're special to me too. I really enjoy the time that we spend together and how supportive you've been throughout everything."

Kari smiled like a Cheshire cat and kissed me.

"I realize how hard it is for you to express your feelings sometimes, so thank you," Kari said. "Look at my baby growing up."

Moments like that endeared me to him. He made it easier to open up because I felt the sincerity in his words and actions.

"There's one more thing that I want to say," Kari declared, appearing more serious now.

My heart started to race. I had no clue what he planned to say, but the whole scene was now feeling a little too dramatic for me to remain calm.

"Okay," I responded.

"I want to see you and only you from now on," Kari announced, with a look that was now as serious as a Catholic priest at confession. "We have only been casually dating up until now. But you are the only one that I think about, dream about, and crave. You are the only person I want to spend time with every day."

All that I could manage to utter was, "Wow."

"So what do you think? Can it be me and you? You and I? Us?" Kari asked. "Can we agree to only kick it with each other?"

I was happy with where the conversation was going. I liked Kari a lot, but I was also a little shocked at the timing.

"Okay," I said after a moment. "Me and you. I like it."

Prior to my move from Los Angeles, I had been growing out my hair. Ivan would fawn over women with long hair so he begged me to let my hair grow. My grandmother always teased that I had hair like Pop Malveaux, dark and beautiful. I liked my natural soft curl pattern, and my hair was manageable so I didn't mind the length. However, after everything that had transpired since my move to New York, I needed a change. I got a pair of scissors from the hall closet and I walked into my bathroom and started snipping. My hair had grown well past my shoulders, essentially to the middle of my back. So once I made the first cut, I had to commit. I started cutting more and more chunks, and big, brown curls fell all over my shoulders and covered the bathroom floor. Normally, a neat freak, I felt like fuck it, I'm doing me and I love it! It was freedom.

Once I finished trimming a little more on the sides, I swept up all of the hair from the floor and hopped in the shower to finish washing my troubles away, along with any stray hairs. I felt so light and free. I had never in life had hair that was less than seven inches long. It was a foreign feeling yet just what I needed. It was springtime and this was my way of spring cleaning and refreshing my spirit. I hoped that my new boyfriend would like my new Halle Berry-inspired look.

Chapter 9

Back in the Saddle

I received an unexpected call to go back to work for one night. One of my PR friends from Los Angeles needed me to cover her client, Romero, at a Jay-Z and Diddy party. Naturally, I jumped at the chance.

I arrived at the party early to check out the scene and tackle any unforeseen circumstances. Romero was a Brazilian model and pretty low-key. I was relieved that I would not have to deal with a crazy entourage. I called his assistant to make sure that they were en route and on schedule. As I figured, they were not. People think that the role of a publicist is expensive lifestyles and glamorous friends. No, that's the role of the star or celebrity. One aspect of my job, especially when dealing with "talent," was usually glorified babysitting.

The red carpet was set to shut down in less than ten minutes. Romero's tardiness had me on edge. The plan for having him attend the party was branding and building his profile as a man on the scene. He needed to be photographed partying at the right places with the right people.

I introduced myself to the frumpy young lady in all black running the carpet. I asked if Jay-Z and Diddy had arrived. Sometimes it was like a crap shot with girls like her. I towered over her with my four-inch, metallic heels asking questions on her red carpet. She could have easily thrown shade and not offered any assistance. Lucky for me, she was cool and dished that she was expecting the music moguls at any moment.

Everyone knew that Jay-Z did not really do a lot of media, so I wasn't expecting him to hang out on the carpet long. Best-case scenario, Romero would arrive around the same time as Jay and Diddy, which would make for the perfect photo opportunity. The photo would get picked up by all of the urban media and blogs, and that would make the night a success.

If only things could always work out in real life how they played out in my mind. Of course this dude showed up after the red carpet was finished and well after Diddy and Jay's arrival, which was so quick that if you blinked, you would have missed it. I wanted to pop Romero upside his gorgeous head, but he was the client and not my little brother. I had to explain to him that since he'd arrived late, we had missed an opportunity.

The scene inside was a combination of industry executives, music heads, and party people in their flyest weekday wear. Once we entered the main level, I spotted the VIP section.

"Look to the left," I instructed Romero. "That's the VIP area and that's where you are going."

He responded with a simple, "Okay, cool."

Romero was one of the sweetest guys ever who had a very genuine sort of nerdy quality about him. He was relatively easy to work with, too. It seemed like he'd fallen into modeling by accident. His true passion was acting and he planned to use modeling as his segue.

We walked over to the VIP entrance and I made sure that he got in and got settled before I dipped off so as not to be a lurker. I wanted him to do his thing and enjoy himself.

His assistant, on the other hand—who I took to calling Slick— must have found himself taking a liking to me because he managed to track me down in the party. At first I thought that they needed something work-related, but I quickly realized that Slick wanted to be in my face.

He was cute, but I already knew the type. He was the childhood best friend slash assistant who probably took himself way more seriously than his boy who actually made crazy sums of money from his natural talent. However, since he was relatively hand- some, with decent conversation, he used that to get the ladies. *Well, not today, not tonight, and surely not with me.* At some point he realized that I wasn't feeling his game as he wandered off to find some unsuspecting breezy.

By night's end, I was tired and ready to go. I did not have to stay the whole time with Romero, but I felt that I should since I was filling in for someone else. I did not want any issues.

As we were walking out of the party, Romero asked me if I wanted a ride. It was only he and Slick rolling in this seven- passenger SUV, so I accepted. My girl Sydney, from The Clique, was in town for work, and I had plans to meet up with her. A ride was what I needed.

When we approached the exit to the club, I looked around to see where Slick was, but I could not spot him. I asked Romero where he was and he had no clue. I told him to hop in the car. I would look out for Slick.

After standing around for a few minutes, I spotted him—he was cupcakin' with a groupie. I should have known, so disrespectful. The way I looked at it, if you were not financing anything, then you made moves quickly and you kept up with the program and you definitely didn't keep people waiting.

He and the groupie girl walked in my direction. They were

laughing and carrying on like two teens after the prom. She had on a hot-pink spandex dress with a head full of synthetic black extensions and uncontrollable boobs spilling out of her dress.

Slick walked up to me. "This is Keisha. She's rolling with us."

He almost said it as if he expected me to challenge him. His tone said *I dare you*, but my facial expression said *I don't care*.

Romero must have connected with his late-night lady friend and decided that he wanted to get dropped off at her place. We dropped him off first. Now it was only the lovebirds and me. Spectacular! They actually seemed to be quite familiar with each other like this was not a first-time encounter. Pink dress was polite but did not say too much.

My stop was next. I planned to meet Sydney near where she was staying at the Hotel on Rivington on the Lower East Side. She was hanging out with some peeps at a dive bar close to her hotel. I wasn't exactly sure where the bar was, so I instructed the driver to drop me off at the corner closest to the hotel.

Slick had to get out of the car in order to let me out. As I climbed out of the farthest backseat, I said good night to Pink Dress. I bid Slick a good night as well. When I pulled away from the hug, he whispered, "Can I call you sometime?"

I laughed and shook my head. This guy was pure comedy. He already had my number from coordinating arrivals earlier in the night, but now he wanted to see if he could use it for purposes other than business. I thought not.

Chapter 10

Baller Times One

The holiday weekend had arrived and Nikki was flying in from Los Angeles. I hadn't seen her since the day she'd dropped me off at the airport in Los Angeles, but it was nothing for Nikki to book a last-minute trip for a visit. She consistently had a plethora of guys in rotation to occupy her time and finance the collection of her frequent flyer miles, luxurious hair enhancements, and designer handbags.

To join in the fun, Sydney extended her work trip through the long Memorial Day weekend. That meant the majority of The Clique was assembled. It was bound to be a weekend of major fun.

The girls arrived at the apartment Saturday evening. Dev and I were ready and waiting to start the weekend festivities with a few cocktails at our place. Nikki and all of her luxurious hair came right in and made herself at home in the kitchen mixing up some specialty drinks while Sydney, Dev, and I all sat around the kitchen's bar sipping on lime-colored, salt-rimmed glasses.

Sydney did not waste any time. "So everyone knows about Ivan calling Scottie, right?"

I looked up from my glass and shook my head. I knew where this was going.

"She's happy with her new boo. Do we really even care that Ivan wants to come crying back now?" Nikki asked.

"Maybe he really realizes that he messed up," Sydney said.

Dev set her glass down and held her hand up. "He wasn't all bad. I definitely liked him as a person. But will Scottie or should Scottie entertain him, that's totally up to her."

"Well, Scottie?" Sydney asked.

"I haven't even called him back yet. I really don't have much to say. I cared deeply for him at one point, but now I feel like he is trying to get me back because I'm trying to move on. It's like he can sense that I have someone else."

"That's probably true," Nikki said.

"I don't want whatever he has to say tainting my relationship with Kari. He is a great guy."

"Then don't call him. Move on," Nikki said, making the conversation final.

Once we were all feeling nice, it was time to head into the city. Before we hit the streets, I tipsy-texted Kari to say hi and to let him know that I was thinking about him. I wouldn't really have time to see him throughout the weekend, but I wanted to show him a little attention. He liked that sort of thing.

It was already after midnight, so the group consensus was to keep it low-key. We headed to Pop Burger where we could get food, drinks, and even mix in a little scene.

Surprisingly, Dev did not arrange to have us meeting up with Mel. She seemed to be getting a little annoyed with him. Maybe it was his lack of effort to incorporate her into his real life. Although he'd said that it was for her own good, she expressed how she felt disconnected from him after the whole arrest ordeal. My advice was to simply let her gut be her guide and only do what felt right when it came to Mel. He seemed to have some dangerous secrets and that wasn't cool.

Dev's phone rang as we walked out of the train station, and she jumped before scrambling to grab it out of her purse. We all watched her answer. She had just told us on the subway ride downtown that she had still been receiving prank calls. The calls had not been enough to make her change her phone number, but apparently, they were becoming threatening now and she seemed a little on edge.

Sydney said, "Is it the crazy person? Give me the phone, Dev. Let me answer."

Dev happily handed the phone over.

Sydney was a gorgeous pint-sized ball of fire. Her silky, black, bone-straight hair flowed down her back and swayed from side-to-side when she walked. But her mesmerizing hazel eyes could definitely be deceiving since shutting down bullshit was her specialty.

"Hello?" Sydney said in her raspy Cali accent.

The line was silent. "Who is this?" the person on the other end of the phone asked in a muffled tone. You could tell that this individual was an amateur but had definitely tried to take precautions and hide her voice.

"Look, you little cunt, nobody has time to play childish games. If you really want to speak to Devin, then come holla at her face-to-face and stop the dumb shit!" Sydney exclaimed. "She'll be at Pop Burger on Fifty-eighth Street tonight. Don't be a punk. You keep hiding behind the phone, but why don't you come out and play?"

Click. Like that Sydney hung up the phone. Instantly, the chatter started and everyone was firing questions at Sydney. Even I would not have gone that far.

"Are you insane?" Dev screamed as she snatched her phone

back. "Who knows what that idiot is capable of doing," Dev said as she continued to flip out. "You just potentially threw us straight in harm's way!"

Sydney tossed her silky tresses over her shoulder and calmly turned to Dev. "Look, if you want this to end, then we call her bluff, simple as that. If this bitch really wants it—'cause you know it's a woman—with you, then we are all here and we have your back. At least it's a public place."

"Should we call the police for backup?" Nikki asked, waving her crystal-encrusted phone case.

We looked at her and rolled our eyes.

My gut was telling me that somehow Mel had something to do with the whole strange situation. My intuition was normally on point, but I did not want to start anything so I kept quiet. The person on the phone would not show up to Pop Burger. That was not a part of her plan. If she wanted to actually confront Dev, then she would likely do it on her own terms and that was the scary thing.

The girls were all worked up. We were a collective ball of chaos walking down the street, Sydney and Dev still yelling at each other while Nikki and I were trying to decide if we should be scared or not.

Out of nowhere, Nikki declared, "I don't know about you ladies, but I'm looking way too cute to fight or be involved in a murder. Call that crazy fool back, Sydney, and arrange this showdown for another night, okay?"

Sometimes she could be so extreme. We were all silent for a moment, digesting the random admission of vanity. Then the roar of laughter ensued. We all laughed uncontrollably at the seriousness with which Nikki made her statement. Even Dev and Sydney had to stop bickering to laugh. By the time we walked up to Pop Burger, everyone had calmed down. We all decided that we were not about to be punked out of continuing our plans for a good night. However, I did text Kari and tell him the situation to put him on alert in case we needed some male backup for the night.

When I asked Dev out of curiosity if she had mentioned anything to Mel, like the phone calls, she said no. I wasn't sure why, but I assumed that she had her reasons.

We walked into Pop Burger like we owned the spot. It was clear that we were all on the same page. If some shit was about to pop off, then we would be alert, confident, and ready to do what we had to do. Either way, Dev would not be in it alone and she knew that.

The DJ was jamming and the spot was packed. The décor always reminded me of a 1970s-raunchy, sex, pervaded bathhouse. The red, felt banquettes and the raw white-oak planks lining the walls and floors screamed hot, steamy, sex cabin. It probably didn't help that during my first time hitting up the location in the meatpacking district, there were snippets of an old-school porn flick being projected onto a wall and playing in a nonstop loop. Porn in public? Only in New York.

My girls and I headed to the lounge area, drinks in hand, and sat down at a table with an excellent view of the comings and goings of the crowd. Nikki turned to Dev. "Dev, are you nervous?"

Dev turned to Nikki, blinked her faux lashes and cocked her head to the side. "Nope, are you?" We cracked up given the comment that Nikki had made earlier in the night. The alcohol had us all feeling carefree.

As it turned out, a guy that Dev and I knew in passing was having his birthday party in the lounge area—he was a major player on the social scene. That's why the spot was packed. I saw a couple of other familiar faces, too. The girls were enjoying the chic New York scene so they mixed and mingled, collecting drink after drink from the throngs of men falling at their feet and vying for their California girl attention.

Around three o'clock in the morning, we closed out our tab. We were spent and the crowd started to wind down. After the waitress finished collecting our signed receipt, she was headed away from the table when a large-framed woman pushed past the frail waitress charging in our direction. It was like something out of a cheerleading movie, the way that we all stood in our sky-high stilettos to confront whatever drama was coming our way.

The linebacker-sized heifer tried to approach Dev, but not before Sydney and I blocked her path.

With an intimidating scowl on her pretty little face, Sydney shouted over the music, "Who the hell are you?"

I couldn't see Dev at the moment but after a few glasses of alcohol, she was likely feeling herself, which was par for the course. I was sure that she was right behind us saying to herself, *I can take this big broad down.*

The big woman shifted her weight to one side, then looked at Sydney. "Wow, I was coming over to speak. Are you her bodyguards or something?"

Sydney didn't let her guard down. "Depends on who's asking," she shot back, throwing a quizzical look back at the big woman.

"Look, I thought that I recognized your friend from the hair shop and I was going to say hello. But it's not that serious."

I felt a hand on my shoulder pulling me back. Dev pushed Sydney and me aside. The next thing I knew, she embraced the girl offering a dramatic, Dev-style hello. We sat there looking like a fake goon squad all worked up for nothing while the two of them chatted for a brief second.

"Whatever," I whispered to Sydney. "Better safe than sorry."

"Exactly. Now let's get the hell up out of here. We've had enough drama for one night."

We made our way back to Jersey and everyone was beat. Girls were dropping out of their stilettos at the front door. Jewelry and makeup were coming off like costumes. Once everyone was situated, I climbed in my bed and lay there staring at the ceiling, thanking "sweet baby Jesus" that we made it home safely and the night did not get any crazier. I rolled over and grabbed my phone off of the nightstand to text Kari that we had made it home safe.

By the time I woke up the next day, the girls were all stirring and Sydney was in the kitchen making breakfast for everyone. She whipped up fluffy eggs, grits, biscuits, and bacon. Light meal but a good start to the day. Even though it was a holiday weekend, I decided to stay home and get on my grind applying for jobs while the girls roamed the city. They would probably end up shopping in SoHo and given my budget—which was just above the poverty line—I thought it best to stay home.

I needed to get focused. A little fun in moderation was cool, but the bigger picture had to stay at the top of my mind. I was ready to get back to work.

I made a list of all companies or things that were even remotely of interest to me. Once I created a decent list, I scoured company websites and checked the career sections.

I applied for every single in-house public relations position that I could find. From record labels to beauty companies and even sports leagues, I was up for anything. By the time the girls got back to the apartment, I had covered a lot of ground and I was feeling accomplished and ready to party. A Sunday night on a holiday weekend in the city was guaranteed fun. With no work the next day, everyone would be in the streets heavy, looking to get a little crazy and have a good time.

We were hitting up Lotus, a swanky hotspot on Fourteenth Street. It was a restaurant by day and club by night. To get ready, we cranked up the music and started the pre-party drinks. Everyone began selecting looks and outfits for the night.

Nikki and Sydney had picked up a few cute items on their shopping spree, so the only trouble they had was deciding between which sexy little number to wear. I had a skin-tight tangerine jumpsuit that I couldn't wait to rock, so there were no decisions needed on my part for once.

Dev and Sydney were in Dev's room throwing outfit options on the bed for consideration when Nikki and I ran into the room with drinks in hand and a brilliant idea.

"So who's down for a little extra fun?" I said.

Dev looked suspicious. "What are you chicks up to?"

"We should play a little game tonight," Nikki chimed in. "Nothing too complicated. It's pretty simple actually. Let's see who can get the most numbers."

Dev paused. She looked as though she was letting the idea register. It didn't take long before she quickly said, "I'm in!" Then she added, "But what's the prize? What do I get when I win?" The room fell silent. We each looked at her with the screw face. She even had to laugh at herself on that one.

The night was getting off to a festive start and we were all geeked to get to the club and let the games begin. Dev had her flask, so we were taking shots on the way into the city.

The conversation on the way to the club consisted of a sole

topic: shit-talking about who would win, what assets we would use, and how many men we could snag. Everyone pulled out extra stops in the wardrobe department because we knew what was at stake—a pair of earrings. It was laughable as designated prizes go, but it was more about the bragging rights. Who would walk away the illest chick with the most game?

Everyone's look was on point. Lashes were luxurious and ready to bat, lipstick was poppin', and titties and ass were spilling out from every angle like bang-boom-pow!

Dev had been texting back and forth with Mel since earlier in the day. She knew that he was planning to go to Lotus as well. On a holiday weekend, Mel was likely to roll deep; his boys liked to do it big. We wanted to get to the club at the same time as Mel so that we could walk in with him, hassle-free. The door would be crazy and that's when the bouncers started acting extra selective with letting people in.

We arrived at the club slightly before Mel and the crowd was spilling over into the street, which was not a good sign. The girls started asking questions about what we were going to do and it looked like Dev was getting a bit annoyed. I told them to chill and let her handle it.

About five minutes later, Dev told us that Mel was walking up on the left side of the club, so we headed in that direction. We had to push through the crowd, and people were the worst when it came to lining up for a club. They would stand there like statues not wanting to lose their spot when in actuality, it didn't matter because nothing was guaranteed. Things were so chaotic. It took a minute for Dev to finally spot Mel.

As I thought, he was with a bunch of guys. It must have been a special night; some of his dudes even brought their trophy women out. I was peeping everything trying to see who was what to whom.

Mel hugged Dev and gave her a kiss on the cheek. "What's good, ma?"

"Trying to see what's up with you," Dev said.

"Wait here. I'll be right back," Mel said.

I watched him make his way to the Arnold Schwarzenegger-looking doorman.

"What is he doing?" Nikki asked. "We better get in this club tonight. I did not squeeze my butt into this Dolce and Gabbana dress for nothing."

"Hush, girl," I said. "Don't trip. We'll get in."

Nikki had never met or rolled with Mel before. She wasn't familiar with his way of doing things. We had never gone to a club with Mel that we did not get into.

Mel came over to Dev and swiftly told her to collect IDs.

Dev picked up on the sense of urgency. "Get your IDs out quick and give them to me."

We all obliged but looked at each other sort of unsure. I was thinking, please don't let these people lose my ID. Dev collected IDs from our group and Mel collected IDs from his group, then he walked away again.

Apparently, the doorman was giving Mel a hassle about the number of people that he was trying to get in. Since it was a holiday weekend, you had to move fast and the doorman basically told Mel that if he wanted to get everyone in—all thirty people— he would have to buy out the entire basement bar. Mel was a boss, so he didn't hesitate. He told the bottle service girl standing next to the doorman, "run it," as he handed her his credit card. It was like the red sea parted. Bouncers were clearing the way and yelling at people to step aside.

"Now that's what I'm talking about," Nikki said at a level that was way too loud. She didn't even know these people. I quickly shot her a glare.

I had never actually been to the basement bar area. I honestly did not know that it existed, but it was definitely the sexiest part of the club. The dim lighting and warm brown tones almost made this spot seem secret and forbidden. The ambiance screamed for people to "Make Love in the Club" like Usher recommended.

As soon as we all got settled at the table of Mel's choice, the drinks started flowing and so did my courage. It was time to start winkin' and blinkin' at some cuties.

I spotted a fly little something by the entrance to the area that we were in. I headed his way. Normally, my girls went by the code: you come together, you leave together. However, this night was a movie in the making, and it was every woman for herself. There was a title at stake and I intended to win.

With my swag on a thousand, I casually looked in the cutie's direction before I made my move. I wanted to establish eye contact first. We briefly met eyes and I subtly looked away. It was time to hunt. I waited until the right amount of people attempted to pass by him and I made my move. I approached the walkway and made it seem as though I had no choice but to get close to him in order to pass. He fell for it. He reached for my arm as I attempted to slide by and said, "Don't pass in such a hurry." It was a lame effort, but whatever, that wasn't my concern.

"Give me a reason to slow down," I snapped back.

"Feisty. I can get with that. What's your name?"

"Scottie," I replied with a slight smile. He was corny, but I needed to seal the deal. "You know what? Put your name and number in my phone and I'll call you sometime. I would really love to chat, but I was on my way to the restroom. Sort of an emergency."

"Cool, cool. I dig it." He definitely was not from New York

speaking like that. Oh well, I would never call him anyway so it really did not matter. I handed him my phone and he did as he was instructed. Number locked and loaded and I was on to the next one.

I noticed Dev pass while I was making my first transaction, so she was feeling the pressure. I spotted her by the bar and went right over to rub it in. "One to zip, baby!"

She shot me a look.

I laughed and strutted off in my strappy, gold sandals.

As I headed up the stairs to the main level, it was a bit dark and I was definitely tipsy, so I decided that I'd better hold on tightly to the railing. I made my way through the crowd, dancing a bit here and there. The music was blaring and the party was live. The bar was jam-packed, too, so I hit the white illuminated glass stairs to the right. I needed to check out the scene from the loft view.

As soon as I found a place to stand, I scanned the main floor and it didn't take long to spot Nikki sitting in a booth with four guys chatting it up. I knew that she was on her game when I noticed the hair flip. Then she offered a subtle touch on the knee of the guy sitting closest to her. Nikki was playing to win, but she unknowingly created the perfect assist for me. I thought to myself, *thanks, girl*, as I hurried down the stairs in her direction.

"Hey, Nikki, who are your new friends?" I asked, with an innocent smile.

The anxious one in the crew stood immediately and extended his hand. "Please, join us."

I followed his lead and slid into the booth being careful to sit up straight, eliminating any potential bulging in my stomach region.

"Would you like a drink?" the anxious dude asked.

"Sure, thank you," I said.

I had been drinking Kir Royales all night, but at that point I would sip on anything. The downside of the tipsy life after a certain point was that I would drink whatever and that was always a recipe for a massive hangover.

Nikki and I clinked glasses as we winked at each other. Time to wrap this up and move on. Nikki got her friend's contact information and I settled for anxious dude. He wrote his number down on a cocktail napkin. There was no way that he would make it into my phone. That may have sounded mean, but the rules of engagement were not always fair.

We headed back down to the basement bar to check in and see if anything exciting was happening. To our surprise, the other girls were huddled around the table taking shots with Mel. I was secretly hoping that Mel was slowing down Dev's action. He wasn't the super-clingy type, but maybe he would have tried to have her on lockdown, for our sake.

Everyone was feeling good and that was obvious. It was like we were all one big happy family. Drinks were flowing like crazy. Everywhere that you turned there were huge bottles of liquor. Mel's friends were getting even friendlier and the girlfriends of some of the guys were even chatting it up. I noticed that one girl in particular kept trying to make conversation with Dev. It seemed a bit strange, but with Mel around, nothing too crazy could pop off. After I took my shot of Patrón, I was ready to collect more victims. I headed out on a mission.

If this was how guys operated when they went out, then I could completely understand why they always had so much fun. While ladies sat posted like wildflowers waiting for a man to approach them, we could have been out there picking who we wanted, testing out the waters and throwing what we didn't like back.

Regardless of how anyone felt, my crew and I were moving around that club like we owned the joint. We were killing the game with the amount of sweet-talking that was going on. I only gave out my number to one cutie. As for the others, I collected the digits so that I stayed in control.

It had to be close to four in the morning and my feet were killing me. All I wanted to do was go home. One of Mel's friends lived in Jersey and agreed to give us a ride, which was perfect. We were all too far-gone to navigate our own way.

Everyone in our party started to make their way to the exit around the same time and we were all borderline drunk. Mel was hanging on Dev like I had never seen before so he must have been feeling good. It looked like he was grabbing at her butt and trying to whisper in her ear, but I tried not to pay attention. That was way more than I needed to see.

When we hit the street, the fresh air felt awesome. It sobered me up a tiny bit and that was exactly what I needed. At least one of us had to be somewhat aware of our surroundings.

Nikki, Sydney, and I were all standing in a huddle waiting on Mel's friend to pull the car around. Dev and Mel were off to the side, talking and smooching.

"I bet Dev didn't win with Mel all in her face like that," I said to the girls.

They cosigned my sentiment. We had a good chuckle since his back was to us and he was in her ear hardcore, completely oblivious to his surroundings.

"What could he possibly be talking about right now?" Nikki asked. "It's too late for excessive chitchat."

"Don't act brand-new," Sydney chimed in.

All of a sudden, Sydney, the shortest one of the crew, went

plowing into Nikki as some headscarf-rocking, hoodrat-looking girl with black Timberlands came barreling by. I caught a glimpse of her face and she looked familiar.

"What the fuck?" Sydney yelled out, but the girl kept moving past Sydney and didn't even react to her.

As we were all talking shit and getting ready to act up, it clicked that she was headed straight for Dev and we sprung into action. *Fuck, how did she find us? It's the crazy stalker bitch.* It was the same woman from a while back who had stared Dev and me down at the happy hour spot.

You could hear nothing but a massive rush of high-heels click-clacking at a rapid pace toward the direction of Dev. There were snippets of a crazy bitch screaming and ranting about hoes, sluts, cheating asses, bitches, and babies. Her volume was on a thousand. Even with all of the chatter from the after-club crowd, you could hear her clear as day. She was acting like a raging lunatic and it seemed as though she had no plans on slowing down or letting up.

This was going downhill fast and it all clicked for me in an instant. She was Dev's stalker. But in actuality she was not after Dev at all; she was after Mel's scumbag ass. That must have been his bitch!

I was instantly nervous and fired up. This woman was clearly ready to do damage. I didn't know what she was capable of, given all the harassing calls to Dev over the past few weeks. What I did know was that people in New York fought dirty. Razor blades, box cutters, and any other dangerous items that you could think of were common in street fights. I couldn't even count how many people I'd seen walking the streets with large, horizontal scars on their faces.

Luckily, the crazy hoodrat went straight for Mel. I heard a loud thud as she bopped his ass in the head real swiftly with something hard. I couldn't tell what it was; it all happened so fast, but he began stumbling instantly. As she continued to flail her fists toward him, we were right there to swoop Dev up and get her out of harm's way.

The look on Dev's face was heartbreaking. She was truly in shock. She was completely clueless. Hell, so was I, for that matter. I was normally the expert detective, but even I did not see any of that coming.

The street crowd stood around looking in awe. It was clear that she wasn't a threat to anyone except Mel. His boys ran over to try to de-escalate the situation before the club bouncers had to step in. A few of Mel's friends looked after him. He was in a daze. The others attempted to get control of the woman scorned and hustle her down the street. She was still screaming and yelling venomous obscenities at Mel as they pushed her away.

Dev was visibly disturbed and rightfully so. The man that she had grown to like and spent so much time with had a woman, and he had been blatantly deceptive. She and Nikki linked arms and walked toward Mel's friend's car. In the midst of his disoriented state, Mel tried to call out to Dev, but she kept walking. She would no longer acknowledge him. He not only had disrespected her by making her the other woman, but he'd also put her in harm's way for the second time and embarrassed her publicly. She was completely done and she did not even have to say a word. We all knew it.

Everyone had just climbed into the car and shut their doors when Mel's boy—the one driving us home—started going off. "Yo, he's a dumb-ass motherfucka, son!"

We all looked around in silence. But then I couldn't resist, as always, and I chimed in with a simple, "I agree."

"Yo, Dev, I'm sorry you had to be a part of all that," his friend continued. "Shit is crazy."

"Thank you for taking us home. I really appreciate it," Dev said, and that's all she offered. I could tell that her anger was starting to set in.

The remainder of the car ride was silent. Once we were in the apartment, tension and anxiety were filling the silence.

"Dev, you cool?" Sydney asked.

"No, I'm not. I'm fucking pissed off!" Dev said as the veins bulged from her neck. "I want to call his trifling ass and curse him the fuck out, but what good would that do? He already knows that he ain't shit. No, what I really want to do is clock his ass upside the head like his chick did. *Blocakah!*"

It wasn't funny at the time, but now that we were home safe and sound, we could laugh our hearts out about that blitz, Rambo-style attack. She got him good.

Nikki shifted the energy back after we had a good laugh. "I heard one of Mel's boys asking how the girlfriend knew where we were. There was speculation that one of the trophy girlfriends must have called her."

"Now that's a trip," I said.

Nikki continued, "So that's probably why she was outside ready and waiting because she had already gotten the play-by-play from inside."

"Dev, I don't know if you remember, but there was a girl by Mel's table that kept breaking her neck to be in your face. She was with the guy who had on the white linen outfit," I explained. "I would bet money she knew what was about to go down."

"Vaguely, I remember thinking that her breath smelled horrid. I wasn't really trippin' off of her, though."

"That goes to show you, never know who's watching," Nikki said.

"Ummm, I know this may not be…uh, perfect timing," Sydney chimed in. "But I still want to know who won the game!"

We all gave Sydney the side eye, but of course we wanted to know as well. So in a state of exhaustion after a chaotic night, we went through our phones and purses to tally up the numbers.

"This is hilarious," Dev said. "After all of the mess that happened tonight, we are sitting here with the sun coming up counting phone numbers for points."

"Well, we need to crown a winner. The girls leave today," I said with a shrug.

"I guess I should be looking at seriously keeping and calling some of these dudes after tonight's revelation," Dev said.

"Couldn't hurt." I smiled.

We were all huddled up on Dev's queen-sized bed when we compared our totals to figure out that Nikki was the winner. We were working off of the honor system and Nikki claimed to have made twenty-three "transactions," so she won by a slight margin.

She squealed with excitement and way too much energy, but we let her have her moment. I was ready to crash so I headed to my boudoir. I threw myself across the bed and lay there exhausted. *What a night.*

Chapter 11

Baller Times Two

My spirits were in a better place since the girls' visit. I had not been as gloomy and emotionally burdened. The last few weeks were eventful and I wanted to try to keep that momentum going. Realizing that I was in a positive space, I made a conscious decision to make every effort not to go back to the negative slump that I had been in.

I'm in New York, a city that people from small towns are dying to experience. I have this opportunity in the palm of my hands, so it's up to me to squeeze it tightly and make the most out of it. Go hard or go home.

Motivation was in the air. I treated myself to a trip to my favorite place for inspiration and clarity, the Brooklyn Museum. It's one of the largest and oldest museums in the country. The contemporary art spoke to my yearning to create. I would stare at contemporary pieces for hours on end. The use of different mediums to make the works come alive always left me feeling joyous. I felt like I could create anything with my hands and conquer my goals.

Working in public relations allowed me to create in a slightly different way, whether it was crafting press releases or coming up with fun promotional ideas, I think that is what drew me to a life of PR. I was wholeheartedly ready to get back in the game.

Day after day I kept pounding the pavement and scouring the

Internet to find the perfect job. My little fingers would tap away at the computer's keyboard keys researching prospective companies, looking for freelance writing opportunities, and checking my email. Sometimes I would get slightly discouraged with all of the auto replies waiting in my inbox. I was dying for a real live person to respond at least once.

Chatting with my Jolie every other day really helped me stay encouraged during the job search. She was very spiritually in tune and always had positive things to say. She would offer up great ideas. Sometimes I wished that I could be more like her, but much of her positive energy and optimism had come with age and learning as she'd gone through life.

During the next couple of weeks, I received interest from mediocre companies and great companies alike. I examined every potential opportunity with a critical eye and took meetings with those that truly caught my interest. Things were starting to pick up.

One random Tuesday I was flicking back and forth between CNN and HGTV when my cell phone rang. Typically only three people called me during the day: my Jolie, Dev, or Kari. I ran to the phone and realized that it was a New York area code but not a number that I knew. I cleared my throat.

"Hello, Scottie speaking," I said in my professional voice.

"Hi, Scottie, I'm Caroline Stinger with Human Resources and I'm calling from The League regarding your application for the publicist position."

You are fucking kidding me. Get a grip and don't scream. This is one of the leading sports leagues; don't act pressed.

"Hi...hi, how are you?"

"Excellent, is this a good time for you?" she asked.

"Sure."

She didn't know that most recently, I had been curled up on the bed watching TV. Of course I could talk. I had nothing but time to talk. She probably expected that I was in an office setting at the moment and needed to slip away into a conference room to chat. Not!

"We would like to bring you in to meet with the hiring manager, Joel Tumblin, and me before the end of the week. Would you be able to come to our office on Thursday at ten?"

"Sure, that works great."

"Terrific. I'll email you shortly to confirm and supply you with all of the details."

"Perfect, thank you so much," I said, trying to temper my excitement. "I look forward to meeting you on Thursday."

After I hung up the phone, I started pacing and talking myself through the excitement. I was elated at the thought of the opportunity. I needed to call my Jolie, then The Clique and Kari—in that order—to let them know the good news.

Thursday came around, and I was beyond prepared. When I arrived to meet with the HR lady at The League's office in midtown, she was ready and waiting for me. Caroline was a petite woman wearing what looked like a JCPenney suit with her hair pulled back in a tight bun. She offered a stern but pleasant smile, then led me to a very drab and basic meeting room off the lobby. You could tell that the space was designated strictly for Human Resources interviews.

Once we were locked in the room with no windows, we discussed a bit of my background and the position. Sports had never really been my main interest, but I thought that it could be fun to give it a try. I did all the proper research to make sure that I didn't make a complete ass out of myself in the interview.

After a successful meeting with HR—that luckily did not involve much grilling on the sports side—Caroline took me to meet with Joel Tumblin, the hiring manager. He seemed like a very genuine guy. Clearly, he was not a recent former athlete. His waistline made his navy blue shirt look as though it were grasping for air. He was a big teddy bear. He offered me a glass of water, which I respectfully declined. Then we went through a range of questions as he told me more specifically about the position.

"Just curious, what are your top three daily go-to sources of news?"

I looked him in his eyes. "*New York Times, Wall Street Journal,* and *USA Today.*"

Joel must have liked my answer. "I think you are a great candidate so I would like to bring you back in to meet with one of my colleagues."

"Okay, fantastic!" I had to give him the extra enthusiastic voice.

As Joel walked me to the lobby, he let me know that Caroline would be in touch to schedule my next meeting.

Like that, I was out of there. Dev's office was not that far away in the Fashion District so I decided to stop by. It was lunchtime so we went to Chipotle to grab a salad. Over grilled chicken, corn, salsa, cheese, and sour cream creations, I ran down every detail of the interview.

"Wow, I hope you get this job," Dev declared. "Man, if you do, we are gonna be in there!"

I chuckled. "Why are you so crazy?"

"I'm so serious!" Dev exclaimed, with almost more excitement than me. "If you get hired, then we have the inside track and I'll finally get to snag me a baller! I better start up my Kanye Workout Plan ASAP."

"Please stop. I really can't take you right now," I said. "Look, even if I get the job, which I don't have yet, I doubt that I'll ever have a chance to hook anyone up. Plus, what would I say? Um, excuse me. Do you want to see a picture of my friend? She is really cute and looking for a baller to wife her. She's been on the Kanye Workout Plan religiously."

Dev rolled her eyes and I laughed. The thought of getting the job had me excited, though. The opportunity to have The League on my resume would be huge, but I didn't want to get too worked up to get let down.

Caroline from HR was very on top of it. By the time that I got back to the apartment, she had already emailed me a proposed time and date for the second interview. As I continued to check my emails, I noticed an unfamiliar name buried among party invites and spam. It was an email from a record label that I'd applied to. The date indicated that it was two days old. They wanted me to come in for a meeting next week as well.

Things were definitely starting to heat up and I was thrilled. I called Kari to tell him the good news. He was equally excited for me.

"Babe, you are killing the game right now," he said. "Who's gonna be calling next? The White House?"

"Please hush," I said, shunning his ludicrous notion. "You are so silly. But really, thank you for being so supportive and enthusiastic about all of my minor wins."

"You are an amazing woman. I want to see you succeed and do major things."

"Thank you, baby."

"You're welcome. Now enough with all of that," Kari said. "Let's celebrate this win. I'll come over and cook you dinner tonight."

"Sounds like a plan to me!" I felt a happiness that was new and scary at the same time.

Kari was such a sweetie. After working all day, he went to the store and picked up the groceries for his special meal. I offered to go food shopping for him, but he declined my offer. He wanted to keep the ingredients a surprise. I respected his wishes and told him to plan to make enough for Dev as well since I knew that she would be home.

Dev had been around the apartment more since things with her and Mel had crumbled. Mel still tried to call her every now and then. She would never answer. At one point, he even got slick and tried to call from other people's phones, but once she identified the voice, she would always hang up just the same.

She hadn't been in a complete funk, though. She had a few dates here and there but nothing serious. She wanted to lay low on the guy tip for a minute. Hence, she found herself home with Kari and me on our dinner date. It was cool, though. They got along well so the three of us always had fun together.

Kari was serious about his meal. He moved around the kitchen like a madman sweating and even talking to himself in short whispers. He didn't want us to get too close to his kitchen and his recipe. So he slaved over the stove while Dev and I sipped on wine and chatted him up from the other side of the room.

"Dinner is served, ladies," Kari finally said, complete with a cheesy grin.

"Thanks, babe. You are too kind to us." I jokingly smacked him on the butt and gave him a thank-you kiss. "You know I like a man who knows his way around the kitchen."

This was one of maybe five meals that he could make. His presentation consisted of smothered chicken breasts, sautéed vegetables, and yellow rice. It was so cute how extra proud of himself he was. As for me, this was more than any man had ever cooked for me. I appreciated the time and effort.

Over dinner, we talked about the potential job opportunities that were now coming my way. Kari and Dev both gave me their feedback as to which job they would prefer me to have. This was all premature, though. I did not have an offer from either company and furthermore, I had not even met with the record label yet.

After dinner, Kari and I cleaned the kitchen before heading to my room for some quality time. I really liked that Kari never had any expectations when it came to sex and me. Sure, he wanted it like any other man, but he was always so easy breezy about things. I never felt like every time we were alone, he was going to put in his best attempt to sex me up.

He liked to cuddle as much as I did. He would hold me close in his diesel arms and whisper in my ear. It always made me feel like I was in a fairy tale. I loved the time that we would spend together and the intimacy that we shared. I also liked the idea of being his girl, though sometimes I would get anxiety about my relationship being too good to be true. I had never had this before. I had a man who cared about me and was always there when I needed him. He had no problem telling me, heck the whole world, how he felt. Our relationship was never a secret to anyone; not his friends, my friends, colleagues or even strangers. Kari had nothing to hide. He would do little things to try to reassure me that he was serious about us, but because of my past, I still had my reservations.

Chapter 12

A Woman With Options

After a month-long interview process with The League and completing multiple writing samples for both positions, I had two offers on the table. With one offer from The League and the other from the record label, I was elated. Only two months prior, I was unemployed, depressed and unsure of my future.

The toughest part was still to come. I had a decision to make. I liked sports, however, I loved music. But The League was willing to pay a higher salary. This would not be easy. I called my Jolie to talk it out. She suggested that we go over the pros and cons of each opportunity. After speaking to both my Jolie and my dad, I had a better idea as to which position I would select. When I met up with Kari, he was very supportive and surprisingly, contrary to personal interests, he did not try to sway me one way or the other.

"Go with what your gut is telling you, baby," Kari said. "You are the one that has to do the work and be happy with it."

If anyone knew the realities of doing the work, Kari, a fellow publicist, did.

"I think I know what I'm going to do, but I want to sleep on it before making my final decision."

"Sounds like a good plan."

I smiled as my head rested on Kari's chest. I wasn't sure what I was smiling about exactly, but I was in a good space in the moment and I could get used to the feeling.

"What do you think about a trip to Atlantic City to celebrate?" Kari asked.

"I've never been," I said. "That would be a perfect getaway weekend before I start the new gig!"

"That's what I was thinking, a nice relaxing trip to start you off right."

It was settled. We were going to Atlantic City.

The next morning, I awoke with a clear head. I was focused on what I needed to do. I called The League to accept the position and my second call was to the record label to respectfully decline their offer. A sense of calm flowed through my body and I breathed a sigh of relief.

Once Kari finished up with his client, we were on our way to mini-Las Vegas. The drive to Atlantic City was not as long as I imagined it would be, maybe two-and-a-half hours at most. When we arrived, I felt like we were in a sleepy, small town, but as we moved closer to the action, I got more of the Vegas, high-rise casino feel.

To my surprise, Atlantic City was situated along a beach board-walk. A casino on the beach was a completely new concept to me.

We pulled into our hotel and it was luxurious. The property was massive so I made it a point to take mental notes of landmarks as we walked through the main floor.

Kari toted most of the heavy bags and went to check us in while I waited in the fancy lounge area, which looked like some rich Fifth Avenue grandmother's living room. When he came over with the room keys, we took one of eight elevators up to the twenty-second floor. Since he insisted on taking care of all the details, I simply followed and let my man lead the way. We kept walking and walking and walking down an extended art deco hallway with minimal light until we finally reached the absolute end. Kari slid his keycard into the door and pushed open one half of a double door, which led to a massive suite fit for a queen. My eyes lit up with surprise.

"Kari, this room is amazing!" There was a panoramic view of the Atlantic City Boardwalk. We still had a bit of daylight on our side so you could see for what felt like miles and take in the beauty of the view.

"I wanted your first visit here to be special," Kari said.

Where did this man come from?

"Well, you definitely succeeded in a major way. Thanks, babe." I grabbed Kari tightly and kissed him in front of the floor-to-ceiling windows.

"Damn, I love how you show me your appreciation," Kari said with a grin.

"Are you trying to make me blush?"

"No, trying to make you love me."

If I were talented enough to make one eyebrow rise, it would have totally been a moment to do it. His comment came out of nowhere.

As the words left Kari's mouth and entered the universe, I managed to keep smiling as I had been before, but inside I was screaming with fear and anxiety. *Love*, I thought to myself. I'm not sure what type of reaction Kari expected, but I didn't quite know how to react. I went in for another kiss. It seemed as though that would be the safest route.

"Do you want me to make you a drink?" I asked. *I sure could use one.*

"Sure, babe," Kari said as he smiled, flashing his pearly whites.

The evening set in and we sipped cocktails while giving each other sensuous head-to-toe massages with Lothantique massage oil. After we were oily and relaxed, we headed to the shower. It was a massive space with dual showerheads, a light-colored marble finish throughout, and a handy little shower bench designed for fun, I assumed.

Luckily, I packed a little get sexy kit so my candles created the perfect sexy time ambiance. Once we entered the shower, I could see that Kari's penis was saying, "Hello, I'm here. Please don't neglect me." It was hard and huge.

I picked up a washcloth to lather his body. I slowly began to massage and cleanse his chiseled frame of the oil. The water was steaming hot. Pulsating showerheads drenched our bodies from both angles relaxing every inch. I was so caught up in my moment of bliss that I forgot to put a shower cap on. Thankfully, I'd learned to maintain and style my short pixie cut. My hair was fine and wavy, so a little product and I would be set.

I continued to wash Kari thoroughly before finally making my way down to his penis, which had been poking me and begging for my attention the entire time. I massaged his manhood with my soapy towel sliding it back and forth, creating a sensation of a wet kitty cat. Kari loved it. He started moaning and groaning and biting me in between kisses.

I knew that Kari didn't want to cum yet, so he spun me around and sat me on the shower bench. He slid down on his knees and put his face in between my legs. This man knew his way around my sweet spot. He licked and suckled like it was his last big bet and all of his chips were on the table. He instructed me to slide to the edge of the bench and pull both of my legs up on the bench. My va-jay-jay was now facing him front and center for better access. Kari was a true pleaser in the way that he never *talked* about wanting to please me sexually—he just did it.

Mere moments after repositioning my body for prime access, the twisting, licking, and swirling of his tongue coerced my body into reaching an epic climax. I started to squeeze Kari tighter with my thighs and my legs suddenly got weak and began to give out on me. I threw my legs over his shoulders for extra support, but when my entire body started to shake from the climactic onset and soft soothing of his tongue, I couldn't take it anymore. I grabbed Kari's head and pulled him up. He looked a little puzzled.

"I want you right now," I demanded in a lustful, *Girl 6* voice.

"You will always get what you want, love." Even that last word could not throw me off-center in the moment. I needed to feel him inside me.

Kari immediately scooped me up and we exited the shower. Our steamy bodies rubbed along each other. He carried me soaking wet to the next room. We fell onto the bed in one swift motion. I wanted him badly. My body was aching. I still hadn't completely stopped shaking.

When he entered my sweet spot, it was drenched and more than ready to welcome him. Kari and I were so in sync that we could predict what the other wanted next. We made crazy, freak-nasty love from the back, flipped upside down, and my favorite, with me on top. I liked being on top because it allowed me to reach a mind-blowing orgasm. I also enjoyed the control and Kari didn't feel any type of way about it because I made him feel ecstasy in the end.

I straddled him while we were both sitting up facing each other and I improvised with a move that was intense. I could feel his heart beating fast against my chest as we grinded and thrust, holding each other as tightly as possible with a combination of sweat and water now dripping from us. We were one big ball of lust.

"Lay back," I instructed Kari and he did just that. As he lay back I began my show.

I rolled my hips and popped my pussy on him like a true porn star in training.

Kari grabbed my ass tight and squeezed it with a look of pleasure just before he was about to explode. I liked to please him as much as he liked to please me. He let out a loud sequence of moans and like that, I put him to sleep.

The getaway was just what I needed. It allowed me a chance to clear my mind and get my body tuned up—a perfect combination for starting fresh. I spent the night before my first day of work getting mentally and physically prepared. I watched *SportsCenter*, read every newsworthy, sports-related article in addition to picking out a black, above-the-knee dress with three-quarter-length sleeves and a black blazer to finish off my typical publicist uniform.

I walked into the high-rise, midtown office building for what was now the third time, but this day was different. This girl was now an employee of The League.

After reporting to Joel, I struggled through the boring, new-hire orientation and fought every urge to doze off. At the end of an uneventful day, I was shown to my desk and given all of my essentials by IT, which included a laptop and a BlackBerry.

I was all set up and settled in when I realized that it was six o'clock. There wasn't anything pressing to do, so I decided to call it a day.

When I got home, Dev wanted to know every detail. I'm guessing that she expected it to be a bit more glamorous than it really was.

"So how was it? Who did you meet today?" she asked enthusiastically.

"My coworkers," I said with a chuckle.

"Okay, smart ass. But that consisted of some players, right?"

"Oh yeah, I intentionally left out the part where I met the New York Talons' entire team in the lobby on my way to lunch."

"Dang! You did? How exciting!"

"No silly!" I said. "That would probably never happen. First off, the teams are spread out all over the U.S. and it's not like they have to come to The League office to check in on a regular basis. The athletes' schedules are hectic and they probably only drop by our offices when it is absolutely necessary."

I did my best to explain to Dev my role and how the PR world works in general. The misconception in entertainment PR is that you simply rub elbows with celebrities and so-called "important" people. Reality check, you write press releases so you better be good with putting words together. You mastermind detailed PR plans that people rarely ever use or refer to. You cold call media that generally act like you are bothering them—but they don't hesitate to act friendly when they need you. Lastly, you kiss ass and play nice with the media people who you actually know and want to continue a relationship with. That pretty much sums it up. There are times that you interact with high-profile people, but it is by far not what most publicists do every day.

My first week at The League was a breeze. The work hadn't started piling up yet. One day, while in the restroom, I ran into a young lady with legs for miles and at least four-inch heels on. If I had to guess, she had been a model at some point in life. Her icy-blue eyes looked as though they could put you in a trance that you wouldn't wake from.

I was at the sink washing my hands alongside the woman I came to know as Lydia when she unexpectedly said, "Hi, you must be the new girl that I heard about."

"Hi," I said with a slight smirk. "I guess so. I'm Scottie. Nice to meet you."

Lydia was not in my department, but our groups worked closely together. I quickly came to know her as an intelligent hard worker from Baltimore who did not take crap from anyone. Eventually, she gave me the background scoop on everyone that worked on our floor. Forming my own opinions based off of my personal interactions with people was cool, but I would not deny potentially insightful information. According to Lydia, a woman named Britney was one to keep an eye on. She was venomous. I hoped that overall, The League employees would not be anything like the treacherous people at my old PR agency.

The head of The League's publicity department was a plump brunette with masculine features and a leftover 1980s hairstyle. Her slick commentary and taskmaster style made it evident that she was a Ms. Know-It-All. Her name was Gail Dean, but people rarely used her first name; they called her Dean. Pretty fitting if you asked me.

My manager, Joel, was easygoing and helpful in the process of getting acclimated. He gave me guidance but left me to my own devices to get my work done. It was my responsibility to learn all that I could about our athletes' lives and who they were as men outside of the game. I was charged with making them seem appealing as well as saleable to mainstream media. The League's special events also fell under my list of responsibilities. I loved the rush of executing a red carpet on event day. There was a sense of accomplishment.

As the weeks went on, the workload increased and I found out that my first event would be the Athlete's Annual. Festivities surrounding the event attracted thousands of fans from around the world. In college, my friends and I would take special trips to the Athlete's Annual so I was familiar with the event from a fan's perspective. However, working an event of that magnitude could prove to be an interesting challenge.

The two months leading up to the Athlete's Annual were hectic as hell, to say the least. The League's style was to learn as you go. Since everything was new for me, there was a huge learning curve and catching on quickly was imperative. I learned instantly that people would only forcibly communicate with those who were outside of their department. If you did not know the right questions to ask in order to obtain the information that you needed, then you would come up short.

Gathering information was like a search-and-rescue mission. Everyone had a very specific job function and you had to go through multiple individuals to get what you needed to complete a task. Some people had been there so long that they seemed to be very sensitive about their role, so you had to make sure not to offend or piss anyone off while trying to do your job.

I found myself working late hours to feel like I was caught up each day, only to turn around and do it again the next day. But I liked the feeling of working toward a specific point of execution.

During the Athlete's Annual, the main events that I was responsible for from a media perspective were the Entertainer's Game and the red carpet, just prior to the main event. Interacting heavily with the events department and the talent department were crucial pieces to the puzzle.

For the Entertainer's Game, I had to find out everything: how many media persons could fit in the venue, what my credential process would need to be, who would be playing in the game, and if the celebrity talent would be willing to do media interviews to promote their participation in the game. The events group held all of the answers and sometimes it could be like waving ice cream in front of a dieting woman to get what you needed.

The red carpet was slightly unpredictable in terms of talent, so I simply had to make sure that we had media on hand to get interviews and shots of whoever decided to stroll down the carpet prior to the game. The origin of my stress was largely due to the fact that this would be my first weekend full of events and I wanted everything to go smoothly.

Kari was starting to witness the immense pressure that I was under as our late-night conversations in bed were dominated by work talk.

"Babe, can you please stop flicking back and forth?" Kari asked. "Leave it on *SportsCenter*. You're driving me crazy."

"You know I always watch my CNN. Don't act brand-new," I said. "But this sports world is not a game. I have to make sure that I know who's doing well. I can't be in the dark when it comes to the Athlete's Annual and who will make the team."

Kari shook his head.

He did his best to be supportive. Kari would hold me in his arms and stroke my back trying his best to make me destress and release some of the anxiety. On occasion, he would offer advice and reassure me that he believed in my rock-star capabilities. Sometimes his words of encouragement were like music to my ears.

"You should take some time out to relax, Scottie."

"I'm trying to prove myself still. I don't feel like I have that luxury yet."

"I'm not suggesting anything extreme. I thought that it would be good to grab dinner with friends. Maybe tomorrow."

"I'm sorry, baby, you're right. Seems like an excellent idea. I haven't been very social lately."

The next night, we linked up with some friends and went to a low-key spot in Hell's Kitchen called Ta Cocina. Their two-for-one margaritas made it one of my favorite restaurants. The drinks were flowing and everyone was chatting and enjoying good company. Most of the group was Kari's peeps. They had become my friends by default.

"I want to make a toast," Kari said spontaneously. "Everyone raise their glass with me. I would like to congratulate Scottie on her new gig at The League. She's doing big things. I'm so proud of her and her accomplishments! To Scottie!"

Kari leaned in to kiss my glossy, frosted, pink lips.

"You guys are too sweet," I said. "Thanks, everyone, for being so supportive."

My unemployment status had been no secret to the crew. They all knew my struggle and they were genuinely happy for me. That is, except for Kari's smart-ass best friend, Kelvin. He always irked the hell out of me. But he was Kari's boy, so there wasn't much that I could say.

"So how long before you leave ma' boy for one of them millionaire ballers?" Kelvin blurted out with conviction.

What the fuck kind of question is that, you asshole?!

Eyes shot up, glasses dropped on the table and suddenly a lively dinner table fell silent. Everyone looked a little stunned. Kari fixed his lips to speak up on my behalf, but I raised my hand to his chest. "I got this."

"Probably about the same damn time that you scrape enough pennies together to move out of yo' momma's house. Ooops! That would mean never," I spat. "By the way, jealousy does not look good on you, Kelvin."

Kelvin and Kari had been friends since elementary school and they were inseparable growing up, like Kid 'n Play, complete with similar names. From what I could see, as they grew older, Kelvin wasn't always a very good friend to Kari. In most instances, he would have something negative to say. People like that could be toxic. It's usually a good indicator that they are not happy with things in their own life or they are harboring jealous feelings. I tried to mention Kelvin's behavior to Kari once, but he made up an excuse for Kelvin. From that point on, I left it alone.

After that awkward moment, everyone tried to go on like normal. I was still seething with disdain for Kelvin, but I did not let him ruin the remainder of my dinner. Eventually, we wrapped up at Ta Cocina and everyone said their goodbyes and went their separate ways. Kari and I headed back to his apartment. I would rarely stay over since he lived so deep in Brooklyn, but on weekends, it worked out fine. We rode in silence until I decided to speak my piece.

"That was a disrespectful thing to say," I commented. "One day somebody is going to smack the shit out of ya boy."

"Scottie, stop it. He was playing."

"Playing! That's your idea of playing?" I fired back. I was starting to get pissed all over again. "You know, you always take up for him. But that was straight-up wrong, it wasn't a joke, it damn sure wasn't funny, and it was flat-out rude."

"Why are you getting so upset? You're kind of acting like he exposed your secret or something."

He raised his voice slightly with that comment and I didn't like his tone nor did I like where the conversation was going. That comment came out of nowhere. I was getting livid. Did he have some hidden feelings that he wasn't telling me about? Had he and Kelvin already discussed this?

"Well, what the fuck? I mean…did you put him up to it? Was

that good cop-bad cop routine where you let him ask me all the fucked-up questions and you sit back and wait for the answers?"

"Of course not! Scottie, don't be ridiculous. If I have something to say, I'll say it my damn self." Kari rubbed his goatee.

"You know what? Whatever. I'm done. Talking to you is pointless right now," I said.

"Seriously, that's how you're gonna act?"

"Pretty much," I said as I rolled my eyes and turned my head to look out at the brownstones passing through my line of sight.

I had nothing more to say to Kari. He was being an insensitive jerk and I wasn't going to sit there and try to reason with stupidity.

When we got to Kari's house, the tension in the air was still thick. He threw his keys down on the glass coffee table and stormed into the bathroom, slamming the door shut. I went straight to his room, slid on my pajamas, curled up in his bed, and shut my eyes. Yes, mad.

The bright sunrays and Kari's snoring woke me up the next morning. After hearing me stir for a minute, Kari finally decided to open his eyes and stretch his long arms toward me.

Without wasting any time, he said, "So, are you still mad from last night?"

"I'm not mad at you. I was hurt that you did not take Kelvin's disrespect serious."

"You're right. I guess I didn't give what he said that much weight."

"It was more the delivery and the setting that made me upset," I said. "Kari, turn the tables around and tell me how you would have felt sitting there being chastised in front of a table full of people?"

He stared off for a moment. "I get it, babe. You're right. I would have wanted to sock him too."

Chapter 13

Athlete's Virgin

The days leading up to the Athlete's Annual in Miami proved to be torture. With all of the last-minute updates to media materials, constant questions via email, and maintaining the guest lists for multiple events, the work ran me ragged and pulling long hours seemed to be expected of everyone. There was definitely a do-what-it-takes mentality and by all means, you did not want to screw up and feel the wrath of Dean. The last thing that you wanted was her flipping out on you, as she had been known to do.

Lydia and I chatted about what parties would be hot and the fun that we were ready to get into. She knew people in Miami, so she was excited to hang out. My girl Bella, also a part of The Clique, had recently moved to the area for business school so I was ecstatic that I would get to see her.

Given that this was my first ride at the rodeo, I had no idea what to pack for the trip. Naturally, I wanted to be cute, while keeping in mind that it was a work trip. I only packed a couple of sassy outfits. When I had attended the mandatory Athlete's Annual orientation at the job, they did not include "freakum dress" on the list of must-haves. But I had packed one anyway.

Kari walked into my room and looked at the piles of clothes stacked all over the bed. "Babe, did they tell you to bring enough outfits for you and the groupies to wear?"

"Hush up." I giggled. "I really don't know what to expect, so I want to be ready for whatever."

"I hear you."

"If I want to secure my future at The League and set my self up for advancement to the next level, then I have to be ready for whatever whenever."

"Well, Ms. Ready Whenever, how are you getting to the airport in the morning? Do you need me to take you?" Kari asked.

"No, The League arranged a car service from here to the airport." I updated Kari on my first-class travel style. "But it gets better. I found out that they chartered a commercial flight for all of the employees. Pretty dope, right?"

"Oh, they're fancy!" Kari laughed.

Then his facial expression quickly turned from playful to concerned. "So do the guys take the same plane as the staff?"

"Uh yeah. They don't make the female employees take a separate flight from the males." I rolled my eyes.

"No, you know what I mean. Stop playing," he snapped. "I'm talking about the athletes, the men that make The League possible."

"Oh, those guys." I wanted him to make it clear what he wanted to know.

"Uh, I can't say for sure, but I highly doubt that any of them would be on our flight."

I sensed that the inquiry was coming from a weird space. I didn't want to make it a big deal on my last night home, so I changed the subject and finished packing.

Later that night, Kari made love to me in a way that he had never done before. He held me extra tight, like if he lost his grip, I would disappear. I figured six days away from each other could have emotions running high.

Morning came quickly. After I gathered my suitcase and black crocodile carry-on bag by the front door, I climbed on the bed to lie next to Kari. His eyes were still closed. When he turned his head in my direction, I kissed his cheek, then his eyes met mine. He smiled and I leaned in to kiss his morning breath.

"Sorry to wake you, babe. I wanted to hear your voice before I left."

"I'm gonna miss you," Kari said softly.

"I'll be back before you know it." I caressed his scruffy facial hair. "I'll call you when I land."

"You better," Kari responded with a smile.

He smacked me on the butt as I got up from my bed. I knew that he was watching so I put an extra sexy sway in my sashay.

When I pulled up to the airport and my driver opened the door of the black Cadillac Escalade to guide me out of the vehicle, I felt like a celebrity. VIP treatment. However, the VIP lifestyle stopped at check-in. The airport was packed. Once I finally got my boarding pass and made it through security, I had worked up an appetite. I whipped out my company credit card and ordered up as much food as a twenty-dollar breakfast allotment would cover.

The flight to Miami was quicker than I expected. The League definitely knew how to set their employees up in swanky accommodations. My group was staying at the Epic Hotel in Biscayne Bay, which was a chic waterfront property. When I walked into the lobby, I noticed a few of my colleagues sitting in a lounge area chatting. I politely waved and continued on to the front desk.

There was signage everywhere promoting the Athlete's Annual and even the room keys had the event logo on them. It was pretty impressive to be a part of such a major production.

Once in my room, I hung up all of my clothes, including my

suits. They were mandatory attire when working a League event. I lined up my nametag, all-access credentials, and hotel keys in preparation for the next day. After making sure that my security lock was on the door, I headed for the shower to freshen up before my dinner date with Bella.

I replied to a few urgent emails, then called Kari before hitting the streets, but to my surprise, he didn't answer. I left him a message letting him know that I'd made it to Miami. I also called Bella to check on her status. She was ten minutes away.

I grabbed my makeup bag and jetted into the bathroom. The lighting was fantastic and horrible all at the same time. It showed me every blemish and imperfection, but there was no time to dwell on what I could not change. Mascara check, eyeliner check, eyebrow pencil check, bronzer check, and last but certainly not least, a swipe of blush.

My outfit was the last beast to tackle. I prayed that what I'd packed would look right. Sometimes things looked better in my head than on my body. Thankfully, I had brought a few mix-and-match options in case. My leopard print pants were slightly challenging to wiggle into. The black tank that I'd brought was loose at the bottom so I could hide any unforeseen stomach spillover, and it cut in a bit by the breast region, giving a little sexy side boob. I had to sit down carefully on the bed in order to slip on my red stiletto booties. One wrong move and the pants of choice would be a wrap.

My phone was buzzing like crazy and I figured that it was Bella so I answered with my earphones not even bothering to look at the screen.

"Hey, boo, you downstairs?"

"Boo?"

"Really? That's how it is when you go out of town?"

"Hello!" I said as I looked at the phone.

I was rushing around and moving so fast that it took me a second to recognize Kari's voice on the other end of the phone.

"I'm sorry, babe. I thought you were Bella. She's on her way to pick me up."

"Sure, tell me anything."

"Stop it. I called you a little while ago."

"I know. That's why I'm calling you back."

"Okay, Mr. At-ti-tude!"

"So where are you ladies headed?"

"South Beach to do dinner and drinks."

"South Beach...hmm...well, have fun. I'll speak to you later."

I heard the sound of the dial tone. *Did he just hang up on me?*

I had options. I could do one of two things, overreact and call him back cursing and flipping out, or give him his space to be annoyed and go on to enjoy my night. I chose the latter. Sprayed on a little sandalwood-and-vanilla scent, gave myself a once-over in the full-length mirror, tousled my short waves to frame my face, grabbed my gold leather clutch, and I was out the door.

Bella rolled up to the valet stand in a drop-top Mini Cooper. It was her style, understated and chic. She jumped out of her ride and ran around to the passenger side greeting me with her arms wide open. We squealed like two schoolgirls and gave each other *The Color Purple*-style hug. I missed my sister from another mother. It had been almost a year since we'd seen each other.

Bella chose to attend business school in Florida so that she could be closer to her father. When she was born, he took one look at his baby girl and said "Bella" in his native Italian tongue. He moved away from California when she was in junior high, which was right after her parents decided to split. Bella had always adored her father even through the tumultuous divorce. Her mother was adamant that Bella would be raised with her in California, and as an African-American judge, she got her way.

Her father was loaded, so he must have given her the assist with the new car. He always spoiled Bella and gave her anything that she wanted. But she never came off as a freeloading brat. She was the sweetest person, with her big, dark-brown eyes and head full of soft, curly, sandy-brown hair.

"I'm so happy to see you. And you look fantastic, honey!" Bella continued to observe. "This new man must really be treating you right."

We slapped high-five.

"Thanks, sweetie! You look amazing as always." I stepped back as I checked her out. "Miami better watch out for you, honey!"

"You are so silly, Scottie!"

Bella zoomed out of the driveway and after a few turns, we were on the MacArthur Causeway with the wind in our hair. The humidity was low and the moon was shining brightly. It was a gorgeous, warm Miami night, which felt so relaxing.

"Where are we headed?" I yelled to Bella, trying to compete with the music and the wind.

She turned the music down. "I was thinking we'd go to the Italian spot on Española Way."

"Great idea! I love that street."

"Okay, good. Afterwards, we can go down to Ocean Drive and have drinks. We'll have a zillion options to choose from."

Bella needed a night out. She did not have any of her close girlfriends nearby and business school had been kicking her butt. A release was long overdue. After dinner, our night consisted of drinks and more drinks resulting in a couple of tipsy tales surrounded by a few good men. We'd made our way to a sexy little rooftop bar with a beautiful view of the Miami skyline.

Bella's eyes were glassy and a tall, muscular man with name-brand gear on from head to toe was relentlessly in her face. He and his boys were posted at a table covered with at least ten bottles, and they invited us to hang out with them. Essentially, I was taking one for the team. I had absolutely no interest in any of the guys since I had a great man waiting for me at home. I decided to text Kari.

Bella and her guy were getting cozy, but it was quickly approaching two in the morning and I still had to get up and report for work in a few hours. I thought it best for me to call it a night. To my surprise, when I went over to break the news to Bella, she was ready to go as well.

"You are in no position to drive," I said as we made our way down to the lobby. "Maybe we should call a cab."

I was definitely tipsy myself, but I slowed down around 1 a.m. and started drinking water to try to level my intoxication out. Even still, I was in no position to drive either.

"Girl, don't worry about it. I got this."

"Oh no you don't! You live way too far to drive intoxicated, and furthermore, my Jolie will kill you if you killed me."

"No, Scottie, my father set up a car service account for me, especially for nights like this."

"Wait, so let me make sure I have this straight. You go out and get too drunk to drive and Daddy already has it set where you call the car service and it goes on his tab, no questions asked?"

"Pretty much. I use the same company that he uses for his business," she continued. "He doesn't, you know, want me taking chances driving drunk."

"I hope you know how lucky you are."

It took the car service no longer than fifteen minutes to pick us up in a luxury SUV with the celebrity tint.

The next morning it would be safe to assume that I hated life. Mornings were not my thing and there was so much work to be done. Joel had already sent me about ten emails. My day would consist of heading to the temporary office in the hotel to try to get a few things accomplished before I had to go to the mandatory community service project.

The project site that I was assigned to was deep in the 'hood. This girl was no stranger to the 'hood, but this was a different type of hood. There I was, standing around with a bunch of people who seemed totally clueless as to the reality. The plan was to work with a local community partner and assist a deserving family in building the home of their dreams. The athletes would show up to take part in the build, do a few press interviews, pose for a few photos, and shake some hands. My assignment was to make sure that the right photos were captured as well as assist the media with getting their desired interviews.

I was pretending to be a pro and working on insulating a wall when a trio of players arrived. The SUV pulled up and they piled out. My mouth dropped wide open as I looked at them from inside the frame of the house. With hesitation I followed my co-worker out of the house to greet them. *This cannot be happening!*

My body almost refused to continue walking as we reached the end of the driveway. This was not the type of impression that I wanted to make on my colleagues. I couldn't envision how this would work out, but I took a deep breath and continued walking toward the players.

One in particular walked right up to me. "What's good, girl? What you doing here?"

"Working, how's it going?" I responded after giving the tall, muscular man, minus the name-brand gear from head to toe, an awkward hug.

I could feel the inquisitive glares piercing my back. They were probably wondering how I knew one of the star athletes on a personal level. Hell, this was my first event with The League! Turns out that Bella's guy friend from the night before was not a draped-up and dipped-out wannabe baller, but an actual baller. I felt silly for not recognizing him that night.

Still in shock, I introduced myself to the other two guys and we all proceeded to walk toward the build site. I still had a job to do. The guys got to work on their designated areas. I could not wait to get on the phone and tell Bella what I discovered. She did not mention anything about her guy being a professional athlete, so I assumed that she was clueless too.

Once I got back to my hotel, the key card could not activate the green light on my room door quick enough. I tripped out of my shoes, grabbed my phone, and spilled onto the bed letting out a long sigh of relief after an exhausting day. Bella's line rang four times before she finally answered.

"Hey, hun! How did you make out today?"

"Girl, never mind me. I got some scoop for you!"

"What happened?"

"Ok, so what did the guy that you were with last night tell you that he did for a living?"

"I actually don't know. I never asked," Bella said with a slightly nervous hint in her voice.

"Why?" she continued.

I recounted the story of how I'd run into her boo earlier in the day. She was as clueless as I had been.

I could tell that Bella's mind was working on full speed. Had this been a few of my other girlfriends, they would have been super-geeked to find out that their new crush was a professional athlete. Not Bella. This only made her think that she would probably be wasting her time entertaining him.

"Now I don't know what to do," Bella squeaked.

"What do you mean? I don't understand the dilemma?"

"He called me earlier and I was going to return his phone call. But now I don't know how to act."

"You're trippin'. Be normal. He is a man like all the others."

"But wait, how do you work for The League and you didn't recognize him last night?"

"I mean, hello? I just started working there. I don't know all of the guys' names and faces. Plus, I was drunk and he was so un-assuming," I continued. "Call him back and stop acting funny."

I couldn't spend any more time coaching Bella. I had real problems to solve and work to catch up on. It seemed as though working the Athlete's Annual was the equivalent to a doctor being on call for twenty-four hours. People would email you and expect a response at all hours of the night, and if you did not respond, that only meant that you would have an even larger pile of potential issues to deal with in the morning. Although I had been having a little fun here and there, I was definitely feeling the pressure.

The next day was Friday and that was the real kickoff for the weekend, starting with the youth games that were happening all throughout the day. I would be helping to escort media around a massive space, similar to a playground for all ages with sports-themed activities, to facilitate interviews. From what I'd heard, it could've been a long and trying day, so I followed up on a few emails before falling asleep watching *SportsCenter*.

The next morning, I woke up bright and early to the Miami sun shining in my room. I had forgotten to close the shades before passing out. I squirmed around in the comfy hotel bed trying to decide what to wear. Knowing that I would be out and about all day I determined that the number one criteria for my outfit had to be comfort.

Breakfast was a necessity before the long day ahead. I saved fifteen minutes to grab food at the lobby restaurant before boarding the company shuttle to the park. I quickly learned that you have to eat when you can because things move so fast that you may find yourself going an entire day without eating, and between no food and little sleep, that's a recipe for an embarrassing situation. Who wants to be laid out on the ground requiring medical attention from the local EMS crew?

When we arrived at the event site, I was thoroughly impressed at the level of the production. There was so much to see. Colorful team signage and festive team flags were flying from posts in the ground. There were multiple stations for autograph signing, areas for kids to participate in hands-on drills and activities, spirit teams running around to cheer people on, and booths where guests could win prizes. It reminded me of a sports-themed carnival minus the cotton candy and funnel cake.

I headed over to the media check-in booth to meet up with my first crew for the day. Television crews were assigned specific time slots in which they could come and film in order to ensure that they would have a designated PR escort during their time at the event. Like I said, PR can easily be a glorified babysitting job.

The local CBS affiliate was up first. We toured every inch of the grounds and they were very satisfied with the footage until they noticed one of the star players from the Los Angeles Sting Rays exiting his car service and walking toward an autograph booth.

"Scottie, do you think that we can get a quick interview with Damien Telfetter?"

"It looks like he is heading over to an autograph booth, but let me check," I said hopefully.

Damien was walking with a balding, short, freckle-faced guy who I assumed to be a part of his business team. Likely his manager, agent, or something in that arena, and on the other side of him was a nice-looking black man who had a little swag but definitely not as much as Damien. Must've been his brother or childhood friend. Athletes were known for having at least one person that they grew up with around at most times. I could only imagine that their presence served multiple purposes. When you were thrust into a world of chaos and money with people waiting at your every beck and command, it helped to have someone around who knew you before; they kept you grounded.

"Excuse me, Damien?"

Of course I was nervous as all hell. What if he ignored me? What if he had a nasty attitude? The situation had all of the potential to be very embarrassing for me, but I tucked away my fears and approached him like I had every right to do so. Meanwhile, I could hear the fans lined up at the autograph booth screaming, thrilled with the anticipation of meeting Damien.

"Hi, I'm Scottie Malveaux and I work in the PR department at The League."

"Hello, Miss Scottie."

This was a good start. At least he acknowledged me. Now that you have his full attention, you better make it quick, girl.

"The local CBS news crew is touring the event and they would like to ask you a couple of quick questions…if you don't mind?"

Damien gave me a raised eyebrow, then looked to the balding, freckle-faced man. "Do we have time?" he asked.

The little bald man nodded his head. Then he looked up at me. "Make it brief."

"You got it." *Asshole*. "Follow me, right this way."

I signaled the producer and camera crew over as I instructed Damien to stand in front of an Athlete's Annual logo. Everyone fell into place and the interview began. The producer came and stood next to me and mouthed the words *thank you*. She was so excited to have secured the interview. If it hadn't been for this opportunity, they would not have locked in such a high-profile interview on their own. Perfect timing.

The interview was harmless and done in less than five minutes. I was the three- to five-minute-interview queen. That's how long I would always tell people that an interview on the fly would take, even if I didn't know for sure.

Damien Telfetter was handsome, but I reminded myself that I was at work and not my own personal meat market. The remainder of the day was cake. I escorted my second crew and they were super low-maintenance; so much so that I ended up getting to cut out a little early because they wrapped up ahead of schedule.

I had not heard from Bella all day, so I called her on my way to my walk-through for the Entertainer's Game. She was floating on cloud twelve—forget nine—this dude had her wide open that fast. I needed to know what the hell he did or said to make her come around.

"Scottie…?" Bella paused like she was at a loss for words. She was giving me all the dramatics.

"Uh yeah. Start talking, baby cakes."

"So...we went out last night. He told me to meet him at the Delano Hotel and I'm not going to front, I thought it was a set-up for the okie-doke."

"But you went anyway."

"Yeah, I rationalized that he probably wanted to meet up for a drink first, and I was right."

Bella went on to indulge me with the details of her date. From drinks at the Delano, he drove them to dinner in his panty-dropper Maserati Gran Turismo. I personally didn't know anyone who owned such a car. He'd asked Bella if she would mind him taking the lead on deciding the restaurant. After two drinks and a ride in a Maserati, she was not in any mood to play the independent woman with an opinion, so she'd conceded.

They arrived at Nobu and Bella mentioned that she got the feeling that he was a regular by the way that the staff greeted him by name and sat them rather quickly in a cozy, somewhat private space. They immediately delivered a dish that was referred to as his favorite starter. The private space gave them a chance to exchange basic information without interruption and apparently his conversation was very real and did not have an air of Hollywood. He asked her questions about her background and how she came to live in Miami. Bella took note that he mentioned how he really liked Miami and always spent as much time in the city as possible.

She liked his attentiveness and she was ultimately pretty smitten with her baller beau. In her eyes, he conducted himself like a total gentleman, which seemed to be slightly surprising to her. When I asked if she would be open to seeing him again before the week-end was over, she giggled and eventually said yes.

Now that her love life was squared away, it was time for me to check some emails and get my work life on point. This was next to impossible with the Entertainer's Game quickly approaching, and by quickly, that meant that it was the following day. Saturday would be filled with last minute requests, questions, and a mound of other bullshit, so I needed to take my final opportunity to try to get ahead of the game as much as possible.

After my walk-through, I sat in the PR office for about two hours straight with no interruptions and knocked out countless emails, figured out the media seating assignments, and emailed staff assignments to the people from my team who were helping me execute everything the day of.

Considering all that I had gotten done for the day and the things that were still running through my head, I needed a drink. It was seven o'clock and I wasn't set to meet up with Lydia until ten to make an appearance at a work-related party. On my way back to the hotel, I instructed the cab driver to stop by a liquor store so that I could grab a bottle of Riesling to sip on while I got dressed.

It felt like heaven being back in my room. My shoes flew off my feet and onto the floor immediately. Naturally, my clothes followed. I poured myself a glass of wine in a tumbler-style glass, which was the only option in the hotel room. The first sip was refreshing like a cold glass of lemonade on a hot August day in Texas. The more that I sipped, the more I regretted committing to go to the party. I decided to call Kari. Maybe he could pump me up enough to want to go out.

"Hey, babe, what are you up to?"

"Not much. At the house chillin'. I was actually thinking about you."

"Aawh, why didn't you hit me up?" I asked. "Oh, probably because you pretty much hung up on me the other night."

"I'm sorry. I was trippin'."

"I know. That's why I didn't overreact. But you still could have called."

"I know that you've been busy. I didn't want to bother you."

"This trip has been hectic. Even more than I expected. But I like hearing from you no matter how crazy things get."

"That's good to know. So what do you have to do tonight? Work stuff?" Kari continued.

"No, I told Lydia that I would go to this party with her. But I got a bottle of wine on my way back to the hotel and now I really don't feel like going."

"Yeah, it's probably best if you stay in, relax, and get some rest so that you can be fresh for tomorrow."

"Well…that's not exactly what I expected you to say. This is my first time working the Athlete's Annual, which would be a huge deal to most people. Plus, I have access to all of the hot parties. Why wouldn't I take advantage of that? I can sleep when I get home."

"Scottie, you have it all figured out, so do what you want. I have to go."

"What's new," I said. "I'll call you later. Bye."

When we got off of the phone, I had an extra jolt of energy from snapping on Kari. I was suddenly amped to go.

Lydia was normally a conservative dresser when it came to the office, but let me find out that she knew how to hit the streets. When I walked up to her in the lobby and she turned around, her swagger was on ten. I was glad that I decided to step it up myself by slipping into my tight fuchsia mini with my fuchsia and teal, sky-high wedges to match the multicolored tank that I was wearing.

We party-hopped hardcore that night. There were parties at almost every major hotspot in the city and my body felt like we hit them all the next morning. In reality, we only went to two places.

First we went with the original plan and headed to the semi-work party that was being thrown by one of The League's corporate partners. It was a good look with athletes all over and hot hip-hop performances, but there were too many coworkers for our taste.

We dipped out to the Grey Goose-sponsored event a few blocks down the street and that was a much better scene—meaning no coworkers in the building. Complimentary cocktails and cuties made the party a hit in my book. Lydia and I sipped on Goose and cranberry until we were tipsy enough to head out.

When I looked at my dying phone and it said a quarter to 4 o'clock in the morning, it was time to call it a night. I had a text message from Kari. It was time stamped from two hours prior and he slid in an apology for his earlier antics. My battery was too low to respond.

Lydia had run into one of her friends and he offered to give us a ride back to our hotel. I could not tell if it was her friend like they had a sexual relationship or if they were platonic friends. Either way, it wasn't my business. I needed to concern myself with getting in that hotel room, forcing myself to drink a crazy amount of water, and taking some pills to avoid a massive headache.

We pulled up to the hotel and praise Jah, I did not see anyone I knew milling around. I thanked our driver and told Lydia good night before I zipped through the lobby and dragged my drunken ass to the elevator as fast as I could.

Morning and real-life responsibilities were going to come quickly, so I tried to pull it together. I finished drinking one of my many glasses of water and climbed in the bed. As soon as my head hit the pillow, the room was spinning. All bad.

The next morning when the phone on the nightstand closest to the window shook me awake with a blaring ring, I knew that it could not be my wake-up call. I rolled over quickly to grab the phone with my eyes only half open, but I missed my target and smacked over a glass of water splashing it all on the bed and my arm. That's when I realized that I still felt like shit. My body required more sleep, but unfortunately, that wasn't a realistic possibility. Even though it was a Saturday morning, I had an event to manage that evening. And regardless, we all had to report to the temporary office in the hotel around nine but definitely before ten.

My feet hit the ground and my stomach did, too. I instantly felt the contents of my stomach trying to creep up my throat. I ran to the bathroom. I only had a short period of time to pull it together and when I caught a glimpse of myself in the mirror, I realized that I looked crazy.

My first order of business needed to be the vending machine down the hall. The insides of my stomach were craving a ginger ale. I managed to breathe my way through the second nauseated feeling. I did not throw up, but I knew that it would be back. I had learned over the years that ginger ale was my best friend on mornings following a night full of drinking.

After a few sips, I felt good enough to hop in the shower. The hot water woke me up and made me feel slightly more alive.

Everything seemed to be taking me ten minutes longer than normal and I couldn't stop dragging. The main focus was making it downstairs to show face in the office. All I had to do was throw on something halfway decent. I could come back to my room and change before the game anyway. When I walked into the office, there was only a sprinkling of people. That discovery made me feel better, so I found a spot, set up my laptop, tried to act normal and actually focus on getting some work done.

Unfortunately for me, that did not work out well at all. I struggled through the first half of the day. Around noon I left my computer in the office and I slid out quietly and made my way up to my room for a quick nap.

I arrived at the arena around five-thirty to print out the advisories for the media and do a few last-minute things. The celebrity participants were already roaming around the arena and the production crew was working hard to finish up. All of the planning and execution that a large-scale event required to be a success still amazed me. Once the game got underway, my crew and I went around facilitating interviews for the athletes and celebrities that were in the audience. The arena was packed. A sold-out crowd watched athletes and celebrities alike compete for bragging rights in a game that was intended to be lighthearted and fun for the fans and participants.

I was headed to arrange an interview for *E! News* when I spotted what looked like Bella's date hugged up with some busty, blonde wig-rocking, diamond-dazzled diva. This guy was in this chick's face heavy. Kissing her on the cheek, touching her face, which looked like it contained the entire MAC counter to achieve her after-five look.

I sincerely hoped that my eyes were deceiving me, but I needed to get closer to really be sure that it was Bella's guy. The catch was, I did not want to get spotted. I casually inched toward the section that he was sitting in and crouched behind a man who was slightly taller than me. Sure enough it was his ass. I knew that my eyes were not playing tricks on me. *Now what do I do?* For the moment, I had to get back to work, so I couldn't do much.

Bella had a genuine heart and although he had no commitment to her, she was falling for him. It would not sit well with her to know that he was hugged up with another woman. Most people understand that when you are dating, there is the potential for both people to be seeing other people. But you don't want to have it confirmed and thrown in your face so that you know about it in detail.

On behalf of my friend, I played it cool, and once the game was over and people were hanging out back of house, that's when I spotted him from the back, or rather I spotted his diva's ass because it was huge. I admittedly took on the role of Inspector Gadget as I needed to find out what the deal was.

I recruited a little help in an effort to make things less obvious, plus, the dude knew my face. Doing a little reconnaissance for me, Lydia made her way into the vicinity of the conversation that he was having with a middle-aged Hispanic man standing to the left of a vomitorium. I observed from afar. It looked as though he was introducing the big-booty chick to the man. Lydia would have the intel on the whole conversation. She was too close to not overhear every single word.

"Your suspicion was right on. He is no good," Lydia told me when she wrapped up her conversation.

"Shut up?" I said incredulously. "What did you hear?"

"That was definitely his girlfriend, and if it wasn't, I don't know why he would have introduced her as 'his girl.'"

"He said that? Damn!"

"Yep," Lydia said with her eyes wide.

"How am I going to break this to Bella? Being out with another chick is one thing, but sporting a chick that you are introducing as your girl is another."

"Tell her to stay away from these athletes. They will get you every time."

I decided that I needed to call Bella right away while the whole story was fresh in my mind. When I called, she picked up on the third ring. Once I knew that I had her undivided attention, I prefaced my story with a statement of understanding as to why she had major reservations about even entertaining the idea of dating a professional athlete. I felt badly for encouraging her to call him, but then again she was grown and able to make her own decisions. I went on to break down the events of the evening.

Bella was not in shock, but she was definitely pissed. She was upset with him for being deceptive and upset with herself for allowing her emotions to believe for one moment that he could be honest. By the conclusion of our conversation, she had decided that she would not ever contact him again and if he reached out to her, she would politely tell him to go to hell. Bella had stepped out of her comfort zone with this guy, but now it was safe to say that she was back on her no-athlete's diet.

The next day, I woke up refreshed and ready to kill it at the final event. My team had their assignments, the media was confirmed and I received the manifest listing which celebrities were expected and where their seats would be.

By the time three o'clock hit, I was rushing around feeling the last-minute event pressure. I hadn't even had a chance to look at the *USA Today* that I snagged from the hotel lobby. With everything else on my plate, I had totally forgotten to type up and print out the press markers, which were essentially name cards for media. They helped media identify where to stand on the red carpet. I whipped them up real quick while I was getting dressed and shoveling room service down my throat.

I got to the location where the plush crimson red carpet was rolled out with fifteen minutes to spare—enough time to get the press markers printed and laid out on the carpet. The velvet rope and stanchions were lined up along the carpet, the bright lights were in place and beaming down, and security was on hand mean-muggin'.

After I taped down the last marker, I coated my lips with my favorite cherry-colored lipstick, and media started to arrive. I greeted people individually and told him or her to look for their spot and line up. As media continuously flowed in, we had a packed red carpet. The only thing left was the pretty faces and chiseled bodies that grace the television screens and the pages of the magazines.

My whole team was on walkie-talkies, and I had one person stationed directly by the VIP drop-off to give us a heads-up as to who was coming our way. Typically, lower-level talent would arrive first so that they did not have to compete with the A-List celebrities for the media's attention.

We were getting closer to game time and people were arriving in what felt like droves when you are managing a red carpet. As I was handing off to one of my colleagues, I felt a tap on my shoulder. I was in event mode, so I turned around quickly to greet someone who I thought might have needed something.

To my surprise it was Damien Telfetter again. I knew that he wasn't playing in the game so I wasn't shocked to see him on the carpet. All of my *SportsCenter* paid off.

"Uh, hey!" I said awkwardly.

We had met at the event on Friday, but it wasn't like we kicked it on weekends. And there I was talking about "Hey." I could've kicked myself for that one.

"What's up?" he said with a cocky, self-assured smile. "Are you gonna escort me down this carpet or what?"

My face must have looked slightly strange.

"That is what you do, right?" He looked at me, then looked at his entourage and said, "I'll meet you guys on the other side. I'm in good hands."

Well, technically, yes, that was my job, but he was speaking to me as though I was his personal publicist and he had me on retainer for special occasions like this. Not so much, and I could tell that a few of my coworkers were sizing up the situation.

Well, shit, now that you put me on the spot, what else can I do? You got this, Scottie; suck it up and knock it out.

I wasn't supposed to be the one nervous on the carpet. People were not focused on me. They couldn't care less about me. They were there to ask this freak-of-nature star athlete questions, not me. I was shook by Damien's approach and his presence for some reason. I had to get my mind right and do my job, though.

I led him down the carpet and made him do every single interview, since he wanted to put me on the spot. When we got to the end, he thanked me and before he walked away, he asked, "Will I see you inside?"

"Maybe," I replied, as I turned to rush back to the other end of the carpet and get back to work.

Before we could finish wrapping up the last of the guests on the red carpet, one of my female coworkers could not wait to ask if Damien tried to talk to me. In all actuality he never asked me out or asked if he could contact me at a later date. Either way, I would have never told her anything anyway. It was not my style to have my coworkers in my business.

I quickly dismissed her question and looked around to see if we had any stragglers before shutting down the carpet.

Once the red carpet was over, the remainder of the night was easy and I was relieved. I facilitated a few interviews for the U.S.

"National Anthem" singer, but that was easy. Now it was time to try to find a seat in the arena where I could at least watch the last half of the game.

I ran to the restroom closest to the VIP lounge before I hit the stands. As I walked toward the east side of the arena, I noticed Damien and a smaller version of his crew coming in my direction. My first thought was to do a pivot turn and head the other way. That could have come off like I was running scared, though. I put my head up and kept my stride. The plan that I hatched in my head within five seconds was to walk past them confidently, speak to him and his crew, and politely keep it moving.

Before I even got to him good, Damien shouted, "So that's how you're gonna act now?" He wanted to make sure I heard him.

I could have played the role and acted completely brand-new like I had no clue that he was talking to me, but what good would that do? In any case, I had planned to speak; he did not allow me the chance.

"Hello again, Damien," I said with a slight hint of attitude.

The nerve of him. What did he expect?

"Look, I know that you're working and all right now, but you should give me your number so that we can talk sometime when you're not as busy."

The hallways weren't buzzing with people like they were during halftime so I understood why he was so open about approaching me. On the other hand, what he seemed to fail to realize was that at the end of the day, he and I worked for the same company. That would look extremely bad on my part if someone caught a glimpse, walked by, or overheard me interacting with a League athlete like he was suggesting. He was handsome, but that's where it had to stop.

"I appreciate the offer but...no thanks."

He had a look of shock on his face that quickly turned to a stiff shrug as if to convey that he did not care. *I guess that must not happen too often.*

After an awkward moment of silence, we both turned to walk away and I heard him say with a confident tone, "You'll change your mind."

I kept walking. I could not and would not feed into that type of ignorant and arrogant attitude. One down and who knows how many more to go—I was no longer an Athlete's Virgin.

Chapter 14

Stripper's Ambition

"So are you going to tell me what your problem is?"

"Scottie, what are you talking about?"

I didn't pass go, I didn't collect 200 dollars, I didn't even stop at home first. I went straight to see Kari after my flight from Miami because I missed his face and his touch.

Now there I was, sitting at his place for a little over an hour and he'd spoken no more than twelve words in my presence. One would think that after not seeing your girl for six days, you would be dying to chat it up, hug, kiss, and simply be engaged with her. I wasn't sure who this imposter was, but I could not wait until we could get back to the regularly scheduled program.

"It's okay," I said sarcastically. I was exhausted and over the game of dismiss-Scottie-to-see-how-long-she'll-take-it. "Look, if you can't be honest and tell me what's up with you, then I'm leaving."

Kari turned to me with a cold scowl on his face. *I must be caught in the matrix because this shit can't be happening.* I couldn't take it anymore. I felt a surge of emotion run through my body, from my toes to my fingertips and I began to unleash.

"I can't take this, I'm tired! I've been on the road for six days straight dealing with these crazy-ass people and this ridiculously demanding job sucking the life out of me. The expectations were extreme and the work was strenuous, so to cope with the stress, I decided to drink my problems away because I felt alone and like no one would understand what I was going through. But I held it all together on the outside looking toward the light at the end of the tunnel, which was supposed to be your ass. The person that I thought genuinely cared! I go out of my way to get to you only for you to treat me cold and shitty? I'm done!" I was screaming and sobbing simultaneously. My vocal cords were hurting and my head was pounding.

The stress and frustration built up from days prior finally erupted. Salty tears were streaming down my face at a rapid pace as Kari rushed over to my side. I was crying uncontrollably. He scooped me into his muscular grip and whispered, "I'm sorry."

I had a head-on collision with my wall of tolerance. I was at my boiling point. Thankfully my breakdown erupted post-trip.

Kari stood in the middle of the living room holding me tightly like he would never let me go and that's just what I needed. After he finally calmed me down, he was ready to talk about what was bothering him.

"I'm sorry that I made you to lose it like that."

I paused for a moment. "It wasn't all you. The way that you were treating me turned up the fire on an already boiling pot. This weekend was the hardest weekend that I've ever experienced in life as far as my career is concerned, and it really took everything out of me."

"But, I thought that you were out in Miami having fun."

"It wasn't all fun. The nights that I did go out, I was essentially trying to escape and release some of the anxiety that I was feeling from the day," I struggled to explain. "Get sign-off on this, make sure you turn in that, check off on X, don't forget Y. This company has crazy expectations and if things are not perfect or close to it, you could potentially get your ass handed to you. It felt like my mind, my actions, hell, *my life* was moving at a rapid speed and I was doing my best to keep up. It was overwhelming."

"I'm sorry, babe. I had no clue that you were under that much stress. Here I was, feeling slightly insecure thinking that all you were doing was partying and flirting with ballers."

"Why would you think that, baby? You know I'm happy with you."

Kari continued to explain. "I was actually annoyed with you because I called to check on you Friday night after we spoke, and you never hit me back. Not even the next day. Do you realize that I haven't talked to you since Friday?"

"I saw the message, but my phone was dying and I was honestly a little tipsy. I planned to hit you when I got back to my room, but I ended up passing out. And as for the players, trust me. The interaction was not that deep. It's not like we were around them the entire time."

"See, I didn't know any of that. I thought the worst. I'm sorry."

"Is that the only reason that you were pissed with me?" I inquired for clarity.

"Yeah, pretty much. I guess I let my emotions run wild."

"You should know by now…I'm not that chick. I get it. There was no way that you could have known how crazy things were if I didn't tell you. That was my fault. But I want you to know that those weren't normal circumstances. Please don't hold that against me."

"I get it too," Kari said, as our eyes locked. "I don't want to fight."

I giggled and wrapped my arms around him. He was so sincere and I did not want to fight either. Since we were back on track, I wasn't even going to mention that Damien Telfetter tried to talk to me. That would have increased Kari's insecurity and set me up for a future fight.

That night, Kari and I had amazing makeup sex, which was the perfect remedy for the week ahead. Unfortunately, the other unappealing aspect of working the Athlete's Annual was essentially working two weeks straight. After we arrived back in New York on Monday, all employees were still expected to show up for work the following day, as well as for the remainder of the week.

It was pleasantly quiet around the office on Tuesday, so I took the opportunity to catch up on some personal emails, which I'd been neglecting. As soon as I logged into my account the words "Erotic Dancer" practically slapped me in the face. It was from Lydia. I wasn't nor had I ever been an erotic dancer, although there was the one time in college when I was low on cash and the thought crossed my mind for a brief moment. Anyway, my curiosity forced me to click on the email immediately.

To my surprise it was an offer to exercise, but in an erotic way. Leave it to Lydia to find the most racy and unconventional form of getting fit. She included the class description, cost, and suggested attire. Learning some new moves could only impress my man and keep him guessing so I was in. I was also secretly hoping that they could teach me how to make my booty bounce like the women in Twerk Team from Atlanta.

Friday could not have come quickly enough. I was ready to get out with my girls, Dev and Lydia, to let loose a bit. I took the number six train to Thirty-third Street and walked over a couple of blocks in search of the studio.

After standing in the middle of the block looking confused for a minute, I spotted it. Not what I expected at all. It was a tiny doorway with an entrance that you could easily miss. This place looked a little sketchy. Despite my hesitation, I clutched my bag and marched up the mini staircase to the elevator. I had come to realize that everything wasn't always what it seemed from the street level in Manhattan.

Once the doors opened to the studio, I was relieved. The décor was very minimal but enough to attempt to make you feel comfortable. Cherry hardwood floors gave a sense of mystery as to what you were about to encounter. The lighting was dim. I assumed that they were trying to get you in the mood to be a freak for the evening.

I had no clue what to expect of our instructor. We walked into Room A and saw a thicka-than-a-Snicker black woman at the front of the classroom with a mirror wall behind her and two rows of floor-to-ceiling silver shiny stripper poles.

"Welcome to class, ladies. My name is Precious," she said with a smile. But you could tell that she did not play games.

"Thank you for joining us for a special combo class. If you pay attention, you will learn a lot within the two hours that you are with us this evening. Now let's get to work."

Dev, Lydia, and I had come sashaying into the class with our highest "come fuck me" heels on, but she quickly shut us down.

"Take the heels off, ladies. We're not there yet."

"First up...stretching. Bend over and touch your toes angling slightly to the left," Precious called out, following up with a demonstration.

It was starting to feel like exercise. After the stretching warm-up, Precious put on a little Kanye West and I tried to resist the urge to bust a move. Her stern expression didn't make it too hard.

"Follow my lead. Watch me in the mirror and do your best to keep up. I don't expect you to be an expert."

First up was a sensual body roll with a twist. I knew how to do what I thought was a body roll, but Precious had us trying to move parts of our bodies that I had never envisioned moving. The entire one-hour class basically built upon a routine so that by the last ten minutes of class, we each had to perform the routine solo. It was nerve-wracking, but all of the other ladies in the class, strangers included, cheered you on so that made it less intimidating.

We had a brief water break, then went straight into the pole work session. Miss Thang had us strutting the pole with our fuck faces and heels on like true working girls. We learned how to do a basic spin. She placed her big butt against the pole and demonstrated how to slide down the pole with one leg in the air landing gracefully at the base of the pole. In total, we learned about four unique pole tricks and we had ample time to practice each. By the time that class was over, my whole upper body was weak.

"Do you guys think that Precious was a former stripper?" Lydia asked as we were on our way out of the studio.

"I don't know, but I sure wondered the same thing while we were in class," Dev said.

"I feel like I learned some good moves that I could use," I said with a slight smirk.

"I bet you did, chick. Just make sure I'm not home," Dev cracked.

We said our goodbyes before heading our separate ways for the evening. I hadn't mentioned anything about the erotic dance class to Kari, in case I was horrible. If things worked in my favor, then I could bust out my new skills unexpectedly.

My confidence was a little high from class so on my way to Kari's, I tried to decide if I was ready to showcase my skills. I liked attention but did not make it a habit of setting myself up to be the center of attention. However, in the hopes that class went well, I did pack a little extra something in my bag to seduce my man if I felt the timing was right.

I used the spare key that Kari let me hold to let myself into his apartment. When I walked in, he was chilling on the couch with his feet kicked up on the ottoman, looking relaxed after a long workweek. I dropped my bag by the door and ran over to hug and kiss all over him. We hadn't seen each other since our Monday night rendezvous after the argument.

"Hey, babe," I said as I planted a big juicy kiss on Kari's plump lips. "I missed you."

"I missed you too, sweetcakes," Kari said, grinning from ear-to-ear before playfully smacking me on the butt.

"I bought some wine for you. I put it in the fridge to chill so it's waiting. Whenever you're ready."

"Wait, you got it for me or for us?" I said with a knowing smile.

"Yeah, yeah, I got it for us," Kari admitted as he gave me a bear hug and kissed me on the cheek.

"Well…I got a little something for you too."

"Oh really?" His eyes widened.

"All right, where is it?"

I winked at my baby as I got up to pour us some wine. "I'll let you know when you're ready to receive it."

On my way to the kitchen, I was trying to decide when the best time would be to bust out my moves. I had to come with something since I had already opened my big mouth. *I think I may need like two glasses of wine and a shower first.*

I went into the living room, sat on Kari's lap, and handed him his wine. We clinked glasses and made sure to look each other in the eyes.

"I'm going to take a quick shower so I can relax, babe."

"Okay, but before you go, I need you to do me a favor." He looked serious.

"Sure, what is it?"

"Give me a kiss."

I cracked up laughing at his silliness and he followed suit. I planted a kiss on his lips that was sensual enough for him to beg me to stay.

"Wait, no, don't go yet. One more."

"They'll be plenty more, babe," I said as I began to walk away. "I need to get comfy first."

I scooped my bag up from its resting spot by the front door and made my way to the shower. I could always count on fresh towels and a clean bathroom at Kari's place. That was the type of man that he was. I'd dealt with men in the past that were fine as hell but nasty pigs when it came to their living space. One thing that I could not handle was a dirty man.

Kari took pride in his one-bedroom bachelor pad. He had been living there long enough to create a cozy atmosphere complete with a huge, comfy, light-brown sofa sectional, impressive kitchen utensils for a man, and a coordinating color scheme of blacks and browns throughout the apartment's décor. Early on, I had inquired about the woman who helped him decorate and he insisted that he did it himself.

Like a typical do-it-yourself man, Kari switched out the original showerhead with a chrome, seven-setting, power-spray handheld showerhead. It was excessive but definitely relaxing so I never complained.

After my spa-style shower, I downed the glass of wine that I'd brought into the bathroom. It was kicking in while I moisturized my body, sprayed on a light scent, and slipped into a black, lace, boy shorts number.

Since I could feel the alcohol settling in, my nerves were calmer than they normally would have been under the circumstance. I came out of the bathroom, which was right next to Kari's bedroom, and ducked behind the door before he could get a whiff of what I was up to. I closed the bedroom door slightly, leaving a little crack. Kari had a stereo system in his room that served as his surround sound when we watched movies. I was sure that he had a little sexy mix CD that we'd made love to before, so I rummaged through the pile of CDs sitting next to the stereo. *I hope he does not come in and think that I'm being sneaky and going through his stuff.*

There was a purple CD that had the word "sexy" written on it and I knew I'd hit the jackpot. I quietly put the CD in and turned the volume down before I hit "play."

"Babe, can you come here for a second?" I called out.

He didn't respond, but I could hear him walking my way so I turned up the music a bit. When he walked in and saw me, his eyes bugged out and he smiled.

"Well, hello…"

"I told you that I had a little something for you. Now sit down in this chair and watch me work."

I must have appeared confident because Kari sat down with not even so much as a goofy chuckle. He was staring at me.

I said, "Do you trust me?"

"Hell yeah."

"Then let me be your guide."

I instructed Kari to close his eyes. I kissed him on the cheek to calm any anxiety. Then I slid a blindfold out of my bag and placed it on his head. I had to leave him sitting there for a brief moment while I ran to the kitchen. I needed another glass of wine to take straight to the head. I had no intentions of being drunk, but tipsy, yes.

"Babe! What are you doing?"

"Be patient, please!"

I cranked up the music a notch more and started to caress Kari's upper body, slowly undressing him. I teased him with a few kisses on the lips, but once I had his shirt off, I suckled on his nipples and kissed every inch of his chiseled chest. I played around a bit more before taking off his blindfold. He had to let his eyes adjust, as I was now topless and standing in between his legs.

Kari smiled. "Damn, baby, you look good."

I winked, spun around, and dropped my ass to the floor before snaking back up between his legs. His facial expression said that he was impressed by my moves and that hyped me up even more. Kari tried to grab me, but I gave him a stern look. "No touching."

He smiled and whispered his compliance.

In my "come fuck me" stilettos, I strutted my sexy walk around his chair with my hand on his head. I loosened his belt, slid it off and used it as a prop. Our instructor taught us how to move while sensually touching our bodies, so I did just that. Of course I improvised a bit, adding my own personal touch. But so far, I could tell that my improv routine was a hit. Kari was practically drooling.

When I spun him in the direction facing the wall, he looked at me, but he did not utter a word. He understood that it was my show. We had learned how to use the wall in class to help exude your sexy.

I spread my legs open slightly and caressed my boobs, butt and, pussycat before dropping into a revealing squat. When I came back up, I decided that it was time to strip off what was left.

After I was completely naked, I moved to undo his pants and his penis popped straight out. When I went down on Kari, I did it like I had never done it before. It was like something came over me during that whole performance and I played the role of a true temptress.

He picked me up, pinned me against the wall and whispered in my ear that it was his turn to take complete control, and that he did. We continued our fun off and on into the next morning.

Chapter 15

Intensity of Young

Britney always played with her fried, white, bleached-blonde, stringy hair when she talked. It drove me crazy. She was the only coworker that I could not stand. She exuded bad vibes, plus Lydia had already warned me about her. I liked to give people a chance, but when you showed me who you were, I paid attention.

I despised the sarcastic and arrogant tone that she used when speaking to people around the office, almost as if she thought that she was better than everyone else. She seemed like the type of woman who was miserable internally. Ironically, she appeared to have a select few senior-level executives wrapped right around her finger. However, it wasn't relevant to me whom she had in her corner. I wasn't feeling her. I made it a point to keep my distance.

When I would pass her in the hallway, she'd look me up and down as if to size me up and see what I was wearing. I stayed fly so she could look until her eyes hurt. But she never spoke.

I was asked to work the night of The League's draft for new players, and I willingly signed up since it would be a new experience. Those of us working were instructed to arrive at the draft center at five o'clock. The actual draft did not begin until seven o'clock, but we were to be there early for the walk-through.

When I walked into the office at the draft center, I saw Britney's frumpy, pale, shapeless figure in the corner looking like she was gossiping. I headed toward the table filled with snacks and goodies to grab bottled water.

As I was chatting with a colleague, Britney walked up and per her usual, she did not say anything to either of us. We continued to talk and I acted as though she wasn't there, though I could tell that she was eavesdropping.

Soon after, it was time for the draft festivities to begin. I headed to my post, which was right next to the stage. The audience was made up of die-hard fans that could not wait to hear the pick selected for their team. They were wearing team paraphernalia and yelling recklessly in anticipation for what was to come. I had been assigned to escort the number four pick through the media circuit once his name was announced.

While I was standing next to the stage waiting for the number four pick to be declared, I felt apprehensive, like they were about to call my name and I had to walk up on that stage in front of the hundreds of people in the audience and the millions watching on TV. My stomach had butterflies. I was attentively listening to the names as they were announced. The entire production was complicated, and I did not want to be the chink in the chain of events.

"With the first pick," The League commissioner began, "the Cincinnati Rangers select...Marion Chambers."

It's starting. Oh goodness, Scottie, get ready.

It was all going so fast. The first name was called. Marion walked up on the stage, he put on his new team's gear, his photo was taken, and then he was handed off to his PR escort to do the media circuit. The media circuit was essentially a press conference, television interviews, radio interviews, online interviews, and a photo shoot all crammed into a couple of hours. Each draftee was required to participate. It was like a promotional tour on steroids.

Security detail was assigned to each PR escort walking players through the media circuit. After the third pick, I gave my assigned security agent a quick head nod. He was a huge man sporting a low-cut fade with an all-black suit that he could have only purchased from the big and tall store. He reminded me of an extra-large version of Blade.

"With the fourth pick, the Portland Pythons select...Rusty Danonbrook."

Since we had no inside track as to who would get picked at what number, I researched the top ten potential draftees so that I would be relatively familiar with whoever came in at number four. Now the suspense was over and I knew that I would be escorting Rusty. He was young enough to be my little brother but nonetheless handsome. Now the young, handsome millionaire with the nicely tailored, navy blue suit was headed my way.

"Congratulations. I'm Scottie Malveaux with The League PR, and I'll be guiding you through the media circuit."

It was obvious that he was still in shock and riding on an understandable high. His dreams had come true. He had been drafted into The League. Life as he knew it was about to change dramatically and this was only the first step on his new journey.

I was pretty sure that he heard my introduction as he responded to what I said to him. But I was positive that he had no clue what I was talking about when I mentioned the media circuit, and quite honestly, I was as clueless as to what to expect. We had run through the circuit during the walk-through earlier in the day. But now the test run was over and things were moving fast. People were buzzing about everywhere you turned, which made it challenging to concentrate.

I instructed Rusty to follow me up the pathway, and we headed toward the jungle that was the media circuit. The security officer led the way and kept the throngs of fans that were calling out to Rusty at bay. The first stop was the press conference room.

"Rusty," I said, pointing. "Go and take a seat at the podium."

I sound like his mother. Oh well, he followed my direction and that's all that matters.

After all of the print reporters asked him a slew of questions—How do you feel about being in The League? Are you excited to play for the Portland Pythons? How will you celebrate tonight?—the moderator wrapped up the press conference and it was time to move on.

The press conference was a warm-up for the live interviews that were about to take place. As we walked over to the live shots area, Rusty became a bit more comfortable with me.

"Man, this is all so crazy and surreal," Rusty said.

"I know. Dreams do come true, right?"

"Man, you have no idea," he said, shaking his head. "When do I get to see my family?"

"They'll meet you after all of your media interviews. So pretty much about an hour and a half from now."

As we were talking we walked into the live shots area which was set up like a bunch of cubbies sectioned off by black drapes to give each television crew their relative privacy.

Rusty asked, "So what do I have to do now?"

I fixed my lips to respond. However, before I could answer, I heard an annoying, high-pitched squeal over my shoulder chiming in.

"I'll take him through this part of the circuit," Britney said in a snide tone. "You've never done this before."

I spoke up with authority in my voice to make sure that she

made no mistake about what I was about to say. "Actually, I can handle it. I'm sure that you have other responsibilities to tend to."

I gave her a half-ass, fake smile and walked away telling Rusty to follow me. I could tell that he recognized the tension in the exchange.

"Y'all got beef?"

"No, I don't have patience for busybodies that are always doing too much."

"Well, you definitely shut her down," Rusty said, seemingly impressed. "I don't want to mess with you, Miss Lady."

I glanced up and shot him a look of confirmation.

"Are you from New York?" he asked.

I quickly responded, "No," figuring that he was trying to size me up.

I knew it was time to change the subject. "Let's start over there with ABC." I pointed in their direction. "They will connect you to the local Portland ABC station, and you'll do the interview with the sportscasters via satellite."

"Okay, cool."

I went over to the station's booth with Rusty in tow. A cute little redhead producer informed me that she was ready for him and it was as easy as that. Once Rusty was settled in the chair and conducting his interview, I glanced over in Britney's direction to see if she had, in fact, found something better to do.

I zoned out for a minute thinking about the fifty different ways that I wanted to curse her out. Then the side of my stomach started to vibrate. It shook me out of my trance. It was my phone. I had it in my suit jacket pocket since I wasn't carrying a purse with me. I pulled the phone out of my pocket. It was a text message from Kari. *Hey babe, how's the draft going?*

I started typing a reply when I felt a tall figure standing over me. I looked up from my phone.

"You're done?" I asked.

Rusty shrugged. "Yeah, where do I go next?"

I guided Rusty through the remainder of the local television interviews and he was pretty sharp on camera. He displayed quick wit and a great personality, which is not typically expected of athletes when they first start out in their professional careers. He also had the fact that he was a sexy young man with a killer smile working in his favor. A nice smile could always make me weak.

Our next stop on the media circuit was photos.

Rusty and I were walking side by side with security leading the way when I took out my phone to hit "send" on the message that I started earlier. That must have inspired him to try a little harder with me. "So where are you from?"

"Excuse me," I said, as though I had not heard the question, knowing full well that I had.

"Well, you said that you aren't from New York. So where are you from?"

"California."

"Okay, Cali is cool. I like Cali."

"Uh huh," I said, looking back at my phone.

"So do you work for The League or for a team?" he quickly followed up.

"I work for The League. Would you like a copy of my resume as well?"

"No. That might be too personal. But I'll settle for your phone number."

Excuse me! You'll settle for my phone number? The intensity of young, this dude was too precious.

"That's cute," I commented with a slight chuckle. I wasn't trying to completely dismiss his advance, but I didn't want to give him the wrong idea either.

"Cute? Really? You gonna hit me with the 'cute' line."

"Look, you're a nice young man. But honestly you're like my little brother's age. Plus, you are about to have so many chicks at your disposal. You'll be fine."

"I'm not talking about all that. I'm trying to get this woman right here in front of me to check for me like I'm checking for her. But if you want to miss out on all this," he said, putting his hands out, palms up, like a presentation, "then that's your loss."

I looked up at Rusty and I couldn't control the urge to laugh. He laughed with me, likely because he could tell that I had no intentions of letting the conversation continue in that direction— which was a slippery slope. I couldn't give in and cross that line for jailbait. And more importantly, I had a man.

To my surprise, my man was waiting up for me after my night finally wrapped. At one-thirty in the morning he couldn't wait to hear all about my adventures and how my first draft experience went. Sometimes his enthusiasm about my job was so adorable.

I was exhausted from all of the walking and standing around all night, but I made him a deal that if he would massage my shoulders, I would give him all of the juicy insider details.

My back and shoulders were throbbing and Kari's hands worked magic to bring my body parts back to life. In keeping with my promise, while I sat between Kari's legs, I spilled every detail from the evening that could even remotely be considered juicy to a man who loved sports.

I did conveniently forget to mention the part about Rusty Danonbrook requesting my phone number for his archives. My better judgment spoke to me loud and clear, and it said that letting a piece of information like that slip out of my lips would somehow cause an unpleasant situation. So I shut the hell up.

"Scottie!"

"Hunh!"

"Were you asleep?" he said as he kissed the side of my forehead.

I was still sitting in between Kari's legs when I dozed off. The last thing that I remembered was an image of Rusty's face. I could picture him so vividly: his smile, his caramel complexion, and his dreamy brown eyes. Something was intriguing about him. I had to rid my mind of those images. It couldn't lead to anything good.

"I'm sorry, babe. I guess I'm beat."

"Let's go to bed then. Come to Papa. Let me carry my girl since she had such a long day," Kari said with a sympathy smile.

I fell into Kari's arms. "You are too good to me."

Chapter 16

The Great Chase

"So did you get a dance or did you watch him get grinded on all night?" Dev asked with a concerned look on her face.

We were hanging out in my room catching up since coming and going was the most that we'd seen of each other in the last few weeks.

"Honey, please, Kari and I went to the strip club to see the dancers. I had no plans to sit around and watch him get dances all night."

Dev laughed loudly. "I heard that!"

"There was this one chick that was bad, though. You could tell she makes major money. I wanted her to stay far away from Kari. I would have paid her ass to stay away if I had to."

Dev doubled over with laughter, but I was halfway serious. I knew that my man was fine. Mama raised a woman who was always a detective and never a fool.

"Well, that's good that you guys ventured out of the norm and had a nice time."

"Yeah, it was definitely entertaining, but the encore at the house was even better!"

"Shut up! Let me find out you busted out some of the tricks you learned in class!"

"Girl, please. I had already tried out a few moves the same night that we took the class!"

"You. Are. A. Mess!"

"Please, I had to make sure to use what I learned while it was fresh on the brain."

"I'm not mad at that, chick." Dev initiated a high-five, then her face turned serious. "Do you trust Kari?"

"Where did that come from? Do you know something that I don't?"

"No, no, no," Dev insisted. "It's just a question."

"He's a good guy, but I'll probably never trust any man completely."

"Is it because of your past? Namely Ivan?"

"Likely. I mean, I trust him only as far as I can see him. Kari hasn't given me any reason to treat him like I don't trust him. But at the same time, I'm not going to be stupid and give him an opportunity to screw me over either."

"But he seems like such a stand-up guy. You two have been rocking with each other basically since you got here."

"True. Don't misunderstand, I do care about him, and I enjoy our time together. I'm going to keep rocking with him. But a person will always have that room for error and for that reason, I situate him like the others—at a distance. But I'll have fun with him while it lasts."

Dev looked at me like I was a cold bitch.

"Hey, I'm not trying to set myself up to be disappointed again."

"Do you still think about Ivan?"

"Yeah. I guess, sometimes I feel like we have unfinished business. But really, if I'm being honest, he probably has a lot to do with why it's hard for me to trust. His deceptive ass fucked ya girl up."

"You'll be fine, chick," Dev said. "You're tough, you always bounce back."

Dev and I sat in the room chatting for a few hours. We drank Riesling while we gossiped and reminisced. I told her all about the encounters that I'd had at the Athlete's Annual and the more recent incident at the draft.

"Did you mention to Kari that the ballers were showing you love?" She chuckled. "I wonder what would have happened if you didn't have a man?"

"Well, honestly, it wasn't even about Kari. I know that sounds bad to say, but it was more so a knee-jerk reaction—how bad would that look if I got caught up in some shit with one of our players."

"Okay, okay," Dev said with a laugh.

"And no, I didn't say anything to Kari," I quickly added.

"You know that you're potentially playing with fire by not telling Kari, right? Never mind, don't answer. I know that you know."

The following Wednesday at work, a select group of people were summoned into a last-minute, mandatory meeting. Having no idea what it was about, each person within the small group looked clueless as we walked into the coldest conference room on the ninth floor. The only communication that we received about the meeting was an email from Gail Dean, our department head, saying that she needed everyone to meet in five minutes.

Finally, after leaving us fidgeting and fumbling with anticipation, Dean walked in with what seemed like the news of death. She had on her signature, oversized slacks with her hair pulled back in a slick ponytail and a permanent scowl on her face. I noticed that she was pretty good at presenting a no-nonsense face at all times, but in the last eight months of working at The League, she had never called this kind of meeting. If it would have been me alone, I would have been positive that I was getting fired.

"I called all of you to this conference room because I just came out of a meeting where I found out that players from the St. Louis Legends, Miami Storm, and Chicago Crows will be in New York two days from now for a special media presentation at our offices. They'll be unveiling the new and improved uniforms. The catch is that the uniform manufacturer hired an agency to manage the media and we were supposed to provide the venue, but their PR agency fell short on delivering. Now we have been tasked with coming in to pick up the slack. We'll have to get on a call with the agency in about an hour to discuss our strategy moving forward, and we'll work with them to execute the best media unveiling possible. This needs to be *excellent.* All eyes are on us to knock this one out of the park."

You could see that most of us wanted to ask why the hell we were just being brought in on the project, but no one would dare ask Dean a question like that.

"Any questions?"

The room was silent. We all knew what we needed to do.

"I'll forward you the PR agency contact shortly," Dean rattled off as she walked out of the room.

Everyone traded looks with each other. We were filled with the anticipation of exhaustion. We quickly moved on from the shock and started going through our next steps and deciding what needed to be done and by whom.

The following two days leading up to the big media presentation were equivalent to a stressful spot in hell. There would be moments where I would look up from the piles of papers that were strewn all over my golden, oak desk and I would sit there to take in the sounds. Even above the low volume of the communal television, you could hear that everyone was working feverishly.

We essentially had to do the job that someone else was supposed to do but in a fraction of the time and with no explanation. Our abruptly modified schedules meant working late nights, taking conference calls, crafting talking points, pitching media, and solidifying a minute-by-minute schedule for the presentation.

I was specifically in charge of coordinating the media interviews for Byron Stalling of the Chicago Crows. I needed to confirm all of the media that had interest in speaking with him as well as escort him through the interviews on the day of the event.

I knew of Byron Stalling, but I had never met him and didn't know much about him other than that he had just signed a $12 million contract with the Crows. My colleague had worked with him in the past and she said that he was sweet and very respectful. Being from Houston, Texas, I could only assume that he had the southern charm working in his favor. He had been in The League for nine years and to my knowledge never had any brushes with the law. From what I read he also did occasional charity work and was well liked by fans. All of the media that I spoke to prior to the event seemed eager to speak with Byron.

The unveiling wasn't until noon, but Byron and the other players were instructed to arrive at our offices by 10:15 a.m. They needed to be properly prepped before the presentation. I received a call from Byron's agent letting me know that he was nearby so I headed to our main lobby entrance with The League security to intercept Byron before fans could have an opportunity to approach him. Our timing was impeccable, as his car service pulled up two minutes after we made it downstairs. I emailed the schedule keeper to inform her that Byron had arrived.

When the driver opened the door of the black-on-black Cadillac Escalade, all I saw was a pair of black Gucci loafers hit the sidewalk. A large, six-four frame followed and my eyes connected with a pleasant gaze that was from none other than Byron. I walked closer to where he exited the vehicle to extend a hand and introduce myself.

I looked up at him. "How are you? I'm Scottie Malveaux. I work in the Public Relations department at The League."

"Hey, nice to meet you."

"Follow me, please." I motioned. "I'll take you inside."

As we walked through the main lobby, a few people recognized him as a star athlete and said hello from a distance. The security personnel at the front desk were all smiles as they buzzed us in and said hello to Byron, too. While we waited for the elevator, I checked my BlackBerry. I read an email from our schedule keeper informing the PR team that all of the guys were in the building. It was just after their call time, which was fantastic and totally unexpected. Since I was assigned to Byron, my first order of business was to take him to his makeshift green room—a conference room—and go over the run of the day with him.

We arranged for the new uniform as well as socks and size fourteen shoes to be laid out in the green room for Byron. In addition, catering set out a nice spread of fruit, eggs, bacon, turkey sausage, oatmeal, muffins, water, and juice. When we walked into the green room, Byron's attention went straight to the food.

"Well, since it looks like you're hungry, I'll go over the details once you're situated."

"You got jokes, Miss," Byron said. "You should probably grab some food too. Then we'll be on the same page."

I gave him the side eye but decided to go ahead and grab a little fruit. Only to make him feel comfortable of course. He sat down at the small, circular table and I sat down opposite him and crossed my legs.

"What's that computer screen for?" Byron asked with intrigue.

"It's the company's internal website, but it's mainly used as an employee directory. If we're in a meeting and need to contact someone internally, it makes things easier."

"So if I needed to find you, I could?"

"Yes, I suppose."

Byron looked down, then looked back up at me. "Those shoes are hot."

"Thank you," I said plainly. I was ready to go over the logistics of the day.

"So Scottie Malveaux, how long have you been at The League?"

This is getting way off track, but I can't be rude. He is trying to make small talk while he finishes his food. But wait, he called me "Miss" earlier and now all of a sudden remembers my full name. Game.

"I'm coming up on a year," I said with an implied period in my tone and facial expression. "So I'll go over the flow of the presentation," I continued, "and you stop me if you have any questions. Start time is noon. All of the media will gather in our press conference room. The League's head of Merchandise, alongside the manufacturing company's President of Innovative Design, will kick off the presentation with a tandem welcome address. During their remarks, which will last exactly four minutes, I'll walk you up to the press conference room where you will be introduced to the audience. This will serve as the official unveiling of the new uniforms. You and the other two players will deliver brief remarks while wearing the new uniforms—think fit, functionality, and maybe even feel. Lastly, we will close out the presentation and move on to the individual media interviews."

"Sounds like you have it all figured out."

"I do, as long as you don't throw any last-minute issues my way," I said with a smile.

"All right, Miss. You won't have any trouble out of me."

"Perfect, that's what I like to hear."

Things were actually going pretty well with prepping Byron. He was surprisingly easygoing. I tried my hardest not to size him up, but those long, gorgeous eyelashes did catch my attention for a brief moment.

While my head was buried deep in my BlackBerry catching up on emails, I realized that it was too quiet. During my first hour spent with Byron, I noticed one thing that he didn't know how to do and that was be quiet. I looked up from my emails and scanned the room to see what had Mr. Stalling so occupied in silence.

"Excuse me? Hello!" *I think I'm a bit confused by what's happening right now.* I got up from the round table raising my voice at least an octave and waving my hand in the air.

"Why are you taking your clothes off?" I was sure that my voice was squeaking like Whitley Gilbert from *A Different World*. A normal person probably would have been embarrassed. Given the circumstances, I was completely thrown off.

"Calm down, Miss. I'm changing into the uniform," Byron said, in his innocent southern accent. "That's why it's here, right?"

I knew that he wasn't actually expecting an answer and I also knew that he wasn't that naive. That deep southern drawl could fool some into thinking him a saint, but the look in his eyes read as though he took slight pleasure in the entire awkward exchange.

Luckily, I interrupted him before he had a chance to unbuckle his pants. It was bad enough that his glistening chocolate chest was staring right at me.

Maybe it was normal for athletes to strut around semi-naked, but I felt slightly uneasy, mainly because I liked what I saw. His body was a work of art sculpted to perfection, and he had a flawless complexion.

"I'll wait outside while you finish changing."

That was a close call. What if someone would have walked in on us and misread the whole situation? They would have had my walking papers written up before I could have even gotten the word "misunderstanding" past my lips.

I checked my BlackBerry again for updates. That BlackBerry stayed glued to my right hand during events because we didn't have the leisure of missing something. Everything was urgent and time sensitive when it came to The League. Events got my adrenaline moving, I liked the thrill and didn't mind the added pressure.

An email popped up from the schedule keeper with the words "TEN MINUTES" in the subject line. It was almost go time. I banged on the green room door with slight force and yelled to Byron, "You've got five minutes to finish up in there before we have to go!"

"Come in!" he yelled from the other side of the door.

I paused for a brief moment as my nerves kicked in. I had no clue what I was about to walk into, and for some reason, this man made me feel nervous like a little schoolgirl on her first day.

"How do I look?" Byron asked as I entered the dressing room.

"The new uniform looks great. Fits you well."

"Cool," he said, grinning.

"Ready?" I quickly added.

"Whenever you are, Miss."

The League offices were rather large spanning many floors. We exited the green room with seven minutes to spare and followed security to the elevators. Upon reaching the door to the press conference room, Byron seemed slightly nervous. I didn't really expect his nerves to be going crazy. I figured that he did public appearances all of the time.

When Jay Perry of the Miami Storm and Devon Owen of the St. Louis Legends walked up, he greeted them with excitement and it seemed as though his anxiety subsided a bit. The presentation had already been in full motion and once each guy was introduced and on the stage, it was smooth sailing from there.

Before I knew it, the time had come for the one-on-one interviews. I walked Byron from the stage to the interview room, which was right next door.

"After this, I'm done, right?"

"Yep, after this, you are free to go."

"Are you gonna wait for me to finish...and take me back to the dressing room?"

"Uh—yeah."

When we walked into the interview room, all of the reporters were standing around salivating and waiting for their chance at a one-on-one with some of The League's most coveted athletes. Byron was well-spoken and engaging; he completed the first five interviews like a true pro. While he was on his sixth and final interview, I heard the door swing open and I immediately turned to see who was entering. My team member Duke looked in my direction and motioned for me to step into the hallway.

He didn't come and track me down for no reason. I had a feeling that I knew what it was about. An interview with one of our executives was set to run online that morning and I could only suspect that the story hit and there was an error in it. An error in a news story was always a major deal at The League and the expectation was that you would get it fixed, and fast. I had not had a chance to check the story because I had been dealing with Byron and the presentation all morning.

I quietly excused myself and stepped into the hallway. "Is everything all right, Duke?"

"No, the *Wall Street Journal* story from this morning was sent around and Dean noticed a mistake," Duke continued. "She called around pissed looking for you, totally forgetting that you were up here working."

"That's fucking great. Let me run down to my desk," I said, not liking the sudden anxiety that was overwhelming my body. "Duke, would you mind monitoring this last interview that Byron is doing? If everything wraps up before I get back, can you escort him back to his dressing room on seventeen?"

"Sure, I got it. Go," he said.

I decided to take the internal stairs hoping that it would be faster. In my haste thumping down the stairs, I ran into Britney, the bitch. She looked at me as if to say, "What's wrong with you?" but she knew better than to ask.

Then I heard her say, "How are things going with Byron?"

This funny-style bitch has some nerve. Don't address me as though we're friends.

I had already passed her so I ignored her question and kept moving down the stairwell.

When I got to my floor, I made a beeline for my desk. I didn't want to go and speak to Dean first. She was a beast and if I went to speak to her without being fully prepared, she would rip my head off and eat it for lunch.

I logged on to my computer and pulled up the story. When I read it, I spotted the mistake immediately. Our executive's title was listed incorrectly. I snatched up the phone to call the reporter.

"Hi, Thomas, this is Scottie from The League. I just finished reading the story and it looks great, but I'd like to see if you would correct a line in the first paragraph for me? I can email you exactly what it says versus what it should say."

"Sure, send it over and I'll take a look at it right away," he said.

"Perfect. You're the best! Thanks, Thomas."

When I hung up the phone, I heard shuffling from down the hall and it seemed to be headed in my direction. I had a feeling that it was Dean. I wasn't in the mood to hear her ranting and foaming-at-the-mouth tirade.

"You need to call your contact at the *Wall Street Journal* and have that mix-up fixed ASAP. Have you talked to them yet? Where are we with this?"

I hate when people fire questions at me. They do it to throw you off and get you frazzled. But it always managed to annoy me. Everyone else in my group was slightly fearful of Dean and it was obvious. She was a corporate bully.

I shot Dean a stern glance. "I just got off of the phone with the writer, Thomas, and he is going to make the correction immediately. The change should be posted within the hour."

"Good. Send me the updated version when it's done."

"Okay."

That was a battle averted. Thank goodness that exchange did not turn into an epic blowout, which I had witnessed her engage in at least six times since my start date. It was never directed at me, but being in the vicinity was bad enough.

I sat back in my chair and drafted the correction email. It was a very simple request so it didn't take long. I looked at the bottom of my computer screen for a time check. It was almost 1:15 p.m. and the interview session with Byron had likely wrapped. For a brief moment I entertained the idea of going back upstairs to check the interview room or his dressing room simply to say goodbye. But I didn't want to seem pressed. Instead, I decided to keep working and block him out of my thoughts.

My throat was feeling a bit scratchy from all of the constant chatter I had been doing, so I headed to the kitchen to get a glass of water. Lydia was at the microwave warming up her lunch. I hung around and chatted with her for a bit. She asked how the presentation went and without a moment of hesitation. I gave her the rundown but intentionally omitted a few details. We were extremely cool with one another, but the general version would do.

On the way back to my desk, I thought about Kari. I realized that I had not heard from him all day. Normally, he would call or text me about absolutely nothing at least a few times before lunch. I decided to text him once I got back to my desk.

When I plopped down in my chair, I noticed that the red light on my phone was blinking. I became excited like a schoolgirl when her crush calls. I knew it was Kari calling to say that he was thinking about me. He was such a sweetie. I picked up the phone and started to smile with a kiddy grin.

"Please enter your pass code," blared through the receiver. I took direction from the automated woman. She told me that I had one new voice message. I hit the number one on the keypad to play the message.

"Hi, Scottie…"

Uh, flag on the play! The voice was familiar, but it wasn't my man's. It was deep, intense, and definitely male, though. I was thrown off and my stomach began to do backflips. It didn't take long for me to recognize exactly who it was. Fear nearly compelled me to hang up the phone. I had no idea what the rest of the recording would say. I wasn't prepared for this.

"You didn't come back and check on me so I wanted to check on you."

Faint.

"I got your number from the computer system that you so kindly showed me. Anyway, it was nice meeting you, and you'll be hearing from me again soon."

Oh hell! What did I get myself into?

I slammed the phone down in the cradle like the FBI was tapping my phone line. Maybe by hanging up quickly, the people tapping my line wouldn't hear what I heard. I was losing it. I was paranoid.

What was he calling me for anyway?!

I needed to regain my composure and go back into my voicemail to delete the message. I picked up the receiver and hit the little mailbox symbol on the phone.

"Hey, Scottie!" Joel said.

I jumped. He was standing by the other side of my desk. My heart was racing like ponies at the track. It was as if someone had caught me cleaning up the blood after a murder. I felt like I had done something wrong.

"I'm sorry…I…I didn't mean to startle you," Joel quickly offered.

With his briefcase still in his hand, I figured that he had just returned to the office from his social media seminar. I'm positive that my reaction made me look like a freak.

"I'm fine, probably my hunger kicking in and making me a little kooky," I said, hoping that he didn't notice how suspicious I looked.

"So how did things go at the unveiling?"

Gosh, if you only knew.

"It went extremely well and the media seemed to really like the uniforms. There should be great stories hitting within the next couple of days."

"Fantastic!"

Once he walked away, I released a sigh of relief and it was time to get back to business: Operation Erase the Evidence in full effect.

I logged back into my voicemail and despite my apprehension, I listened to the message one last time. I shook my head rapidly from left to right in an attempt to clear the dirty thoughts and scandalous possibilities from my mind.

After work, I headed home to relax and unwind. It had been an eventful day that I could not have planned or anticipated. Dev was home, so we chatted and got caught up. I desperately needed the girl talk and I hadn't even realized how much so. Red wine wasn't my thing, but Dev popped open a bottle and I gladly gulped from my glass. Throughout our entire conversation, I never once mentioned the voicemail. Dev asked me twenty-one questions about the overall event and the players, even Byron specifically, and I told her everything…except about the voicemail.

Once I felt the stresses of the day slipping away, it was time for a steamy hot shower and a date with my bed. When a girl is tipsy, the normal routine flies out the window.

I walked up the stairs from the basement bathroom dripping wet and shuffled my way through the living room into my boudoir. I plopped my damp butt on the bed to try to focus on my next move when my phone rang. My chest fluttered with fear and nervous tension. Interactions with phones over the last twelve hours had not exactly served me well. I was jumpy. Kari's name popped up on my screen.

Oh shit.

I couldn't ignore his call.

"Hey, babe," I answered.

"Hey, Scottie."

Humm, that was an awfully dry greeting to offer someone whom you haven't spoken to all day.

Now I wasn't certain that answering the phone wasn't the best idea.

"How was your day?" I asked, trying to lighten the mood.

"It was okay. But you don't really care one way or the other."

"Damn! Like that? Really?" I had no clue where the attitude was coming from, but I couldn't appreciate it and he was definitely fucking up my high. "So that's how you feel tonight, Kari?"

"Pretty much."

"So why the hell did you even call me?"

"I'm asking myself the same thing." There was a brief pause, then Kari added, "Act like I never did."

All I heard was a click. This motherfucker hung up in my face. My first reaction was to call his punk ass and curse him the fuck out. How dare he! You don't call me with an attitude from jump, not state your issue, and then hang up in my face. I didn't know him to be a drug user, but he must have been on that shit. That could have been the only explanation for his erratic behavior. I was pissed and I still had the phone in my hand ready to dial. But I was also tipsy and tired. I figured I'd deal with his madness in the morning.

Chapter 17

My Star

Kari received no communication from this girl. My pride forced me to allow a few days to pass after he left me speaking to a dial tone. He called, texted, and emailed, but I wasn't impressed by his little elementary tantrum. I decided to make him sweat.

My BlackBerry buzzed. I picked it up from my nightstand to check my email. I froze. This could not be happening. I looked at the sender's name for the most recent email, then I blinked to clear my eyes. Maybe I'd misread something. Hell no, the name clearly said B. Stalling. I clicked on the message since my nosy nature would not allow me to hold off a moment longer.

The email did not have a salutation. It jumped straight to the point. *"This could be completely strange and awkward, but I may or may not have memorized your email address from the directory at your office. Honestly, I can't get you out of my mind. I liked what I saw. I want to know more about you. I respect your decision either way, but I hope to hear from you."*

My mouth dropped open at some point during my reading of the email and my jaw had not managed to close. I was surprised at the audacity of this guy. But at the same time, I was flattered. I had no clue how I should react, what was appropriate, or what my next move would be. I couldn't manage to get a grip on the million-and-one thoughts racing through my mind.

Do I tell anyone about this? Get a second opinion.

I sprawled out on my bed, knees bent toward the ceiling and my eyes staring straight up. I needed to think.

Despite my awareness of the reality, something was appealing about Byron. He seemed highly calculated. I knew that if he had access to my email via my profile, then he was also able to see my cell phone number. Sending an email to my work address was risky, though not as risky for him as it was for me.

The situation was a doozie and I needed to call in reinforcements. I rolled over, grabbed my cell phone, and dialed up my Jolie. She would not be able to solve my problem or tell me exactly what to do, but that's not what I was looking for. I needed someone to talk through the madness with me.

"Hello?" she answered.

"What's up? What are you doing?"

"Hey, honey, not much. How ya doin'?"

I let out a long exasperated sigh. It was extremely dramatic and I was fully aware. "I have a dilemma."

"Oh hell. What's going on?"

My Jolie lived for details. I took a deep breath and began to explain the entire scenario starting from my meeting Byron. I could sense that once my Jolie realized where this story was going, she was a bit relieved. She probably thought that I had really bad news from the way that I started the conversation.

"Umph. That Byron Stalling is something else, hunh." I could tell that she was shaking her head.

"You can say that again."

"I saw him in one of my magazines not too long ago."

"I'm sure that you did. The media loves him."

"So what about Kari?" she said with way too much concern for my liking. "He seems like a nice man from what I know and when I speak to him on the phone, Scottie."

"I'm well aware. But hello, we are not talking about him right now."

"Okay, okay, so what are you going to do?"

"I have no clue. Hell, I'm not married. So I'm essentially free to entertain other men. For all I know, Kari could be doing the same thing. He seems like he is legit, but you never know. For more reasons than one, it would be a huge risk to entertain Byron's advances, though."

"Your father is trying to say something." I could hear him yelling in the background. "Dad says, 'Don't limit yourself, babygirl.' He probably wants tickets to a game." My Jolie continued, "Well, you're normally pretty good with judging character and knowing what's best for you. I say follow your gut and do what you think you should do. You know that it's not for me to say go one way or the other. I'm here for you no matter what you choose, honey."

"I know…and you're right. I'll call you later and let you know what I decide. Thanks for the chat."

My Jolie was right. Byron was something else, but the way that Kari had been acting lately, he wasn't a saint either. Kari was a factor in the back of my mind, but if he kept up his crazy antics, we would be over soon.

I reasoned with myself that everything would be clearer in the morning. At least I hoped it would be. Regardless, I wasn't going to be rushed into making any hasty moves. Before my head hit the pillow, I forwarded Byron's email to my personal email address and deleted the original. I couldn't take any chances.

I woke up the next morning feeling good. The warm sunrays broke through the slits of my eyes to reveal the bright light of a new day. I lay in my cozy, plush bed with only my thoughts and complete silence. Although I had a restful sleep, the clarity that I hoped for had not appeared. I had to be at the office in an hour so I hopped out of the bed to start my day, grabbing my phone off my nightstand as I did it. I shook my head. I had three missed calls from Kari. Glad that I kept my phone on silent overnight.

I couldn't wait to get into the office. At least the demands of my workload would distract me from my reality. During my commute, I tallied up the pros and cons of the situation and mostly fantasized about the pros.

Dev and I were chatting on IM in between my checking emails and transcribing an executive interview. She was telling me about this new guy that she recently met at a Summer Stage concert. I was excited for her. Mel was now a distant memory, but I knew that she desired the attention and adoration of a man.

11:17 DEVinly1: Scottie—he is such a cutie!

11:17 SassyScottT: Umph...do tell me more! How old, kids, where does he live?

11:18 DEVinly1: Born and raised in Brooklyn, no crumb snatchers, and he is twenty-eight.

11:19 SassyScottT: That's what's up. So when are you guys going out?

11:22 DEVinly1: I don't know...he hasn't asked me yet.

11:23 DEVinly1: What do you think?

11:23 SassyScottT: Well have you guys been communicating?

11:24 DEVinly1: Yes. I gave him my number that night and he texted me the next day which was yesterday. We were texting all day but no mention of a date.

11:25 SassyScottT: Ok...ok...well, give it another day. Maybe he is trying to feel you out and make sure that you are comfortable meeting up...

11:25 DEVinly1: True. I hope that he doesn't wait too long.

11:26 SassyScottT: If he does then you take the advice that you gave me and you take the control.

11:27 DEVinly1: I did say that...lol. We'll see.

I was logged into IM through my Gmail so the forwarded message from B. Stalling kept staring at me. I felt like it was calling out to me and I couldn't avoid it, but I wasn't ready to deal.

After lunch, the mailroom called to inform me that a large package arrived under my name. They were making sure that I was at my desk before bringing it up. I thought nothing of it, but I had not done any online shopping lately so it wasn't something that I had ordered. Being in PR at The League, it wasn't unusual to get unexpected goodies, but when the mailroom guy walked up pushing the large box on a dolly, I thought for sure that it could not be for me.

He unloaded the box, instructed me to sign his pad, and politely walked away. He left me alone with my huge box of the unknown.

My desk line rang and the caller ID revealed that it was Kari. I ignored his call; I had to see what the hell was inside the box.

I busted that bad boy open. The standard brown shipping box went almost up to my waist and it was filled with black-and-white tissue paper sprinkled with gold flecks. I tore through the paper, but it wasn't until I got about halfway through that the true contents were revealed. What appeared to be a Jimmy Choo shoebox was staring at me.

Who is this from?

Before I peeked inside the shoebox, I searched around for a card, or a note, or something. But I couldn't locate a single indication as to the identity of the sender. The box didn't even have a return address on the outside; only my name and work address. Kari had fucked up, but I knew that this gift could not be from him. It wasn't his style. It was too flashy.

I dug back in the big box, pulled the shoebox out, and shook the top off. Nicely placed on top of a fly-ass pair of Jimmy Choo, black python, leather, gladiator, multi-strap sandals, was the note that I had been searching for. I flipped over the gold note card. Written in black ink, the message read: *"Your shoe game is official, so I wanted to send you a little something else that you could get into."* I could have fainted. No one had ever given me a gift this expensive. I was sure that these babies had to have cost over a thousand dollars.

It was no mystery that my Santa Claus was Byron. Although he did not sign his name, there wasn't anyone else in my life that had money to burn on that level. My days had been completely unpredictable and filled with unexpected events since I'd met him. Still confused as to how I should have felt, I could not deny that his latest gesture had taken flattery to another level. I'd never had someone trying to woo me in such an extravagant manner. Sure, men sent me flowers and offered sweet gestures while we were dating. But so far, I had not even so much as told this guy that I was interested in him. I could have interpreted the situation in one of two ways: either he was delusional and aggressive, or romantic and determined.

Either way, the shoes could not stay in plain view, so I carefully placed the Jimmy Choo shoebox in the bottom drawer of my desk. As far as I knew, no one even noticed what had transpired with my unexpected package. People were face down in their computers and hard at work.

Instead of plowing through my work as previously planned, I

found myself daydreaming, and it wasn't a mystery as to who held the leading role. I had even started thinking of outfits to wear with the shoes. It wasn't like I could send them back or anything. After all, who would I send them back to? I had no return address.

Secretly I felt like a princess. I enjoyed the thrill of it all, but I couldn't continue being nonresponsive to everyone. I needed to finally face Kari and address Byron. The commute home was filled with tempered anxiety. I jammed out to the most crunk music that I could find in an effort to try and redirect my energy and shake the sordid emotions. Anyone in my head that day would have been exposed to one hundred-and-one wavering thoughts, solutions, and scenarios. I was so indecisive.

When I walked into a silent apartment, I knew that Dev wasn't home. That was excellent. I could blast my music and fix myself something to eat before sitting down to think heavily about my decision.

In an effort to get my mind off of my reality, I watched a little mindless entertainment on TV while I ate. I flicked to MTV and *The Real World* was on which made me squeal with joy. I loved that show and all of the drama that came with it. In college, I had even gone so far as to audition to be a cast member. I didn't make the cut. But that evening I was happy to get invested in someone else's craziness and not think about my own for a little while longer.

Two of the girls on the show were fighting. I was trying to figure out the scenario when they cut to one of the girls in the confessional. She was pissed and she went on to say, "I don't care what they think of me. It's my life and I'm going to live it how I want."

In a weird way, what she said spoke to me. I only had one life to live and I should have been able to follow every desire and live life how I wanted. It was time that I started living for me. Every decision that I would make in life may not have been right, but it was mine to make and I would own it.

In that moment, I decided that I would respond to Byron. I wasn't going to overthink it. I would write what came to my mind and let it flow. I logged in to my Gmail, found the forwarded email from my work address, and hit "reply." I switched out the receiving field and began to compose my message.

I followed his lead and responded in a similar fashion—no salutation. I went in.

"Clearly you are accustomed to getting your way and doing whatever it takes to ensure that things work out in your favor. I won't front. I'm flattered and I like the shoes, but you can stop sending things to my office. I'm not quite sure what you think you want from me. Do you even know?"

Short and simple, then I hit "send." I purposely hit "send" quickly so that I could not rethink my response and overanalyze my words. I was straightforward, and I told him I wanted to know what his angle was. Essentially, why me?

I knew that he wouldn't respond in the next five minutes, so before I could play that game with myself where I continuously refreshed the inbox page, I logged off. Next up was Kari. I was still confused as to why he'd showed his ass the other night, but now I was ready for an explanation so I called him. He answered damn near on the first ring as if he had been waiting by the phone.

"Hi—Hello? Scottie?"

"Yup, it's me."

"I'm so glad that you finally called me back."

"Is that right?" I rolled my eyes.

"Yes. I was a complete asshole to you the other night and…I…I apologize."

"That's for sure.

"It was misdirected anger. I'm sorry."

"Look, why don't you start from the beginning? I'll be honest, I was super pissed at you, but now that I've had a chance to calm down, I want to hear exactly what the hell was going on."

"I can respect that," Kari said in his mellow, nonconfrontational voice. "I had a bad day and I was in a foul mood, then I realized that I had not heard from you all day. My thoughts were going crazy and getting the best of me. I started thinking that most of the time, I'm the one that always calls you first. There I was having a bad day and my girl had not even called to check on me—not once throughout the day. I thought that you were being selfish. But now I realize that it wasn't really about you. I was already pissed, but since I couldn't go off on my client, I tried to take it out on you and that wasn't fair. I know it wasn't."

"You damn right it wasn't fair!" I interjected, feeling a rise in my blood pressure. "I guess you totally forgot that I had a big event at the office that day. I'm sorry that I wasn't around to cater to you and kiss your ass, but I was busy working too."

"No! That's not what I was saying. Don't blow this out of proportion any more than you already have."

"Oh! So now it's on me!"

"No, no, no…I apologize for initially even coming at you the way that I did the other day. I fully admit that I was in the wrong. I don't want to keep fighting with you. Can you please accept my apology and let's move on?"

"You know what…I've had some time to think over the few days that we were apart…and…I'm not sure about us anymore. I think that we should take a break. I liked feeling like I was completely and totally on my own. Since the beginning of my living in New

York, I've been with you. I need to try this on my own now. I really do care about you and I don't want to lose you as a friend... but I need some space."

"Damn, all of that over a minor misunderstanding...really, Scottie?" I could hear the stress in Kari's voice. "I mean do you even care about us? Do you love me like I love you?"

"That misunderstanding made me realize how much I care about *me*...and right now I think we need to chill for a little while and see where our relationship will go from there."

"You're a cold piece of work. You know that?"

The phone line was silent. I had no response since that wasn't the first time I'd heard that accusation, but I wasn't about to confirm his statement.

Kari continued, "The way that you were acting...I thought that you were never going to talk to me again. But then I figured that I was being dramatic. Now you tell me you want a break?"

"I'm not saying that I want you out of my life. I need to fall back from the intensity of the relationship for a bit."

"Is there someone else? Tell me if that's what it is. Don't try to play me for a fool, Scottie."

That wasn't what I expected him to say.

My voice was a little squeaky as I quickly responded, "No, don't even go there."

"If you say so." Kari responded with a twinge less bass in his voice. "Look, I'll play by your rules, so you tell me how you want this thing to go. But for now, I'll talk to you later."

"Perfect."

I heard a familiar click. I sort of felt like he hung up on me again, but this time it was warranted, and honestly, there was nothing left to say.

Chapter 18

Hip-Hop Heart

I heard rumors that Kari had been hitting the streets heavy. I even caught wind of him being spotted with a blondie. That was totally out of character for him, but I wasn't his woman anymore so I had no right to be concerned. We had only spoken once since the break and I didn't ask him any questions in an effort to respect his feelings. I wanted him to take time to do his thing because I had definitely planned on doing mine.

Speaking of doing me, Byron didn't email back right away; it took him two long agonizing days to respond. I checked that email account religiously wondering what could be taking him so long. When he finally responded, I was relieved. I called my Jolie to give her the play-by-play. I had already told her that Kari and I were taking a break. She had no reservations about telling me how big of a mistake she thought that I was making. Kari was such an ideal guy in her eyes.

"Well, he finally responded," I'd said to my Jolie.

"And?"

"He's coming to the city for a commercial shoot and he asked if he could take me out."

"So is this going to be like a date?"

"I'm not even trying to entertain all that at this point. It'll be our first time hanging out so we'll see how it goes."

"As I said before, I trust that you know what you're doing."

"I do...I do. All right, I'll talk to you later!"

I couldn't find an outfit to wear to work. It was crucial that I pick the right look since I was meeting up with Byron after work. The plan was to meet him at his hotel around seven o'clock, which meant that I wouldn't have time to run back home and change. My excitement made it impossible to concentrate and come up with a fly-ass outfit.

That night, after sifting through everything that I owned and trying on countless outfit combinations, I finally settled on the old faithful: all black everything. Even though I had no clue where the night would take us, it was impossible to go wrong in all black.

The following day I could barely look my coworkers in the eyes. I felt like they would be able to read my secret thoughts. I stayed glued to my desk as much as possible. A few people made comments about how cute I looked, but that wasn't out of the ordinary on a typical workday.

As six o'clock finally crept around, I ducked into the women's restroom to freshen up.

Teeth crisp and clean? Check.

Fresh coat of mascara? Check.

Lipstick? Check.

Bronzer and blush? Check.

Smell goods? Check.

I covered all of the majors. Now I was ready to embark on my adventure.

Since I was rocking my sexy heels, I thought it best that I pass on the train option and simply hop in a cab. Byron's hotel wasn't far from my office, but a girl could not get her mean strut on in the city streets, in turn, messing up the taps on her thousand dollar heels. No ma'am.

The cab driver stopped directly in front of the hotel lobby entrance. I wasn't ready. I could see the doorman standing outside of the cab waiting to greet me. This was all too real and now the fear was starting to kick in.

I extended my hand with the money in it toward the cab driver, and I noticed that my entire arm was shaky. I almost stepped on the doorman's foot as he was trying to open the door for me. I was a paranoid wreck. I was such a mess that I quickly decided one of two things would happen: either I would pull it together and fake it like I was that bad chick, or I would turn my ass around immediately and head to the Port Authority and catch a bus back to Jersey. I stood in the lobby for two seconds to decide. The next thing I knew, a burst of confidence came from some mysterious place in my body and I was energized. I strutted through the lobby with a steady stride and my heels click-clacked as I approached the front desk.

"Hello, I'm here to see William Reid," I said to the tall brunette with piercing, blue eyes at the post behind the front desk.

"Sure, one moment," she replied with a strong accent, possibly Russian.

"Mr. Reid will be down to greet you shortly."

"Thank you."

I walked over to the lounge area to take a seat. I figured I should save all of the feet time that I had left—unless I planned on having him carry me at some point. It felt odd asking for a fictitious name at the front desk, but I did as instructed. I knew the deal. He was a well-known athlete. Lucky for me, he wasn't the type that the paparazzi followed around regularly.

"Hey, sexy."

My stomach dropped like I was going down the first major dip on the Goliath roller coaster at Six Flags Magic Mountain. I recognized the voice, so I stood and turned around to greet Byron. He looked good. Actually, damn good. Oh the wonders of what a little money and excellent grooming could do for a man.

I smiled. "Hi, Byron."

He leaned down to embrace me and the whiff of his cologne was mesmerizing. I tried to play it cool, though.

"Ready?" Byron asked.

"Sure," I quickly responded.

We headed outside to the awaiting car service. The doorman swiftly opened the door to the SUV and as I got in, he winked at me. I smiled back. I imagined that he was telling me "Get it, girl," since I knew that the little old man with the white hair was not trying to be fresh. Once we were settled in the car, Byron put his hand on my knee and asked if I was hungry. I wasn't starving, but I knew that I could eat a little something so I said yes.

"My man, take us to the Waverly Inn, please."

Oh hell no. I looked at Byron and he was totally clueless.

"Byron," I said in a soft tone, "We can't go there."

"Why not?"

"I'm not sure if you are aware of this, but since I work for The League…"

In an instant, it became clear. "My fault, I wasn't thinking. I don't want to put you in an awkward or compromising situation."

"Thank you."

"Give me a second. Where else can we go?"

"How about The Stanton Social on the Lower East Side? Have you been there before?" I asked. The paparazzi would not be staked out there.

"No, let's do it."

We arrived at the restaurant with no reservation and no entourage, but the manager seemed to be quick on his toes. He politely interrupted the hostess and informed us that he would show us to our table. Maybe it was Byron's height or his familiar face. Either way, the special treatment we received was something I could get used to. The manager led us upstairs to a cozy booth just big enough for Byron to squeeze into.

"What type of food does this place have?"

"They serve a variety of tapas dishes. The food is really good. If you like seafood, I would recommend the red-snapper tacos."

"So you brought a man of my size to a place that serves small plates?" Byron said.

I laughed. I hadn't even thought of it that way. He was a good sport about it, though.

"I guess I'll have to order ten of everything."

"Okay, now you're being excessive."

"I like being excessive sometimes," he said with a smirk. "I thought you figured that out already."

Staying true to form, when he ordered, Byron instructed the waitress to bring us four of everything off of the food menu. By the time she came over to offer us dessert, we had a table filled with half-eaten plates of food and had no room for dessert. Instead, we continued our conversation about our favorite albums.

"I rock with artists that are consistent, like Jay-Z and T.I.," I said. "They never disappoint."

Byron said as he looked around like he was scanning the room for someone, "I feel you."

"Are you all right? Expecting someone?" I questioned.

"No, not at all," he said with a stern confidence. "So, how do you feel about Mary J. Blige?"

"Love her. She's like a big sister in my head. I can remember dressing like her and knowing the words to all of her songs when I was growing up."

Byron laughed.

"Don't laugh at me! You run this game about wanting to know more about me, I tell you, and then you laugh!"

"I'm sorry, my bad. You're right," Byron said as he grabbed my hand. "How about this? Are you still down to keep the night going after we finish up here?"

"That depends."

"Well, if you decline, then I'll have to go see the Jay-Z and Mary J. concert solo."

He let the comment hang in the air as if he expected me to beg him like a little child who wanted a piece of candy. What he didn't know was that I had already been to the show the other night with two of my friends. Of course I wanted to go again with him, though. Inside, I was geeked, but my response had to be cool and collected.

"That would be absolutely no fun going alone, and since I'd hate to set you up for a miserable night…I guess I can accompany you."

"You're feisty. I like it."

The driver was waiting outside of the restaurant as soon as we exited. We headed uptown riding along the Westside Highway listening to Jay to get us in the mood. I resisted every urge that I had to text Dev and tell her who I was with and where I was going. She knew nothing about Byron and now was not the time to let that cat out of the bag. So I sat back, bobbed my head to the beats and enjoyed what seemed like a fantasy ride.

We pulled up to Madison Square Garden in the heart of mid-town Manhattan where gobs of people, cars, cabs, bikes, and buses were moving at a rapid pace. There I was on a secret date in one of the least discreet locations one could ever designate. This was one of the biggest hip-hop/R&B concerts to hit the Garden, so we knew that there would be paparazzi lurking around the VIP entrance. Byron told me to get out of the car first and he handed me my ticket. He said that he would have the driver circle the block before dropping him off and that he would meet me inside. As I went to grab the door handle, he called my name. I turned back to look at him. I blinked my long, black lashes and before I knew it, his lips were touching mine. It was one of the sweetest kisses ever.

Byron found me once he made it inside. We grabbed drinks backstage before heading to our floor seats where the view of the stage was amazing. The show was about to start so the house lights had begun to dim. The Dream was the opening act and he was good, but I was ready for my girl Mary to hit the stage.

"Are you okay?" Byron yelled into my right ear.

"Yes, thank you," I said, trying to keep it short and sweet since it was hard to hear.

When Mrs. Mary J. finally stepped on the stage, she looked as fierce as ever. All black everything like me. She had on her fly, trademark, thigh-high boots, hair was styled in a blonde bob, and she started hitting her signature Mary moves.

Jay and Mary on the stage together felt right. Byron and I both sang and rapped along like two teenagers at a B2K concert. I liked the fact that he did not zone out on me. He was into the music yet completely aware of the fact that I was by his side. I didn't want the show to end. I was having so much fun.

Before the finale song concluded, we made our way toward the backstage area. I wasn't used to this quasi-celebrity life, so I followed Byron's lead.

"I need to stop at the ladies room."

"Okay, I'll wait right here," Byron said.

I left Byron standing in the hallway, which was filled with tons of people. Everyone who was anyone was at that show. I tried to make my restroom stop as quick as possible, but apparently, I wasn't fast enough. By the time I walked out, there was a big-booty broad hanging all over Byron like they were old friends. I stood there and observed for a second because I didn't know what the situation was. For all I knew, she could have been his girl or his plaything. Either way, I did not have claims to him, and I could not afford to get mixed up in any drama.

The girl was smiling and rubbing up and down Byron's chest. He wasn't making enough of an effort to stop her either. Byron must have felt me staring at him because he looked in my direction and abruptly pushed the chick out of his way so that he could head toward me. I was annoyed as hell. I knew this was a bad idea, but I had to test the waters.

"Scottie, I can already tell what you're thinking. It wasn't what you think, though."

I screwed up my face. "Oh really," I said. "It doesn't matter anyway because you're not my man."

"She was some whack-ass groupie."

"I knew this was a bad idea. Let's go."

As we were walking through the hallway toward the exit, I noticed what looked like a familiar face in the distance. It took me a second to process where I knew her from, but when it clicked, there was no mistaking. It was Britney, the stank-attitude-having bitch from work.

Fuck! I can't let her see me with Byron. She'll suspect something and she has a big-ass mouth.

We were about to pass the entrance to the side of the stage and

I had to think fast so I looked back at Byron and said, "Thanks. I gotta go."

He looked puzzled, but I left him standing there because I didn't have time to explain. Britney was approaching quickly and it looked like she could have spotted me before I ducked off to the side. I click-clacked as fast as I could and went through a couple of black production curtains that I had no business being behind. I had to get away…from him and from her. I needed to get to an exit that would let me out with the general crowd; that way I could blend in and lose them both for sure.

Once I reached the street level, I hailed the first cab that I saw and hopped in as fast as I could. I didn't know why I was still paranoid, but I was. On top of everything else, it was late and I had to go to work in the morning. I wanted to get home as quickly as possible. I hated dropping the cash on a cab to Jersey, but under the circumstances, I had to make an exception.

The whole ride home my phone kept buzzing in my purse. Byron was blowing up my line, but I didn't answer. He started texting me apologies and asking me to please pick up the phone. I decided that I would deal with him when I was ready. I had no real grounds to be pissed about the groupie situation, but it had rubbed me the wrong way.

I laid my head back on the seat, looked out the window, and wondered what Kari was up to. He loved Jay-Z and I knew that he would have had an amazing time at that concert had we gone together. I wouldn't have had to deal with groupie incidents or hiding from coworkers. I couldn't help but wonder if I'd made the right decision, especially every time my phone rang and Byron's number showed up. After a few more of his calls, I did the unthinkable. I turned my phone completely off for the night.

Chapter 19

Get Away

The following morning at work was miserable with a twist of torture on the top. Once I arrived, I wished that I had called in sick, but it was too late since a couple of people had already seen my face. I had a slight hangover. It felt like there was a little man with a hammer inside my head having temper-tantrums every few minutes. I wasn't in the mood for the friendly fake hellos and good mornings of office life.

My cell phone buzzed off the hook when I finally turned it on. I had three text messages and ten voicemail messages.

Really, Byron?

Almost every message started with, "Scottie, I'm really sorry." He was profusely apologizing and to my surprise, there was also one long voicemail from Kari. He was stumbling over his words and pausing for extended amounts of time; apparently, he was checking up on me.

As far as I was concerned, all men could kiss my big toe at that moment. I needed a hearty sausage, egg, and cheese sandwich to shake the ills that I was feeling. I walked into the cafeteria with every intention of getting in and out fast. While I was waiting for Roberto with the rotten front tooth to finish up my breakfast sandwich, I heard my name being called from behind.

"Good morning, Scottie."

It's definitely not a good morning if you're speaking to me.

I turned around to acknowledge the voice. I should not have been surprised to see that it was Britney the bitch.

She's up to something because she never speaks willingly. I really don't feel like dealing with her right now.

"What?"

"Wow, did someone wake up on the wrong side of someone else's bed this morning?"

This little trick is really trying to get under my skin.

She naturally thought that everyone was a whore as she was. I tossed her *thee* nastiest look that I could conjure up and rolled my eyes real stank-like to top it off. I wasn't in the mood for her bullshit.

"How did you enjoy the concert last night?"

"What?"

"I said…How. Did. YOU. Enjoy…the concert last night?"

"I don't know what you're talking about."

"That's strange. I could have sworn. Didn't I see you backstage?"

"Nope, wasn't me," I responded, mustering up a bit more bitch-don't-fuck-with-me bass in my voice.

I strutted off in my turquoise-and-red Reebok exclusives, leaving her low-budget ass standing by the $2.99 bowls of cereal. I didn't have the time or the patience to continue an elementary exchange with such a simple-minded individual.

Britney was an insecure little girl portraying the role of a confident woman, but I could see straight through the facade. It usually took her family money and the promise of sexual favors or material items to get men to stomach her for an extended period of time from what I'd heard.

I plopped down at my desk and put my head down on my folded

arms. The old-school Dell computer mounted on my desk chirped with a new email message. But I couldn't care less who it was or what it was about. Concentrating on work was not an option. I needed to feed my belly first. While I was eating, I checked my Gmail to kill time and I almost choked on my breakfast sandwich. The email stood out like it was typed in big bold red letters. The subject line read "E-Ticket Confirmation" and it was from JetBlue Airways.

What the freak?

I hadn't booked any trips so something was definitely suspicious. I clicked on the email without being entirely sure what I would find.

I scrolled down to look at the details of the flight itinerary. It wasn't spam.

A departure from JFK airport with an arrival in Barbados...in three days.

I couldn't act like I was clueless. As soon as I let everything process for a moment, I knew who was behind all of this and who bought the ticket. But why was he so damn extreme? Leaving multiple voicemails was one thing, but dropping serious coins on a plane ticket was another. I was beyond surprised and this gesture was borderline crazy...or romantic, depending on your frame of reference. None of this was normal, though. This was the type of fantasy ridiculousness that happened to reality stars on TV and not to a chick like me.

What the hell do you do when someone tries to buy you an apology? This was one that you couldn't exactly give back. Byron was intriguing and his methods may not have been conventional, but the trip was obviously a gesture to make up for the incident. Little did he know I wasn't really stuck on that or mad. It was too much going on. I needed to talk to him and see where his head was.

Sending him an email instead of a text seemed like the best idea, since clearly his ass was on the computer like nonstop, making transactions from shoes to airline tickets. The email was short and to the point, no subject, only a simple, "call me after seven tonight."

I hit "send" so fast that I hadn't even carefully considered what I'd said. Oh well, I figured. That meant that the ball was in his court and now I would have to wait on his call.

For the remainder of the day, I planned to live in my moment of fantasy since I had no clue how this whole trip situation would turn out. I started visually sorting through my outfits for Barbados and taking a mental note of what I didn't have but would need for the trip. I conjured up all types of sexy little outfits and I could already feel the Caribbean sun on my skin.

As soon as I exited the bus on my way home, I called my Jolie. I was bursting inside as I had been dying all day to tell someone about Barbados.

"Are you ready for this?" I screamed, immediately after she said hello.

"Scottie?"

"Yeah, it's me. You will not believe this."

"What happened? Did you get fired?"

"No! Be quiet for a second and I'll tell you."

"Okay, what? This better be good."

"Today I'm checking my personal email at work and there was a confirmation email for an airline ticket that I knew I didn't buy, but I opened it anyway. It was a round-trip ticket in my name to Barbados?"

"Who the hell bought that? Wait, was it a joke…or a scam?"

"No! It was a legit ticket. I think Byron bought it."

"Oh hell. And what do you mean you think. You didn't ask his ass? Why would he do a thing like that without asking you first?"

"I have no clue, but people do crazy shit all the time. I hit him up and told him to call me tonight, but I didn't mention anything about the ticket."

"Umph. Well, ain't that some shit," she said in disbelief. "Are you gonna go? Hell, I would. You are young, you got it going on, baby, and you only live once. Be careful if you do decide to go. And be sure to keep your dad and me on speed dial."

"I'm not sure yet. I'll call you later tonight with an update."

"All right, honey."

When I walked into the apartment, Dev announced that she was home before I could even get a word out, "Hey, girl!" She seemed to be in a good mood and I was almost certain that she wanted to chat. The only problem was that I was distracted. All I could think about was Byron and the phone call that I was expecting. I knew myself and that if I chatted with Dev too long, I would be tempted to spill the beans about everything. It wasn't that I couldn't tell her what was going on. But since I wasn't even sure what the hell I was doing with Byron, I did not want to involve Dev or anyone else from The Clique.

A glass of chilled white wine was calling my name. I needed to calm my nerves. As I poured my glass, it occurred to me that I should at least mention the possibility of going out of town to Dev. She was my roommate, after all, and I couldn't keep her completely in the dark.

We stood in the kitchen talking about nothing and I tried to casually mention that I might go and visit the family in Cali for the weekend. I played it off like I was a bit homesick and my dad was looking into buying me a ticket. Conveniently, at the tail end

of my big fat lie, my phone rang. I looked at the caller ID. It was
an unknown number. My stomach dropped. It was Byron. I told
Dev, "I gotta take this." Then I scurried into my room and closed
the door.

"Hello?"

I turned the TV on to create a bit of distractive noise in case
Dev could hear me talking.

"Hey, babe."

Is he hitting me with "babe" already?

Minor pet peeve when guys did that, especially too soon. I
wanted to say, "I'm not your babe," but I gave him a pass and got
straight into specifics.

"So what was up with that email?"

"You wouldn't call me back. I know I messed up, but I really
wanted to see you again. I had fun with you the other night. I
want a second chance."

"That was a really bold move buying a ticket for someone without consulting with them. Do you do that on a regular basis?"

"No, but I felt like I had to do something to get your attention.
It worked, didn't it?"

"Yeah, but what makes you so sure that I can or will drop everything and hop on a flight with you?"

"I'm not sure about anything. But I'm hoping."

The line was silent.

"Look, I gotta go," I said.

"Wait…will you at least think about it?" Byron pleaded, sounding
like a sad puppy dog.

"Yeah, I'll think about it."

I hung up the phone and screamed softly into my pillow. I played
it cool on the phone acting disinterested, but the truth was that I
wanted to say, "Hell yeah, I'll go with you to Barbados or anywhere

else you want me to go." My bags were as good as packed. But with a man used to getting everything he wanted all the time, I had to make him wait it out. I wasn't going to be easy.

My phone rang interrupting my excitement. I didn't expect to see the name that popped up on the caller ID. I had totally forgotten to call Kari back. With slight hesitation, I went ahead and picked up. "Hey, Kari."

"Hi, Scottie. Did I catch you at a bad time?"

"No, not at all. What's up?" I wouldn't dare tell him that the chipper sound in my voice was due to my pending vacation.

"Not much"—Kari cleared his throat—"I'm not even gonna try to play it cool. I really want to see you. I miss you."

There was an awkward pause. I wasn't expecting his call let alone the direction of the conversation. My mind was in another place and I had to think quickly. He started talking again before I could respond.

"Can I take you out this weekend?"

"I…I actually have plans. I'm going out of town with Dev on a little impromptu getaway."

I had no clue why I'd just volunteered all of that information and lied on top of that. It wasn't my intention to start lying to Kari, but it had flowed from my lips so effortlessly. I had always been very upfront and honest with him throughout our relationship, but since we were not together, I didn't want to hurt his feelings.

"Oh…okay…that's cool. I get it. Everyone needs a little getaway sometimes, right?"

I could hear the sadness in his voice.

"Well, you ladies have fun and maybe we can get together when you get back."

"Thanks…let's try to make that happen," I said sincerely, "I'll call you next week."

I really did care for Kari. He offered me amazing stability and my desire to see him still lingered. But there was a stronger desire to explore the unknown. I had only fantasized of dating a powerful man with unlimited resources who would shower me with gifts and give me all of the attention that a girl could ask for. I welcomed the new adventure.

Two days later, I finally let Byron know that I would accompany him on the trip. My first-class seat was amazing—feet stretched out, a copy of *Essence* magazine, and music bumping in my earphones. Life was good. I sipped on libations to start the vacation off right and loosen up a bit. I was nervous as hell. I seriously had no clue as to what type of situation I was about to walk into, but I tried to stay optimistic. Byron was on a flight landing about an hour after mine from Chicago.

Baggage claim was packed, but I spotted a man dressed in a crisp black suit holding a sign that, to my surprise, had my name on it. The letters were scrolled across his white board. I realized that Byron never failed to have it all figured out.

The driver took my bags as we walked to the car. The warmth in the night air hit me like a welcome blanket since I had been freezing on the airplane. The driver confirmed my destination and we were on our way.

Barbados was so beautiful, even at night. The radiant, dark-blue skies and palm trees instantly made me feel relaxed. As we passed one flawless beach property after another, I tried to imagine myself living in such a peaceful environment permanently.

"Miss...miss...we have arrived at your destination, The Crane Resort."

I had completely zoned out. "My apologies, sir, thank you very much."

I exited the car to take in the lavish view. The resort property looked like the front of a Beverly Hills estate. I walked around to the back of the car to hand the driver a tip for his service, but he politely pushed my hand away. "Thank you for your generous gesture, ma'am, but all of your expenses have been settled."

"Good evening, Ms. Malveaux," the bellman said as he grabbed my bags. He instructed me to follow him inside. He pointed to the right. "Our lovely front desk attendant will take excellent care of you. Enjoy your stay."

The visibly pregnant front desk attendant was pleasant as she welcomed me to the resort and provided a few tips for moving about the property comfortably. She handed me keys to a two-bedroom suite. She didn't know how much the words "two-bedroom" were music to my ears. In the back of my mind, the sleeping situation had totally been an area of concern since I didn't want to find myself in an awkward position on night one.

I walked into the suite and it took every restraint in my being to contain my excitement so as not to embarrass myself in front of the bellman. Once he left, I squealed with glee and began to venture about the space.

The entire suite had an Old World charm about it. Every inch had a mix of dark-colored wood with stark white accents.

The bathroom was even extravagant, complete with a massive sunken Jacuzzi bathtub fit for two. I could hear the waves crashing when I stepped out onto the balcony. I couldn't wait to see the view of the beach in the morning's sunlight.

Before getting too relaxed and caught up in the serenity of my surroundings, I thought it best to freshen up a bit. I hopped in the shower hoping that Byron would not arrive as I was getting out. I wasn't prepared for interaction on that level yet. Although, I was realistic, I knew what the expectations would be for someone tricking off money and taking you on a trip to Barbados.

It took Byron longer than I thought it would to arrive. The anticipation drove me to drink. When he texted me that he'd landed, I was halfway dressed, but by the time he walked in the hotel suite, I had been listening to music and trying to calm my anxiety for fifteen minutes.

"How was your trip?" Byron said as he walked toward the couch where I was lounging. "You look nice."

"Thanks, the trip was good." I stood and responded with a smile. "You took good care of me."

"It was my pleasure."

Byron looked like dessert to a girl who had been on a no-sweets diet for months. He extended his massive, chiseled arms toward me and I quickly fell into his firm embrace. Even after a long flight, he smelled good. I could feel his hulking muscles almost squeezing the life out of what little upper body muscle I had. Then he pulled back a tiny bit and looked down at me. "Are you hungry?"

That wasn't what I expected him to say, but I was happy he had. "I'm actually starving."

"Then let's roll."

I felt like a shy schoolgirl at the touch of his oversized, warm hand grasping mine. We headed toward one of the resort's restaurants, which seemed to be closed by the looks of the dim lighting. As we got closer, I looked at Byron waiting for him to realize that it was closed. But then, the doors swung open revealing a bald, petite man whom I later identified as the maître d'. He greeted us like we were the local King and Queen.

The restaurant dining area that we walked through was filled with hints of Asian fusion décor. Our table provided a supreme view of the tropical landscape just beyond the panoramic window. Byron was a complete gentleman as he pulled out my chair. Soft island music played in the background as he looked over the menu.

"Do you see anything that you like?" Byron asked.

"I actually hadn't really looked. I was captivated by the view," I said dreamily.

"It's amazing, right?"

"Absolutely. It looks as though there is a full moon. Look at the way that the light shines on the water in the distance," I pointed out.

Byron winked and flashed his sparkling white grin. "You know what they say about a full moon."

We dined on a five-course meal complete with interesting conversation and flirtatious banter in relative seclusion. I was stuffed and completely relieved that I didn't try to squeeze myself into an overly sexy, tight-fitting dress for the night. I figured that dress would serve me better at least one day into the trip anyway… pull out the big guns. My low-cut, flowing, multicolored maxi dress was perfect for our first low-key night on the island.

"I know I sound like a party pooper, but my body is beat," Byron offered as we exited the restaurant. "I've been doing some intense conditioning this week. Gotta be ready for preseason, love."

"It's cool. We can go back to the room and chill out." My week had been pretty crazy as well so I was completely satisfied with relaxing in the lap of luxury.

We walked into the suite to find the beds turned down and a complimentary bottle of champagne.

"Are you up for a little bubbly?" I asked Byron.

"I'm down if you are."

"You open the bottle and I'll get the glasses."

"Let's toast to us," Byron said.

Two glasses of champagne and a little cuddling on the cozy terrace led to passionate kissing. Tongues were tussling and swirling with lust. Hands were slowly exploring foreign territories. Things were quickly getting intense. Byron placed his index finger under my chin and tilted my head so that our eyes met.

"I'm about to go take a shower before this goes any further," he said.

"That's probably a good idea."

"I'm always full of good ideas, love."

I grinned at him. "Seems that way."

Byron took my hand as he sat on the edge of the chaise lounge. "You clearly know that I'm feeling you, but I'm not trying to pressure you about anything. Make no mistake about it, I would not mind taking things to another level. But I got us separate rooms because I want you to feel comfortable. When you are ready, let me know."

I was surprised by his candor. "I appreciate your extra effort to make me feel comfortable. I really do."

It seemed as though the smart professional athletes had learned a lesson or two from the Mike Tyson and/or Kobe Bryant scandals.

Byron stood and winked at me before disappearing into his room. It was evident that he was excellent at running game. He didn't know that I would not be falling for it on the first night.

The morning sun forced my eyes open bright and early. The ocean view was paradise. My complexion was in need of a serious golden boost, so breakfast by the pool was the first item on my agenda. I put on my hot-pink bikini with the sequined flower on the left boob, slathered on enough SPF to avoid any potential sunburn, and left a note for Byron to join me by the pool.

An elaborate glass elevator with breathtaking views of the endless sea and white sand beach carried me down to a life of luxuriating by the water. I ordered breakfast and checked my cell phone. Kari had called five times, never once leaving a message. My Jolie left a message, but I had already called her back to let her know that I'd made it. And Dev left a message: *"Chick, call me back. I gotta tell you about my run-in with Kari just now."*

"Fuck!" I said aloud, totally oblivious to the fact that other resort guests surrounded me.

I started wracking my brain. *What would I say? How could I spin this?* I called Dev immediately.

I wasted no time after she answered. "Hey, I got your message. What happened?"

"Oh nothing," Dev responded very distantly.

"What do you mean nothing? You said that you ran into Kari. What happened?"

"Oh yeah, I did. No big deal."

"No big deal? But your message sounded like there was something to report?"

"Look, there wasn't! He didn't even ask about you," Dev snapped.

I noticed Byron headed in my direction, so I quickly wrapped up my call. "That's strange. Look, I gotta go. I'll holler at you later."

Byron took his seat next to me and kissed my cheek. "Who was that?"

"Excuse me?" I turned to look him in his eyes, quite taken aback.

"Who were you on the phone with?"

"Not that it's any of your business," I said, playfully rolling my eyes. "It was my roommate."

It's a little hard to snap on someone who'd just spent who knows how much money taking you on a lavish, last-minute vacation. However, something about his question did not sit well with me. I would save that conversation for a later date. What I needed to figure out was my explanation for Kari. If I still wanted to keep things in a good place with him, I had better come up with a feasible story.

"So what would you like to do today, love?" Byron said, snapping me back to reality.

"I thought that it would be nice to spend a relaxing day by the pool."

"That's cool. It's whatever you want to do. I'm gonna need an umbrella, though. My family is from the islands, but I'm not built for all of this one-on-one with the sun," he said, rubbing his beard.

"Well, a girl like me is, and our attendant is the slim little dude with the dirty blond ponytail to the left of the bar."

"You are so damn feisty," Byron said as he smiled at me.

We spent the day lounging, dipping in and out of the pool, and enjoying each other's company. Byron told me stories of his childhood adventures growing up in Houston. His parents were still together, but his voice was filled with an air of resentment toward his father for what seemed like past issues of infidelity. He spoke as though he were still the little boy trying to protect his fragile mother. I did my best to respond with minimal commentary, as it was better to simply listen rather than comment.

Byron was starting to become sexier by the moment—especially after a few glasses of rum punch.

"The sun is about to set. We should take a walk along the beach," I suggested.

Byron looked at me with a gleam in his eyes. "Let's do it, love."

I stood and grabbed a couple of towels from the towel bar.

"Bring your glass for a sunset toast," Byron instructed.

"Look at you, Mr. Romance."

"When in Rome…." Byron laughed.

Byron and I walked down to the white, sandy beach. We found a quaint little spot by a huge black and gray rock to spread out our resort towel. He popped open the bottle of Veuve Clicquot that he'd purchased from the pool bar. As the sun began to set, Byron made a toast. "Here's to continued success and new relationships."

Our glasses clinked as our eyes locked. His rich chocolate skin had a flawless glow in the Caribbean sunset. His long, dark lashes blinked as he gazed deeply into my eyes. The fullness of his juicy bottom lip grazed mine before our kisses fully met.

"I always prefer to seal my toast with a kiss when I'm in the company of a gorgeous woman."

"That's sweet," I said. I knew that he probably said that to all of the ladies, but it was my time and that's all that I would worry about.

Before Byron could utter another word, I leaned in and pressed my lips against his. I suckled on his plump bottom lip and ran my fingers through the slightly scruffy beard that was growing in. His cologne lingered in my senses and I felt the passion rising to new heights with each exchange of tongue flickering. Our lips were interlocked and our tongues twirled with the moisture of lust. Tonight there would be no referee; we were both ready to play straight through to the final buzzer.

He softly pressed his lips against my neck before moving down the center of my chest. "Are you sure this is what you want?" Byron asked.

"Positive," I replied with sheer confidence.

The bulge in Byron's navy-blue swim trunks was rising and calling for attention. I obliged by sliding my hand down the front of his shorts and grabbing a hand full of his erect manhood. It would take two hands—or more—to fully manage the Mandingo warrior caged in his trunks.

He untied and removed my swimsuit top in one fluid motion, laid me back on the beach towel, and began caressing my breasts juggling as much as he could handle with two hands. He licked and sucked me into submission. The sun had completely set and aside from a glimmer of light in the distance and the reflection of a full moon, we were relatively sheltered in darkness.

Byron's tongue slid over every inch of the inner portion of my thighs, the warmth from his heavy breathing caused an eruption of creamy wetness to ooze from my body. I was anticipating his arrival. Byron threw my legs over his shoulders and went deep-sea diving into my private ocean of sweet white waters with his tongue. He caused convulsions in my body that were foreign and unnatural. My left foot almost caught a cramp from the repeated reaction to a magical pleasure I'd never known. Byron wasn't a selfish lover; he liked to please as well.

After I was fulfilled—which gave him great pleasure—we moved on to the final minutes in the game. He was up by one so I climbed on top of him to solidify a strong finish. With my legs on either side, I bucked back and rode his Mandingo adding in extra swirls for added pleasure. He gripped my ass. I felt him thrusting deep inside of me. Byron's eyes stayed locked on mine until he could not hold his gaze anymore. His eyes rolled back in ecstasy. He moaned and let out sounds of pleasure.

We attempted to brush the sand off of one another while smooching and giggling at our risky escapade. Trying to avoid any awkward encounters, we crept along the back pathway to our suite. Byron kept smacking my ass to rush me along. Our massive shower would be the scene for round two.

As the sun was beginning to break day, Byron rolled over in my direction and pulled me into his comforting grasp. I'd cracked the sliding glass door open before we wore ourselves out and fell asleep. The soothing sound of the ocean in the morning was tranquil. The atmosphere, coupled with the comfort of being snuggled up in Byron's arms, was paradise.

Chapter 20

Fly Away

"Fuck that, Scottie! You fucking lied to me!" Kari yelled. "I ran into Dev at Slate. You sure weren't vacationing with her."

"Let's be clear. You need to calm down and stop cursing at me. We're in public, Kari." My voice was a little above a whisper so as not to draw any additional attention to an already uncomfortable situation. The low lighting and relatively romantic ambiance at Tillman's lounge was a deceptive reality for the circumstance. "I didn't lie to you. You're getting all worked up over nothing."

"Oh, it's nothing? You run off to God knows where and lie to me about who you were with, but I'm overreacting, right?" Kari spat back through tight lips and clenched teeth, never taking his eyes off of his glass of Scotch.

"Please look at me," I attempted to shift Kari's gaze in my direction, "At least give me a chance to tell you what was going on."

"I'm listening."

"I've had a lot on my mind lately. You know that I've been working really hard to earn a promotion since I got to The League and I needed to get away and clear my head. I found a last-minute deal to Barbados and when I mentioned it to Dev, she was down. But her finances didn't work out the way that she thought they would, so she couldn't go after all. Once the plans changed, I really didn't think that I needed to double back and explain all of that to you. I took off."

"See, that's part of the problem." His eyes were fixated on me. "I don't think you care enough about me or our situation to explain things to me, ever." I could hear the frustration in his voice slipping into exhaustion. "You dish out whatever you want whenever you want and I'm supposed to take it. Scottie, I'm not your ex. I'm not out to hurt you or do you wrong."

Damn. Did he just go there?

"That's not fair." I didn't want to come at him too harsh by saying what I was really thinking—"that's bullshit"—because that would only make things worse.

"I'm sorry, Kari, for everything that I've put you through. I know that I can be difficult to deal with. If you're not feeling this"—I motioned to me and him—"then I totally understand and respect your feelings."

"Here you go being extreme again. I didn't say that."

"Then tell me what you are saying."

"Communicate with me. Treat me how I treat you. Give me the same respect that I give you. That's it. That's all I have to say."

I could barely see Kari's eyes. As I sat in silence with Kari, I realized that I had feelings for both men. My emotions were being pulled in two different directions. I hadn't come to a place that I wanted to let either disappear from my life. Until I could sort out my feelings and identify my true desire, I resolved that I would live in the moment.

After the screaming silence filled our space for far too long, I turned to Kari. "I care about you. I really do. Thank you for always being straight up with me."

I searched his eyes for a glimmer of hope.

"I'm going to work on communicating better," I continued. "It's an area of development." I said that with a smile, hoping that would lighten the mood.

Thankfully, after a moment of pause, Kari flashed his gleaming white smile and lifted my hand from the table placing the palm of my hand on top of his. "Let's get out of here, Scottie."

"It's an easy question, Scottie. Do you want to see me or not?"

Byron had unexpectedly called my work line, which always made me nervous.

"You know I want to see you," I whispered.

"Okay then. I'm flying you out this weekend."

"What exactly do you have planned for me while I'm there?"

"Look, don't worry. You'll have a damn good time in my city, love," Byron said, with an air of confidence exclusive to him. "Chicago will show you nothing but a good time as long as you're with me."

Byron made the arrangements as promised and before I knew it, the wheels were up and my next stop was Chicago O'Hare Airport. Unfortunately, one lie begets another and the only people that knew of my true destination and location were my parents. My Jolie warned me of playing with fire, but the intensity of a multiromance lifestyle suited me well. I rationalized that men participated in the same game of chance all the time without an ounce of hesitation or remorse.

Byron didn't have conditioning training so he decided to pick me up from the airport himself. He was waiting in the loading zone, but apparently, the airport police started a starstruck fuss when they asked him to take a photo outside of the car in lieu of giving him a ticket.

Look at him. Relishing in the fanfare. He looks good doing it too.

Black Armani aviator sunglasses with a black fitted V-neck T-shirt hitting every chiseled indentation in his physique perfectly. Simple yet uber sexy.

Byron saw me heading toward the car with the Louis Vuitton Pegase roller bag that he sent to my office after our trip to Barbados. So like a gentleman he interrupted the photo spectacle to walk around to the passenger side and greet me. His burly arms enclosed me while his soft lips gently kissed my cheek.

"How was your flight, love?"

"It was good."

Byron winked as he held the door open. "Get in. I hope you're ready."

I got into the passenger side of his cocaine-white Bentley Continental GT and tried to contain my excitement. I was ecstatic. A few onlookers still lingered about, but I was relieved when I realized that the paparazzi hadn't received the heads-up on Byron's airport trip.

Byron sped off, tires screeching, with his hand gripping my thigh. He seemed confident that he would not be hassled by the police.

Our first stop was Michigan Avenue. Byron loved anything up-scale and designer. I adamantly disagreed with him about the purchase of a Burberry signature patterned button-down shirt. It was hideous and too flashy in my opinion, but he loved it.

I tried on a few sexy little dresses at a small posh boutique. The selection was quality yet minimal; code for expensive. I flipped over every tag while in the dressing room and they all spoke to me loud and clear. "You'll have to use your rent money to afford me."

"Which one did you like best?" the busty saleswoman with too much collagen in her lips asked.

"All of them, Miss," Byron chimed in on my behalf. "We'll take all of them."

He tossed his black card on the counter and turned to me. "Did you see anything else that you liked?"

I tried to mask the shock that was brewing inside of me. This was all too easy. Normally, when things come too easy, there's a catch. I leaned in and whispered as close to his head as I possibly could, which was more like his upper bicep, "No, but you really don't have to buy these dresses for me."

Before I could finish, he shot me a look.

"Thank you for shopping with us today," the saleswoman offered. "I hope that you enjoy the dresses honey," she said, as she walked smiling from around the register and handing me a huge pink shopping bag.

Like that, we were out of the store and back in the Bentley headed to Byron's place. We pulled up to a high-rise building along the lakefront. The valet greeted Byron by name and asked if he would be in need of his car later in the evening. I vaguely heard Byron mention dinner plans as I was trying to grab my bags. The doorman quickly came to my aid insisting that I let him handle it.

We rode the elevator hand in hand to the "PH" level. The elevator doors opened to his white marble foyer. His penthouse was gorgeous. It was laid, complete with floor-to-ceiling windows, a huge elegant, black sectional sofa, stark white walls, touches of sterling silver artwork throughout, and sunlight hitting every inch of the space down to the plush white fur area rug. This place definitely had a woman's touch, and I was certain that kids were not in the picture. Everything in me hoped that it was his mother's doing and not some crazy bitch due to bust in at any second.

I heard a noise coming from the kitchen and I looked at Byron. "Is someone else here?" I whispered.

"Yeah. My chef."

"Chef?"

"Yes, chef. He's making us lunch. It should be ready soon. I called ahead."

Byron kissed me on the shoulder and started walking toward what I could only guess was the master bedroom. "Make yourself at home and relax, love."

I followed his lead and put my things down in his room. While I got myself situated, he left me alone to marvel at the room and its splendor.

Wow, now that's one hell of a bed.

The gigantic bed in the center was clearly the focal point of the bedroom. It had to have been custom-made.

"Babe, lunch is ready!" Byron called out from the distance.

"Coming!"

We sat down to a gourmet lunch complete with hand-rolled sushi as a starter. I felt like I was on an episode of *Lifestyles of the Rich and Famous.*

"I made dinner reservations at a restaurant that I'm sure you'll love."

"Is this one of your regular spots?" I asked.

"Not regular. I like to go when I'm in the company of someone special."

"Don't try to make me blush." I smiled.

After lunch, we explored every inch of his bed. I crossed my fingers that the chef made a quick exit and didn't hear my screams of passion. Although, the curtains were wide open—if the chef didn't hear me, surely the neighbors could see me, but I didn't care.

Movies watched us and we watched them on and off for the rest of the afternoon. Our dinner reservation was for eight o'clock, so we began getting ready about an hour prior—starting off with a dual steamy shower. Byron couldn't keep his hands from probing my body and that slowed down our progress. My sweet lover popped a bottle of Armand de Brignac champagne to start the night off right while we dressed.

I already knew that my new burgundy mini dress fit like a glove, so I snapped the tags and laid it out on the bed while I slathered cocoa butter on from head to toe. Byron, to no surprise, walked out of his dressing area the size of a studio apartment and was fitted in Dolce & Gabbana looking like he was about to walk a red carpet. The suit fit him well. He looked as sexy as the first day that we met.

"Somebody is looking pretty dapper."

Byron dusted off the shoulders of his jacket. "Thanks, love. I put on a lil' somethin'-somethin'."

"You are a mess!" I said with a giggle.

"But you like it," he said, as he walked over, grabbing my naked body and pulling me to him for a soft kiss.

I slipped into my dress and took the last sip of my "Ace of Spades" before we headed downstairs hand-in-hand to the waiting chauffeured car. Byron thought it better to call up his driver since we had already been drinking. He didn't want any trouble with the law or The League. When behind the wheel, intoxicated athletes were like a magnet for police.

The driver pulled up to a luxurious steakhouse at the east end of the West Loop. He held the door open as we exited the SUV. Byron offered me his hand. I stepped out in my gold embellished stilettos with a six-inch heel.

The host showed us to our table immediately. The dining area was filled with patrons. From my peripheral view, I noticed a few people take a second glance as we passed their tables.

"So, is this your first time?"

I looked at Byron with confusion written all over my face. "Excuse me? First time for what?"

I knew that he couldn't be talking about my first time at a restaurant, or a high-end restaurant, or a steakhouse, or on a date, or anything else of that nature so I needed him to tell me what the hell he was talking about. His vague question came off a tad strange.

"First time dating someone like me?" Byron replied, very matter-of-fact.

I wasn't expecting this. Now I felt a bit silly for my initial thoughts.

"Interesting question," I noted. "Yes…this is my first time."

"So…"

Byron was mid-sentence when I spotted a well-dressed black woman in what looked to be her mid-twenties entering the dining area. She entered alone, which I found odd. This restaurant was not the type of establishment where you readily dined alone.

Where is her date? Maybe he's not far behind. Sometimes I'm too nosey for my own good.

Byron was still talking, but he couldn't keep my attention. The well-dressed woman was headed directly toward our table and there was no mistaking her eyes, which were fixated on Byron. He seemed oblivious.

Fuck me! This has to be a joke! Is this his fucking woman? I will not participate in an embarrassing hoodrat scene in this restaurant. Oh HELL, I forgot my mace in New York.

This wasn't my first time at the hoodrat, baby momma rodeo. I looked to the right of Byron as the woman walked up and stood next to him. His eyes rapidly shifted from mine as he looked over at her statuesque frame. I could tell that he knew her. I watched as he stood and greeted her. "Sava, I'm glad that you could make it, babe."

Babe! What kind of babe is this? Babe like Hollywood-schmoozing babe, or like "I sleep with you on a regular basis" babe, or like "I want to sleep with you on a regular basis" type babe?

My face contorted into an obvious quizzical expression.

"Scottie, this is Sava. She's going to join us."

"Join us?"

"Yes, join us. Don't be rude, love."

This dude had me twisted. He had not seen rude. I was roughly two-point-five seconds away from overreacting in a major way, which would likely turn into a scene that this restaurant had never seen before.

Byron shifted to the middle of the booth while Sava, dressed in a scarlet-red, plunging neckline dress, took her spot at our table. Byron attempted to spark up small talk and Sava ate right out of his hand. Her squeaky voice responded to his every comment. I sat silently. I was overwhelmed.

"How do you two know each other?" I questioned.

Byron placed his hand over Sava's and she looked down. He turned to me and tried to use his free hand to grab my hand.

Who the hell is this dude? Money Mike the pimp?

"Scottie, don't..." Byron tilted his head and stared into my eyes as he calmly said, "Go with the flow."

I got up abruptly from the table, grabbed my bag and excused myself. I needed two seconds alone to try to process this new reality that I was currently being tricked into. I walked outside of the dining area. "Where is the restroom?" I asked the host.

"First door on the left."

As I rushed down the hallway, I held back tears of anger, which burned my eyelids and begged to be released.

How did I get myself caught up in this mess?! How could I have been so stupid and naive?

I walked into the last stall and sat down on the pristine white toilet seat. My head fell into my hands and my palms were wet with tears.

"Scottie?" I heard a squeaky voice call out.

No this broad did not follow me into the fucking restroom!

"Get the fuck out and leave me alone!" I yelled.

"But Byron told me to come and check on you."

"Fuck you and fuck Byron, you sick and twisted freaks!" I screamed. "You can tell him to find another fool."

I heard the doorknob click. I realized that I was truly an even bigger fool than I knew for sitting in the restroom crying like a baby. It was time to get the hell out of there.

I opened the bathroom stall and turned toward the door to leave, but to my shock Byron was blocking the door. My legs froze as a rush of fear came over me. I hadn't heard him come in. This shit was getting crazier by the moment.

"What the hell are you doing in here, you fucking sicko?" I played off my fear and projected my voice as loudly as I could.

"Lower your voice," Byron demanded as he walked toward me.

With my right index finger extended in his direction and rage in my eyes, I walked right back at him. "Get the fuck out of this damn bathroom! Now! Who the hell do you think you are? What the hell do you think you're doing?"

"Calm down and stop overreacting. Now, me and my girlfriend are going to sit down and finish our dinner and I suggest that you join us."

Byron backed up against the door as a woman on the other side pushed the sturdy slab of wood into his back and attempted to walk in. "Hello? What's going on in there?"

"Don't make this worse than it already looks," I said to Byron as I took my opportunity and pushed past him to walk out of the restroom door.

I bolted out of the restaurant like a woman fleeing for her life. My heels clicked across the pavement as fast as they could move. I scurried down the street, but I didn't get the feeling that Byron was behind me. I flagged down a cab and looked over my shoulder as I got in.

"Can you take me to…to…it's a huge condo building by the water. I'm sorry…I'm…"

"Miss, I can't understand where you want to go," the little shriveled up old man said in a raspy, two-packs-a-day type of voice.

"I know…I know…just a second."

Think, Scottie! How the hell do you not know where you're staying? Pull it together.

"I think it's on Lake Shore Drive." My mind was scrambled. My vision was cloudy and I felt like someone had kicked me in the stomach.

"You know what? Can you take me to O'Hare airport?"

Chapter 21

Reality Slap

Monday was a welcome thrust back into the reality that I was familiar with. I couldn't sit down at my desk and get situated before the phone rang. Not bothering to look at the caller ID, I answered.

"Scottie speaking."

"Hi, Scottie, this is Caroline Stinger from HR. Do you have a moment to stop by my office?"

"Sure, when?" I asked.

"Now would be fine. Thanks, see you soon."

I headed to the elevator unsure of what the meeting with HR could be about. My gut told me that something was up though. The elevator chimed. As the doors opened, Britney the bitch walked out.

"Good morning, Scottie!" she said.

I felt like I was being *Punked*, but I offered a dry, "Hey."

I could hear her laughing in the distance. Shaking my head, I pressed the elevator button to close the door and proceeded to HR.

I was a spaced-out wreck after my meeting with HR. I tried to maintain a composed exterior, but it was challenging. Around midday my desk line rang and I answered, although it was an unidentified number. "Scottie speaking."

"Scottie, stop acting childish!"

It was Byron. I slammed down the phone. I had already been called into a meeting with HR and legal first thing in the morning on account of my stupidity for messing with his trifling ass. They wouldn't tell me who tipped them off, but I suspected Britney the bitch.

"Hey, girl," Lydia said, interrupting my thoughts as she sauntered up to my desk with a chipper smile. "How was your weekend?"

"It was cool...low-key," I lied, fighting every temptation to disclose the sheer trickery that I had been a party to.

My phone rang again. I looked at the caller ID. "I have to take this."

"All right, I'll holler. Let's catch up and do happy hour after work if you're free."

"Sounds good," I responded to Lydia's back as she walked away. "Hello?"

"Scottie, can you meet me in twelve B?" Joel asked.

"Sure."

"Five minutes ago, Dean called an impromptu meeting. Something about a star player and his concerns about his image."

"I'm on my way."

The last time Dean called an impromptu meeting, we were thrown into a last-minute situation which resulted in my meeting Byron. I wasn't sure that I was ready for another impromptu Dean meeting.

As I approached the conference room, I noticed that the door was closed. I had no clue what I was walking into, but I figured that they had started without me. I gave a slight double tap on the door before twisting the handle.

"Scottie, come on in," Dean said, with so much enthusiasm in her voice that it instantly made me uncomfortable. "I was just introducing Byron Stalling to the group."

Maybe I should slap myself. This has to be a bad dream. She couldn't be introducing me to the slimy, sex orgy-having motherfucker that I just left in a Chicago restaurant with his little freak nasty chick one day ago! No, this cannot be happening!

Shit just got real.

I nervously turned to my left, in the direction that Dean motioned toward. I tried to internally prepare myself for what I was about to see. Get my emotions in check to face a recent former lover who was now toying with my career. A lump the size of a boulder constricted the vocal cords in my throat and my voice was barely recognizable as I tried to drag out the words, "Hello, Byron."

At that moment, I realized that I had been playing a game that I was not prepared to win. If I could have turned and made a lightning speed exit to the nearest door, I would have done so. I felt like the room was closing in on me and my hand trembled with fear and anger when I was forced to extend it and shake the hand of the man that I now upgraded to the level of dangerous and insane.

"Hello Scottie, pleasure to see you again," Byron said, his raspy voice reminding me of Darth Vader. "We have met before, correct?"

"Uh-um, yes…I think so."

"Scottie?" Dean called my name.

"Yes." I snapped back into reality. This was happening and now I had to deal with it.

"Are you all right?" Dean questioned with judgmental eyes.

"I'm…I'm…fine. Thank you."

"Great. I wanted the team to meet Byron as he has come to us with some great projects that he will be working on in the future, and you all may be called in to assist at some point."

I nodded. "Okay."

"Thanks for dropping in," Dean said.

"It was my pleasure," I replied with a smile. I managed to make my face tell the same lie as my words.

The conference room door closed and my feet carried me as fast as they could to the women's restroom down the hall.

Was this a set-up?

I pressed my back up against the cold gray steel of the bathroom stall grasping for air. Tears of stress and fear filled my eyes. That was one of the toughest acting roles in the made-for-TV drama that was my life. I had to sit there in Byron's face—in front of my department head—and act like I vaguely remembered him knowing that we had been sleeping together. I wanted to slap the taste out of his crazy-ass mouth for coming to my office and putting me in such a compromising position.

Sitting at my desk, I couldn't stop staring at the digital numbers counting down the seconds to 6 o'clock. It was like a buzzer. As soon as the clock struck six, I dashed out the door on a mission. Predictable Byron was probably staying at his usual hotel under the same alias, so that was my destination.

The front desk clerk called up to his room and before I knew it, I was on the elevator. I rehearsed what I would say all day leading up to this point, but now my thoughts were blank. I didn't have a script so I would let my anger be my guide.

The door opened as I raised my hand to knock. Before he could part his smug lips to let a peep come out, I went in.

"What kind of deranged idiot are you?"

He opened his mouth as if to respond.

"No, you let me finish. You think the world revolves around

your arrogant ass, but not this chick's world. And furthermore, I thought I made it pretty clear that I'm done with you. D-O-N-E. You keep calling my job, then you show up in a meeting with my boss like a crazy-ass stalker. What the fuck is up with that?"

I held my hand up to interrupt his attempt to speak again and he looked shocked.

"Contrary to popular belief, you can't buy everything that you want. The only way that I better ever see your face again is if it's on TV. And if I do, I'm turning that shit off."

I spun on my heels to walk away, but I could feel Byron's eyes piercing my back. Before I could put enough distance between us, his beastly hand yanked my left shoulder causing me to stumble backward and almost hit the ground.

"You crazy motherfucker!" I hollered out as I tried to get up, hoping that someone would hear my yelling before this scene got any worse.

"No, you're crazy for trying to play me and leave me!" Byron yelled.

I could feel the spit from his rage raining down on my face. I had to think quickly.

I remained crouched low as a protection stance. When I felt him hovering over my back, I gripped my purse handle until my nails dug deeply into the leather and I swung my arm in the air with all of my might aiming straight for his head. When I heard the thump, I knew that it was time to run. I couldn't wait around for a reaction. I was happy that the bottle of vino that I'd picked up around the corner from the office had come in handy. I took off running as fast as I could.

I heard a plea in the distance. "Scot...Scottie, wait...I have your things...your suitcase!"

He was pitiful in his one last, high-pitched cry for attention.

"Do you want it?" was the last thing I heard him call out as I fled.

I rounded the corner toward the elevator like a track star and let my silence do the talking. I pounded on the buttons as hard and as fast as I could. It didn't matter which elevator came first, up or down. I was shaking and my adrenaline was rushing. I needed to get off his floor.

Chapter 22

Try Me

I was wallowing in the sorrow of my horrible choices in men and my phone started vibrating like crazy. It was Kari. "Hey, Kari! I'm glad you called. Before you say anything…I want to admit that I've been acting silly and careless lately, but I miss you. I miss having you as my constant, my person, and my friend."

"Damn. I wasn't expecting that." He sounded miserable.

"Why do you sound like that?"

"Like what?"

"Like someone died." Realizing what I'd just said, I hoped that wasn't the reason for his call. I resolved to shut up and listen.

"I have something to tell you and I don't even know where to start or how to say it."

"Say it, babe. You're scaring me." Now I knew that whatever he was calling to say could not be good.

"You should come over," I continued. "Maybe it's best to talk face-to-face about whatever it is that's got you so upset."

"All right, but is Dev there?"

"No, I haven't seen much of her lately. It's fine. Just come."

"Okay, I'll be there shortly."

I paced around for an hour with my stomach in knots. I heard the buzzer and I knew that the showdown was about to begin. I opened the door for Kari, but my emotions had a vise grip on my tongue.

He started spilling his guts immediately. "I had sex with some-one."

I suppressed every urge to interject and ask if he had come over to tell me that he was moving on to the next chick.

He took a big breath and kept going. "It was after I figured out that you lied to me when you went out of town. I went out, got drunk and I slept with someone. I was so wasted that I didn't even remember what happened. But now she's telling me that she is pregnant."

Kari took a step back and let the words linger in the air for fear of my reaction.

I was too stunned to speak.

"Scottie, listen to this tape of my conversation with her. It will likely answer all of your questions." He hit "play" on his cell phone and I listened intently:

"Pregnant?" Kari said.

"Yes."

The dead air on either side of the line was eerie, and so was the woman's voice.

"What...do you...how can that be?"

"Kari, don't do this."

"We barely had sex from what I can remember, and quite frankly I was so wasted that for all I know, we didn't even have sex at all."

"You can't be serious! I was wasted too. Hell, you kept pushing drink after drink on me. You were the one that said you needed to talk and I was trying to keep you company while you drowned in your sorrows like a bitch over Scottie!"

"What-the-fuck-ever!" Listening to their exchange, I could hear that Kari was starting to get upset. *"We can't do this. This is just wrong."*

"Well, that sure didn't stop you from sleeping with me unprotected, now did it?"

"Look, Dev. Let's calm down and talk about this in a civilized manner."

Kari made his best effort to change his tone. Dev willingly provided every single detail that she remembered from that night and as I continued to listen to her voice on the recording, my body felt weak.

I thought I was going to be sick.

I couldn't believe that my whole world was slowly unraveling day-by-day. First, The League lawyers and HR interrogated me, then Byron ambushed me at my office, and now this. As I stared deep into Kari's eyes, the hurt that I felt formed a lump in my throat so big that it was impossible to swallow. I turned my back on him and walked into the living room.

"Please, say something to me," he pleaded. "This calm demeanor is freaking me out."

My skin felt hot and I saw red. I picked up the glass vase holding the fresh-picked, yellow tulips that I loved so much, and I hurled it at his head. I didn't throw it fast enough because he managed to duck. I charged him and started screaming profanities and throwing blows to his body. He held his hands up in defense before finally managing a grip to restrain my arms after what seemed like twenty minutes of tussling. He pinned me down on the couch with what felt like his entire body weight on top of me.

"Calm down, Scottie! Calm down and I'll let you go!" Kari yelled.

I continued to try to resist until I couldn't anymore. My body was weak and worn. My arms hurt and my throat was strained. I fell silent. I was in a daze. I felt like I was in the *Twilight Zone*.

Kari called out to me, "Scottie? Scottie?"

He finally let me go and I stood and walked to the window. I glared out into the streets.

I managed to project strength in my voice while suppressing

tears. "Kari, what do you want me to do? Or say?" My outer appearance was now cool, but inside I was destroyed.

"Something, baby. Anything."

"What? To make you feel better?"

Kari shook his head in despair. "No, not at all."

I sat in silence, thinking. So many questions were running through my head. I started firing at him.

"Were you guys cheating the whole time we were together?"

"No," he responded, with shame in his voice. "It was the one time and it was after you and I took our break."

"Who came on to who?"

"We got drunk together after we left Slate. I needed someone to talk to. I was pissed at you. And I guess it just happened. Honest to God, I don't remember everything."

"You were mad at me so you fucked one of my best friends." I could feel my outer cool slowly slipping away. "That's pretty fucking low," I continued. "This is classic!" I was infuriated, once again unable to contain my anger. "'Communicate with me and give me the same respect that I try to give you.' That's what you said to me, right?!" I screamed through pained vocal cords. "Isn't that what you asked of me?"

I didn't give him a chance to respond. "Getting the next bitch pregnant, that's a whole lot of respect right there." I had to fight every urge not to crack off the edge of a wine bottle and slice his ass up. "You know what? Fuck you and the whore that crawled up on your sick dick. Good luck with your bastard child!"

Kari's brown skin was pale. His eyes were low and filled with looming tears. He looked like a broken man.

In a low, somber tone, he spoke. "I'm sorry. I'm sorry for everything. By the time I figured out what Dev and I had done, it was too late. Everything was already out of control."

Glaring at Kari from across the room with my arms folded and my body stiff, I felt emotionless. I stared off out the window contemplating my next move.

Interrupting my thoughts, Kari cleared his throat. "So are you going to go ahead and tell me about Byron now?"

At first I thought my heart had stopped. Then it suddenly sped up and started palpitating wildly at the mention of Byron's name. I snapped my neck to look at Kari. He still looked pitiful, but his eyes showed a disdain that wasn't present before.

"What are you talking about, Kari?"

He gripped his left hand over his right fist. "Don't play me, Scottie. You've been running around with him and thinking that I wouldn't find out while you strung me along."

"You're being ridiculous," I said halfheartedly. Truth was, I was tired. Tired of running from my emotions, tired of running from love, tired of hiding, tired of lying, tired of the deception— genuinely tired. I'd been running since I'd left Los Angeles.

"Kelvin told me that he thought he saw you at the Jay concert with Byron, just after our sudden breakup, which was right after you met him at work, if I recall correctly. Then you took a secret trip that you lied about. It all makes sense. Not to mention the unusually expensive things you've been popping up with."

I dropped to my knees at Kari's feet. I slowly raised my head and was face-to-face with his balled up fist. Still seated, he was looking at the floor when I began pleading, "Kari, please. I'm sorry, I'm so sorry. It's over with him. I was blinded. I can admit it now. I was trying to live out some elaborate fantasy that I thought I wanted. I don't know how I got wrapped up in all of it so easy, but I never wanted to hurt you."

"I know how, you watch too much fucking TV and you want to be those bitches. It looks fun, but that shit's not real. You had a real man in me and you couldn't see that! All I ever did was love you, but I was hesitant to tell you because I didn't want to scare you away and look...you ran away anyway."

A single tear fell from Kari's eye. I reached toward his face, but he brushed my hand back. I collapsed on the floor in tears as he got up to leave.

"Kari! Kari! Wait, don't leave like this!" I begged.

Kari was unresponsive to my plea. My next move was not calculated...it simply flowed from the pain that I felt in my soul. "Kari, I love you."

He paused. With his back to me, he mumbled something under his breath. Then, his steps continued toward the door, as rapid and deliberate as they had been before.

Chapter 23

Trust Me

"Welcome to Los Angeles. The current temperature is seventy-two degrees. We hope that you enjoyed your flight and we thank you for flying with Delta Airlines."

The plan was to use the entire five-hour flight to relax, but I couldn't block out the tears, the images, the yelling, and the pain. The scenario replayed over and over in my head. It was a short film, a drama, featuring me and starring Kari. It had been weeks since we last spoke.

I walked up the breezeway and finally made the call that had been the most recent cause of my anxiety.

"Where are you?" I questioned, without nearly considering a traditional greeting.

"Well, hello to you too, stranger."

"I need to see you. Today. As soon as possible." I felt my heart thumping through my chest as I spoke. Unsure of what he would say, I added, "It's important."

"Okay." That simple answer spoke to me in a way that I hadn't expected.

"Great...lunch...one o'clock...Urth Caffé on Melrose," I said.

"I'll see you then."

I gathered my suitcase at baggage claim, then headed to the

Enterprise counter to pick up my rental car. With that, I was rollin'. Top down on the silver convertible with my freshly dyed, jet-black, barely-there hair not quite blowing in the wind. I was on my way.

This girl was back in La La Land and happy. I missed the city that I once shared an intense love affair with. The air in my city was different. The sun was shining brighter. I felt at ease.

I cranked up Power 106, and my jam of the week was rattling through the speakers. "A Milli, A Milli," I rapped along with Lil Wayne like I was on *Star Search* looking for a contract.

An old, wrinkled-up woman in her Mercedes pulled up next to me and I could have sworn that she looked over and gave me the side eye, but it didn't matter. I was in my element and I was feeling like "A Milli."

Melrose was packed as usual. Luckily, I was able to snag a corner table on the patio, after an Asian, earthy, flower child-looking chick with dreads wrapped up her afternoon herbal tea and ginger root cookie fest. The constant flow of traffic and people was what I wanted to break up any potentially awkward or weird moments that were soon to come.

In the distance I spotted long, sandy-blond dreads swaying with a familiar stride. From what I could see without looking too pressed, he definitely maintained his sexy since the last time that we were together.

I quickly dug in my purse for my pocket mirror. I needed to triple check my lips, face, and hair before he got any closer. It had been over a year since we'd last laid eyes on each other and almost as long since we'd last spoke. For what I had to say, I needed to look damn good.

I stood in my fall-brown Aldo pumps making me eye-to-eye

with Ivan. He looked good. My stomach fluttered, but I kept calm and greeted him with poise. "Thank you for coming on such short notice. It's good to see you."

Ivan, on the other hand, wasn't doing so well at hiding his cards. "You look fantastic! It's been so long. Look at you…shoes are amazing and matching your blouse, always on point. I see New York has been keeping you as stylish as ever."

I smiled. "Thanks, I do what I can."

"I'm loving the short cut, too. I would never have imagined that you would cut all of your hair off. It works really well with your face, though." Ivan reached over and touched my cheek.

I instantly felt conflicted. "Let's sit down."

"So what brings you to L.A.? Are you back for good?"

I laughed at the assumption that I could be calling him because I was moving back. "No, not for good. I'm actually here on a quick trip for work. So I'm only in town for two days."

"Well, I'm glad that you made the time to see me."

"I had to…"

And as I was about to delve into the reason for the impromptu lunch meeting, the waitress interrupted to ask if we were ready to order. I went ahead and ordered my salad. Ivan ordered a sandwich.

"As I was saying, I had to see you." I looked into Ivan's eyes as I had a year earlier. "I've grown a lot in this past year and I've also learned a lot about myself. I met an exceptionally sweet, thoughtful, and handsome man who truly cared for me."

I could see Ivan developing a quizzical look on his face, but I maintained a steady and calm tone.

"But," I continued. "I didn't know how to receive him and allow him to treat me well because all of the shit that you put me through."

Ivan looked taken aback. He tried to speak but I interjected. "Wait, let me finish. I don't want you to misunderstand. I'm not here to bash you. I also have to take responsibility for what I allowed you to do in our relationship...or whatever you want to call it. That's why I'm here. To take responsibility, to make peace."

Ivan seemed shocked at the course of the conversation. I could tell that this was not at all what he envisioned. "I'd be lying if I said that I saw this coming," Ivan confessed. "So...you're telling me about your new man and on top of that telling me how horrible I was to you?"

"You can take it however you'd like. But for me, it's not about you; it's about me, and that's my sole purpose. When I left so abruptly last year, I thought that I was doing the right thing by getting away from you. But I didn't realize that I was holding on to things from our past that held me back from truly moving on and from allowing myself to accept someone good into my life. Because of my burdens, I couldn't open up and give of myself because I couldn't trust that the person's intentions were solid. After so much time spent hoping and wishing that a person would be right and treat you right...you eventually get let down so much that you think everyone else has to be just as wrong and ill-intentioned as the previous person that you were with."

"Wow, Scottie. You went real deep on me," Ivan said, as he played with the hairs in his perfectly lined goatee. He sat quiet as though he was thinking of what he wanted to say next.

I tried to relieve some of the pressure. "Ivan, I have love for you and I always will. I didn't call you here for you to really say anything. I needed you to hear me."

"Well, I heard you. Loud, very clear and without hesitation. I heard you," he said, with an inflection of sadness.

I walked away feeling like for once, Ivan and I had an understanding. We were finally on the same page, and that was a relief. In the future, I didn't envision that we would be friends calling each other on weekends, but we left the relationship in such a way that we could be cordial to one another with a mutual underlying respect.

I didn't have to work until the following day so I simply wanted to check into my hotel and lie by the pool. Even though it wasn't exactly summer, it still wasn't New York weather.

The room was gorgeous and definitely surpassed my standards. I flipped on the flat-screen television to catch a bit of entertainment news while I changed into my swimwear slash loungewear.

The words blared through the television speakers crisp and clear: "Byron Stalling has been arrested and charged with stalking, unlawful entry, and battery."

My canister of Carol's Daughter body butter splattered all over my legs as it fell to my feet. I ran to the TV and they had an awful-looking picture of Byron plastered on the screen. He looked like he hadn't slept in days and his facial hair was wild and unkempt.

After they went to commercial, I stood looking at the screen in a daze.

That could have been me.

I started thanking God aloud as I crawled on the bed sobbing quietly. I wasn't sure why I was crying, but it felt like a release.

The lure of celebrity, fame, power and money was what I thought I'd left behind when I moved from Los Angeles. But I guess it will follow you wherever you allow it. Lucky for me I didn't catch a beat down behind it.

I was so ready to get back to New York. I missed my new home and all that it had to offer. After I finished up my work the following day, I headed straight for the airport. My chocolate Franco Sarto riding boots thumped down the breezeway. I was excited to tuck into my window seat. My mission was to write a letter and email it to the man who it took me entirely too much time and heartache to realize that I loved.

THE END

About the Author

Ahyiana Angel is a Cali girl who has turned the Manhattan streets into her playground. This sassy storyteller is a former sports entertainment publicist at the National Basketball Association (NBA). Ups and downs with dating, love, career, and friendships inspired her to create a lane of her own with the popular blog "Life According To Her." As a freelance writer Angel's work has been featured on Essence.com, XOJane.com, SingleBlackMale.org, and ClutchMagOnline.com, among others. Angel has a Bachelor of Science in Business Administration and Marketing from California State University, Long Beach. She loves traveling—especially frolicking in Caribbean sands, embarking on new adventures, and she's up for trying almost any interesting food or cuisine. Keep up with Ahyiana at www.AhyianaAngel.com

Social Media:
 Twitter: @Ahyiana_Angel
 Instagram: @Ahyiana_Angel
 Facebook: Ahyiana Angel

On the web: www.AhyianaAngel.com

Acknowledgments

God put the dream in my heart and the drive in my spirit to complete this work of fiction. I thank God for the dream and the passion to push it to completion. I owe a huge thank you to my parents, Jocelyn and Thomas Owens, for being extremely supportive with every decision that I made along this journey. To my brothers, Thomas Jr., Devon, and Jalen, I love you more than you know. My grandparents weren't aware of this, but they were a part of the motivation in getting this project completed and published. My grandfather had to drop out of school and work in the fields in Texas to help support his family. My grandmother sacrificed her dreams for her family. They worked hard and provided a wonderful life. This is for you!

My family, from the Owens side to the Francis side and beyond, I love you all. Special shout-out to my Sunday afternoon at Grandma's house peeps: Aunt Peggy, Aunt Shawn, Auset, Amdwat, Amarw, Aunt Bert, Carlos, Charles aka Kphra, Cole, Cayden, Domo, Jasmine, Jason, Jakinda, Joey, Richard, Raynell, Shamica, and the next great Chef, Stephanie. She's my cousin, confidante, whip-cracker, sounding board, motivator, and most importantly my sister, Miss Kristen Turner. I'm so grateful to have you in my life.

A warm hug and thank you to Charmaine Parker for believing in me, being patient with me, and taking time out of your hectic schedule to sit with me. Thank you to Zane for seeing the potential in my work and stamping it with her seal of approval. Appreciation and thanks to my talented photographer friend Sean Pressley. He captured the spirit of who I am as an artist through photos. Dawn Michelle Hardy, my superstar agent friend, who took the time to sit with me, brainstorm with me, and really provide guidance in this world of publishing that was all so new. I thank you, Rakia Clark, because from the moment that we first met, you saw my vision for this project, and you were willing to work with me. You are my amazing editor rockstar! Thank you to Sir Charles "Chuck" for the introduction.

To my Fab Five Plus One Ladies: Contasia, Kristen, Sennie, Tamara, and Trenika, I love you and appreciate the support throughout the years. You will forever be my college boo thangs. Sennie, thank you for the late-night chats and especially for pushing me. Special love to our newest addition, little Taylor Aubrey Stone. My New York Loves: Francesca, Renee, Sennie, Mechelle and Sewit, you rock my world! Thank you for being patient with me during this process and pushing me to keep going and not hang out. My London Town Gals: you welcomed me into the clique and I loved every minute of the time we spent. Nicole, you are one of the sweetest people I know. I can never thank you enough for seriously holding me down while I lived in London. Myleik, we go back to Wilshire Blvd. dreaming, and you showed me more than you know. I still have the farewell package you sent me off to New York with, thank you for believing in me. My DMV girls Allyson and Leesha, who held me down during my many trips to make this thing work, I appreciate you. LaShawn, thank you for sending me the email that sparked the DMV trips. Big hugs and thanks for your support to all of my friends from Los Angeles to New York.

Thank you to all of my NBA Family for being so supportive... you know who you are ☺. To all the readers of my blog, www.LifeAccordingToHer.com, and those that supported my Sippin' Sassy events from New York to London, I appreciate you and thank you for rocking with me from the beginning of this journey!

— *Allow yourself to feel the fear, then do it anyway* —

Discussion guide available at www.AhyianaAngel.com